EX LIB

VINTAGE CLASSICS

A GUN FOR SALE

Graham Greene was born in 1904. On coming down from Balliol College, Oxford, he worked for four years as sub-editor on *The Times*. He established his reputation with his fourth novel, *Stamboul Train*. In 1935 he made a journey across Liberia, described in *Journey Without Maps*, and on his return was appointed film critic of the *Spectator*. In 1926 he was received into the Roman Catholic Church and visited Mexico in 1938 to report on the religious persecution there. As a result he wrote *The Lawless Roads* and, later, his famous novel *The Power and the Glory*. *Brighton Rock* was published in 1938 and in 1940 he became literary editor of the *Spectator*. The next year he undertook work for the Foreign Office and was stationed in Sierra Leone from 1941 to 1943. This later produced the novel, *The Heart of the Matter*, set in West Africa.

As well as his many novels, Graham Greene wrote several collections of short stories, four travel books, six plays, three books of autobiography – *A Sort of Life, Ways of Escape* and *A World of My Own* (published posthumously) – two of biography and four books for children. He also contributed hundreds of essays, and film and book reviews, some of which appear in the collections *Reflections* and *Mornings in the Dark*. Many of his novels and short stories have been filmed and *The Third Man* was written as a film treatment. Graham Greene was a member of the Order of Merit and a Companion of Honour. He died in April 1991.

ALSO BY GRAHAM GREENE

Novels

The Man Within
It's a Battlefield
The Confidential Agent
The Ministry of Fear
The Third Man
The End of the Affair
Loser Takes All
The Quiet American
A Burnt-out Case
Travels with my Aunt
Dr Fischer of Geneva or
  The Bomb Party
The Human Factor
The Tenth Man
Stamboul Train
England Made Me
Brighton Rock
The Power and the Glory
The Heart of the Matter
The Fallen Idol
Our Man in Havana
The Comedians
The Honorary Consul
Monsignor Quixote
The Captain and the Enemy

Short Stories

Collected Stories
Twenty-One Stories
The Last Word and Other Stories
May We Borrow Your Husband?

Travel

Journey Without Maps
The Lawless Roads
In Search of a Character
Getting to Know the General

Essays

Yours etc.
Reflections
Mornings in the Dark
Collected Essays

Plays

Collected Plays

Autobiography

A Sort of Life
Ways of Escape
Fragments of an Autobiography
A World of my Own

Biography

Lord Rochester's Monkey
An Impossible Woman

Children's Books

The Little Train
The Little Horse-Bus
The Little Steamroller
The Little Fire Engine

GRAHAM GREENE

A Gun for Sale

WITH AN INTRODUCTION BY
Robert Macfarlane

VINTAGE BOOKS
London

Published by Vintage 2009

16 18 20 19 17 15

First published in Great Britain by William Heinemann 1936

First published by Vintage in 2001

Vintage
Random House, 20 Vauxhall Bridge Road,
London SW1V 2SA

www.vintage-classics.info

Addresses for companies within The Random House Group Limited
can be found at: www.randomhouse.co.uk/offices.htm

The Random House Group Limited Reg. No. 954009

A CIP catalogue record for this book
is available from the British Library

ISBN 9780099286141

The Random House Group Limited supports The Forest
Stewardship Council (FSC), the leading international forest
certification organisation. All our titles that are printed on
Greenpeace approved FSC certified paper carry the FSC logo.
Our paper procurement policy can be found at:
www.rbooks.co.uk/environment

Mixed Sources
Product group from well-managed
forests and other controlled sources
www.fsc.org Cert no. TT-COC-2139
© 1996 Forest Stewardship Council

Printed and bound in Great Britain by
CPI Cox & Wyman, Reading RG1 8EX

Introduction

A Gun for Sale starts with a bang. 'Murder didn't mean much to Raven. It was just a new job.' It is an opening which places us unmistakably in the world of the detective thriller – the world of the gung-ho gumshoe, the sassy moll, and the smiler with the knife, where dialogue is as hard-boiled as a twenty-minute egg, and the action moves quicker than whisky over ice. In those first lines, we can hear a practice run of the celebrated beginning to Greene's *Brighton Rock* (1938): 'Hale knew, before he had been in Brighton three hours, that they meant to murder him.' We can hear, too, advance echoes of unnumbered dark-minded thrillers, all the way down to James Ellroy's 1997 masterpiece, *The Cold Six Thousand*, which starts, abruptly: 'They sent him to Dallas to kill a nigger pimp named Wendell Durfee.'

It places us, to be absolutely precise, in the world of noir. You will be familiar with the images of noir, even if you do not know the films and the novels which make up the genre. Two silhouetted hit men in overcoats and fedoras approach a diner. A G-car cruises at walking pace down a street. A faceless figure in a belted coat stands in a white circle of street-light. A man cups a hand round a flaring match. 'Film noir' was first used as a phrase in Paris in 1946, when French cineastes were looking for a label for a new type of Hollywood product. In the late 1930s, the feel-good world of mainstream Hollywood had begun to spawn a dark filmic alter ego. Noir cinema moved in a world of fear, neurosis, and depthless dishonesty. Its 'heroes' were sleazy private eyes, informers, hit men, gangsters or crims. Policemen were bent, institutions were authoritarian tending to evil. The setting was sordid, confused, almost always urban. Dialogue was terse. There were few verbs, and no happy endings. Action drove character, not the other way round. Everything was cast in extravagantly stylised greyscale, with sudden Caravaggio-contrasts of light and dark.

The 1940s was the decade of the classic noir films, the 1930s the period when the genre was forming in cinema and in literature. *A Gun for Sale* was part of that formation. 'All you need for a movie', in the loaded phrase of neo-noir director Jean-Luc Godard, 'is a girl and a gun'. It was out of these two ingredients that Greene made his fifth novel.

The 'gun' is an assassin called Raven, who is hired to kill the Czech Minister for War. Raven returns to England after a successful hit, only to be paid off in stolen notes by his contact, Cholmondeley, and nearly arrested as a consequence. Bent on revenge, and unaware that his assassination has tilted the world towards war, Raven tracks Cholmondeley down to the Midlands city of Nottwich. En route, he takes hostage the novel's 'girl', Anne Crowder, who happens to be the partner of a detective-sergeant named Jimmy Mather. Mather sets off to Nottwich after Raven, who is himself chasing Cholmondeley and his shadowy pay-masters. As this double-pursuit tapers to a violent climax, so the world edges closer to war.

A Gun for Sale was published in 1936; in 1942 it would be adapted into the less subtly titled *This Gun for Hire*, with a script co-written by the American pulp master W.R. Burnett (author of *Little Caesar*, *High Sierra* and *The Asphalt Jungle*). The promotional poster for the film showed Alan Ladd as Raven, standing in a grainy bright angled light, and casting a corvid shadow onto the white wall behind him. Greene did not approve of Burnett's script, but he can hardly have objected to the existence of the film, for his novel – like its 1934 predecessor, *Stamboul Train* – was clearly written with a eye to adaptation.

Cinema's influence on *A Gun for Sale* is visible everywhere. It is there in the B-movie strap-lines: 'His most vivid emotion was venom'; 'He had been made by hatred'; 'He bore the cold within him as he walked'. It is there, too, in the frequent cutaways, and in the long panning shots through the streets of London and over the suburbs of Nottwich. And it is there most obviously in the dozens of sudden leering close-ups:

the zoom-ins on expressions, objects and body parts – the 'furious dewlapped face' of Mr Davenant, the harelip of which Raven is so violently ashamed, the 'jewelled fingers' of Cholmondeley, or the alien gas masks in which the medical students perform their strange carnival.

The thriller movie is the first of the two great cultural influences which converge in *A Gun for Sale*. The second is the adventure novel. Greene often spoke of H. Rider Haggard, Marjorie Bowen and John Buchan as among his favourite writers. It was from Buchan's *The Thirty-Nine Steps* – with its pursuit scenes over the moors of the Scottish borders, themselves a homage to Robert Louis Stevenson's *Kidnapped* – that Greene learned how to pace a chase, and learned also how powerful excitement could be as a way of bringing the reader to attention. These writers showed Greene that, as he once put it, 'action has a moral simplicity which thought lacks.'

Greene's adventure novels, however, diverged from their Edwardian antecedents in one important respect. The spy thrillers of Buchan and his like featured impeccably clubbable heroes: chaps with a patriot's sensibility and an ethic of fair play. Greene's, by contrast, starred anti-heroes – men driven by self-interest and self-loathing – of whom Raven is the first and one of the darkest. This was a necessary revision: the old, reassuringly simple value-systems of the Edwardian-era thriller, it seemed to Greene, could not hold in the predatory, paranoid, rudderless 1930s. In 1936, Greene wrote, Britain was 'no longer a Buchan world':

Patriotism had lost its appeal, even for a schoolboy, at Passchendaele, and the Empire brought first to mind the Beaverbrook Crusader, while it was difficult, during the years of the Depression, to believe in the high purposes of the City of London and of the British Constitution. The hunger-marchers seemed more real than the politicians.

For all its firecracker action and popular influences, *A Gun for Sale* is an intensely literary novel. While Orwell was mastering his style of artful plainness, and while Auden was coupling left-wing messages to popular verse forms, Greene was combining the tricks of the thriller-writer with the subtleties of the belletriste. His ambition – like so many British writers of the 1930s – was to hitch high-culture ambitions to the higher-powered vehicles of low culture.

Greene's literary hand can be seen in the novel's careful patterning: the images – red berries, sourness, facial disfigurements, speech slurs – which recur, speaking to one another across the novel, and amplifying its themes. So, for instance, Sir Marcus, the villainous armaments mogul, hides a scar beneath his beard; a flaw which binds him symbolically to his nemesis, the harelipped Raven. Then there are the numerous images of globes: the light-fitting like a 'dull globe' in Anne's room, the 'naked globe' which illuminates Dr Yogel's grubby surgery 'globe', the earth which seems to move like 'an icy barren globe, through the vast darkness' – an image which quietly but deliberately invokes the post-apocalypse world of Byron's poem 'Darkness', where 'the icy earth/Swung blind and blackening in the moonless air'. All these globes are there, of course, to prime us for the repercussions of Raven's actions. We slowly come to know what Raven never does: that his assassination of the Czech minister – passed off as the act of a Serbian militant – has been commissioned by Sir Marcus precisely in order to trigger global warfare, and thus boost the fortunes of the armament industry's fortunes. This is a world of Lorenz-Effect geopolitics, where a single assassination can trigger the slaughter of millions.

The fears which preoccupy the characters of *A Gun for Sale* – of imminent world war, of possible gas attacks, of sinister political powers – would all have been real and present fears to Greene's first readers. Greene's choice of an armaments manufacturer as the villain of the piece was particularly timely. Left-wing political theory of the early 1930s had come increasingly to lay the blame for war past and war future at the door of capitalism, which was held to have contaminated state morality with finance. In particular, such theories denounced the massive interlocking interests of governments and the arms companies – Vickers, Krupp, Skoda, Schneider-Creusot. A series of dramatically titled books detailing this hypothesis were published: *Death and Profits* (1932), *The*

Bloody Traffic (1933), *Salesmen of Death* (1933). Of these the best known was the dispassionate but damning *Merchants of Death: A Study of the International Armament Industry* (1934) by H.C. Engelbrecht and F.C. Hanighen, which triggered a 1935 Royal Commission on 'the war traffic' in Britain.

The figure of Sir Marcus – a spiritless but deadly destroying angel, for whom spilt blood is as nothing compared to a rocketing share price – would therefore have been a familiar to the public imagination, as would the excited and nervous gossip which fills the novel – in the newspaper office, on the street, in Dr Yogel's surgery – about the killing which is to be made in 'munitions shares'.

Almost everyone in *A Gun for Sale* is wounded, venal, vengeful or all three. One thinks of salacious Mr Davis, preying sexually on his showgirls, or the sharp-elbowed women who jostle outside a Nottwich jumble sale, waiting for it to open: 'They are quite capable', Greene has the nervous vicar note, in one of the novel's rare flashes of humour, 'of storming the doors'. Those few moments of compassion which do occur are nested within nastiness: the display of arid love, for instance, which passes between mean-minded Acky and his meaner-minded wife, when they are confronted by Raven.

Of these many bitter characters, the bitterest is Raven himself: our murderer and our detective, our hero and our villain. Hatred, Greene writes melodramatically, 'had constructed [Raven] into this thin smoky murderous figure in the rain, hunted and ugly . . . He had never felt the least tenderness for anyone.' Raven is not even evil, just perfectly indifferent – and this is what makes him all the more alarming.

Greene at one point describes Raven as carrying 'a chip of ice in his breast'. It is a phrase which inevitably recalls the famous observation in his autobiography *A Sort of Life* (1971) that 'there's a splinter of ice in the heart of a writer'. Greene recalled being in hospital as a child, being treated for appendicitis, when a ten-year-old boy was brought in to the ward with a broken leg. The parents were told they could go home, but shortly after they had left, complications set in. The parents were summoned back; the boy died. While the other patients shut out the sounds of the mother's cries of anguish with their radio headphones, Greene watched and listened. 'This was something,' he concluded chillingly, 'which one day I might need'.

The similarities between Raven the assassin and Greene the novelist stretch beyond their shared pitilessness. Both also show a deep disdain for the pieties of liberal humanism. *A Gun for Sale*, indeed, can be seen as the start of Greene's long-running attempt to destroy what Hywel Williams nicely described as 'the ethical religion of the English: a decadent liberal Protestantism sliding into secular do-gooding agnosticism.' Against the robust nineteenth-century trio of the progressive, the humane and the universal, Greene relentlessly pitted the squalid, the crooked and the fugitive. His major novels, beginning with *Stamboul Train* (1932) and intensifying in *A Gun for Sale*, confront and continually affront the persistent liberal-minded English belief that truth and decency are always obvious to those endowed with a rational and optimistic goodwill. This is why motives in Greene's novels are always mixed, why the good are sometimes damned and sometimes not, and why the wicked often end up, if not blessed, at least free. His characters exist in a moral world where goodness and badness do not exist as opposed and separate states, but shade into one another by fine degrees.

This ambiguous pessimism – or clear-eyed realism – runs right through to the end of *A Gun for Sale*. Anne and Mather are in a train carriage returning from Nottwich to London. Watching the countryside pass them by in reverse, both know – as the first readers of Greene's book would have known – that a world war has not been prevented, only postponed. 'This darkening land,' thinks Mathers as he gazes out of the window, 'flowing backwards down the line, was safe for a few more years.' Three, to be precise.

Robert Macfarlane, 2005

Chapter 1

1

MURDER didn't mean much to Raven. It was just a new job. You had to be careful. You had to use your brains. It was not a question of hatred. He had only seen the Minister once: he had been pointed out to Raven as he walked down the new housing estate between the small lit Christmas trees, an old grubby man without friends, who was said to love humanity.

The cold wind cut Raven's face in the wide Continental street. It was a good excuse for turning the collar of his coat well above his mouth. A hare-lip was a serious handicap in his profession; it had been badly sewn in infancy, so that now the upper lip was twisted and scarred. When you carried about so easy an identification you couldn't help becoming ruthless in your methods. It had always, from the first, been necessary for Raven to eliminate a witness.

He carried an attaché case. He looked like any other youngish man going home after his work; his dark overcoat had a clerical air. He moved steadily up the street like hundreds of his kind. A tram went by, lit up in the early dusk: he didn't take it. An economical young man, you might have thought, saving money for his home. Perhaps even now he was on his way to meet his girl.

But Raven had never had a girl. The hare-lip prevented that. He had learnt, when he was very young, how repulsive it was. He turned into one of the tall grey houses and climbed the stairs, a sour bitter screwed-up figure.

Outside the top flat he put down his attaché case and put on gloves. He took a pair of clippers out of his pocket and cut through the telephone wire where it ran out from above the door to the lift shaft. Then he rang the bell.

He hoped to find the Minister alone. This little top-floor flat was the socialist's home; he lived in a poor bare solitary way and Raven had been told that his secretary always left him at half-past six; he was very considerate with his employees. But Raven was a minute too early and the Minister half an hour too late. A woman opened the door, an elderly woman with pince-nez and several gold teeth. She had her hat on and her coat was over her arm. She had been on the point of leaving and she was furious at being caught. She didn't allow him to speak, but snapped at him in German, 'The Minister is engaged.'

He wanted to spare her, not because he minded a killing but because his employers would prefer him not to exceed his instructions. He held the letter of introduction out to her silently; as long as she didn't hear his foreign voice or see the hare-lip she was safe. She took the letter primly and held it up close to her pince-nez. Good, he thought, she's short-sighted. 'Stay where you are,' she said, and walked back up the passage. He could hear her disapproving governess voice, then she was back in the passage saying, 'The Minister will see you. Follow me, please.' He couldn't understand the foreign speech, but he knew what she meant from her behaviour.

His eyes, like little concealed cameras, photographed the room instantaneously: the desk, the easy chair, the map on the wall, the door to the bedroom behind, the wide window above the bright cold Christmas street. A small oil-stove was all the heating, and the Minister was having it used now to boil a saucepan. A kitchen alarm-clock on the desk marked seven o'clock. A voice said, 'Emma, put in another egg.' The Minister came out from the bedroom. He had tried to tidy himself, but he had forgotten the cigarette ash on his trousers, and his fingers were ink-stained. The secretary took an egg out of one of the drawers in the desk. 'And the salt. Don't forget the salt,' the Minister said. He explained in slow English, 'It prevents the shell cracking. Sit down, my friend. Make yourself at home. Emma, you can go.'

Raven sat down and fixed his eyes on the Minister's chest. He thought: I'll give her three minutes by the alarm-clock to get well away: he kept his eyes on the Minister's chest: just there I'll shoot. He let his coat collar fall and saw with bitter rage how the old man turned away from the sight of his hare-lip.

The Minister said, 'It's years since I heard from him. But I've never forgotten him, never. I can show you his photograph in the other room. It's good of him to think of an old friend. So rich and powerful too. You must ask him when you go back if he remembers the time – ' A bell began to ring furiously.

Raven thought: the telephone. I cut the wire. It shook his nerve. But it was only the alarm-clock drumming on the desk. The Minister turned it off. 'One egg's boiled,' he said and stooped for the saucepan. Raven opened his attaché case: in the lid he had fixed his automatic fitted with a silencer. The Minister said: 'I'm sorry the bell made you jump. You see I like my egg just four minutes.'

Feet ran along the passage. The door opened. Raven turned furiously in his seat, his hare-lip flushed and raw. It was the secretary. He thought: my God, what a household. They won't let a man do things tidily. He forgot his lip, he was angry, he had a grievance. She came in flashing her gold teeth, prim and ingratiating. She said, 'I was just going out when I heard the telephone,' then she winced slightly, looked the other way, showed a clumsy delicacy before his deformity which he couldn't help noticing. It condemned her. He snatched the automatic out of the case and shot the Minister twice in the back.

The Minister fell across the oil stove; the saucepan upset and the two eggs broke on the floor. Raven shot the Minister once more in the head, leaning across the desk to make quite certain, driving the bullet hard into the base of the skull, smashing it open like a china doll's. Then he turned on the secretary; she moaned at him; she hadn't any words; the old mouth couldn't hold its saliva. He supposed she was begging him for mercy. He pressed the trigger again; she staggered under it as if she had been kicked by an animal in the side. But he had miscalculated. Her unfashionable dress, the swathes of useless material in which she hid her body, had perhaps confused his aim. And she was tough, so tough he couldn't believe his eyes; she was through the door before he could fire again, slamming it behind her.

3

But she couldn't lock it; the key was on his side. He twisted the handle and pushed; the elderly woman had amazing strength; it only gave two inches. She began to scream some word at the top of her voice.

There was no time to waste. He stood away from the door and shot twice through the woodwork. He could hear the pince-nez fall on the floor and break. The voice screamed again and stopped; there was a sound outside as if she were sobbing. It was her breath going out through her wounds. Raven was satisfied. He turned back to the Minister.

There was a clue he had been ordered to leave; a clue he had to remove. The letter of introduction was on the desk. He put it in his pocket and between the Minister's stiffened fingers he inserted a scrap of paper. Raven had little curiosity; he had only glanced at the introduction and the nickname at its foot conveyed nothing to him; he was a man who could be depended on. Now he looked round the small bare room to see whether there was any clue he had overlooked. The suitcase and the automatic he was to leave behind. It was all very simple.

He opened the bedroom door; his eyes again photographed the scene, the single bed, the wooden chair, the dusty chest of drawers, a photograph of a young Jew with a small scar on his chin as if he had been struck there with a club, a pair of brown wooden hairbrushes initialled J.K., everywhere cigarette ash: the home of an old lonely untidy man; the home of the Minister for War.

A low voice whispered an appeal quite distinctly through the door. Raven picked up the automatic again; who would have imagined an old woman could be so tough? It touched his nerve a little just in the same way as the bell had done, as if a ghost were interfering with a man's job. He opened the study door; he had to push it against the weight of her body. She looked dead enough, but he made quite sure with the automatic almost touching her eyes.

It was time to be gone. He took the automatic with him.

4

They sat and shivered side by side as the dusk came down; they were borne in their bright small smoky cage above the streets; the bus rocked down to Hammersmith. The shop windows sparkled like ice and 'Look,' she said, 'it's snowing.' A few large flakes went drifting by as they crossed the bridge, falling like paper scraps into the dark Thames.

He said, 'I'm happy as long as this ride goes on.'

'We're seeing each other tomorrow – Jimmy.' She always hesitated before his name. It was a silly name for anyone of such bulk and gravity.

'It's the nights that bother me.'

She laughed, 'It's going to be wearing,' but immediately became serious, 'I'm happy too.' About happiness she was always serious; she preferred to laugh when she was miserable. She couldn't avoid being serious about things she cared for, and happiness made her grave at the thought of all the things which might destroy it. She said, 'It would be dreadful now if there was a war.'

'There won't be a war.'

'The last one started with a murder.'

'That was an Archduke. This is just an old politician.'

She said: 'Be careful. You'll break the record – Jimmy.'

'Damn the record.'

She began to hum the tune she'd bought: 'It's only Kew to you'; and the large flakes fell past the window, melted on the pavement: 'a snowflower a man brought from Greenland.'

He said, 'It's a silly song.'

She said, 'It's a lovely song – Jimmy. I simply can't call you Jimmy. You aren't Jimmy. You're outsize. Detective-sergeant Mather. You're the reason why people make jokes about policemen's boots.'

'What's wrong with "dear", anyway?'

'Dear, dear,' she tried it out on the tip of her tongue, between lips as vividly stained as a winter berry. 'Oh no,' she decided, 'I'll call you that when we've been married ten years.'

'Well – "darling"?'

'Darling, darling. I don't like it. It sounds as if I'd known you a long, long time.' The bus went up the hill past the fish-and-chip shops: a brazier glowed and they could smell the roasting chestnuts. The ride was nearly over, there were only two more streets and a turn to the left by the church, which was already visible, the spire lifted like a long icicle above the houses. The nearer they got to home the more miserable she became, the nearer they got to home the more lightly she talked. She was keeping things off and out of mind: the peeling wallpaper, the long flights to her room, cold supper with Mrs Brewer and next day the walk to the agent's, perhaps a job again in the provinces away from him.

Mather said heavily, 'You don't care for me like I care for you. It's nearly twenty-four hours before I see you again.'

'It'll be more than that if I get a job.'

'You don't care. You simply don't care.'

She clutched his arm. 'Look. Look at that poster.' But it was gone before he could see it through the steamy pane. 'Europe Mobilizing' lay like a weight on her heart.

'What was it?'

'Oh, just the same old murder again.'

'You've got that murder on your mind. It's a week old now. It's got nothing to do with us.'

'No, it hasn't, has it?'

'If it had happened here, we'd have caught him by now.'

'I wonder why he did it.'

'Politics. Patriotism.'

'Well. Here we are. It might be a good thing to get off. Don't look so miserable. I thought you said you were happy.'

'That was five minutes ago.'

'Oh,' she said out of her light and heavy heart, 'one lives quickly these days.' They kissed under the lamp; she had to stretch to reach him; he was comforting like a large dog, even when he was sullen and stupid, but one didn't have to send away a dog alone in the cold dark night.

'Anne,' he said, 'we'll be married, won't we, after Christmas?'

'We haven't a penny,' she said, 'you know. Not a penny – Jimmy.'

'I'll get a rise.'

'You'll be late for duty.'

'Damn it, you don't care.'

She jeered at him, 'Not a scrap – dear,' and walked away from him up the street to No. 54, praying let me get some money quick, let *this* go on *this* time; she hadn't any faith in herself. A man passed her going up the road; he looked cold and strung-up, as he passed in his black overcoat; he had a hare-lip. Poor devil, she thought, and forgot him, opening the door of 54, climbing the long flights to the top floor, the carpet stopped on the first. She put on the new record, hugging to her heart the silly senseless words, the slow sleepy tune:

> 'It's only Kew
> To you,
> But to me
> It's Paradise.
> They are just blue
> Petunias to you,
> But to me
> They are your eyes.'

The man with the hare-lip came back down the street; fast walking hadn't made him warm; like Kay in *The Snow Queen* he bore the cold within him as he walked. The flakes went on falling, melting into slush on the pavement, the words of a song dropped from the lit room on the third floor, the scrape of a used needle.

> 'They say that's a snowflower
> A man brought from Greenland.
> I say it's the lightness, the coolness, the whiteness
> Of your hand.'

The man hardly paused; he went on down the street, walking fast; he felt no pain from the chip of ice in his breast.

Raven sat at an empty table in the Corner House near a marble pillar. He stared with distaste at the long list of sweet iced drinks, of *parfaits* and sundaes and *coupes* and splits. Somebody at the next table was eating brown bread and butter and drinking Horlick's. He wilted under Raven's gaze and put up his newspaper. One word 'Ultimatum' ran across the top line.

Mr Cholmondeley picked his way between the tables.

He was fat and wore an emerald ring. His wide square face fell in folds over his collar. He looked like a real-estate man, or perhaps a man more than usually successful in selling women's belts. He sat down at Raven's table and said, 'Good evening.'

Raven said, 'I thought you were never coming, Mr Cholmon-deley,' pronouncing every syllable.

'Chumley, my dear man, Chumley,' Mr Cholmondeley corrected him.

'It doesn't matter how it's pronounced. I don't suppose it's your own name.'

'After all I chose it,' Mr Cholmondeley said. His ring flashed under the great inverted bowls of light as he turned the pages of the menu. 'Have a *parfait*.'

'It's odd wanting to eat ice in this weather. You've only got to stay outside if you're hot. I don't want to waste any time, Mr Chol-mon-deley. Have you brought the money? I'm broke.'

Mr Cholmondeley said: 'They do a very good Maiden's Dream. Not to speak of Alpine Glow. Or the Knickerbocker Glory.'

'I haven't had a thing since Calais.'

'Give me the letter,' Mr Cholmondeley said. 'Thank you.' He told the waitress, 'I'll have an Alpine Glow with a glass of kümmel over it.'

'The money,' Raven said.

'Here in this case.'

'They are all fivers.'

'You can't expect to be paid two hundred in small change. And it's nothing to do with me,' Mr Cholmondeley said, 'I'm merely the agent.' His eyes softened as they rested on a Raspberry Split at the next table. He confessed wistfully to Raven, 'I've got a sweet tooth.'

'Don't you want to hear about it?' Raven said. 'The old woman . . .'

'Please, please,' Mr Cholmondeley said, 'I want to hear nothing. I'm just an agent. I take no responsibility. My clients . . .'

Raven twisted his hare-lip at him with sour contempt. 'That's a fine name for them.'

'How long the waitress is with my *parfait*,' Mr Cholmondeley complained. 'My clients are really quite the best people. The acts of violence – they regard them as war.'

'And I and the old man . . .' Raven said.

'Are in the front trench.' He began to laugh softly at his own humour; his great white open face was like a curtain on which you can throw grotesque images: a rabbit, a man with horns. His small eyes twinkled with pleasure at the mass of iced cream which was borne towards him in a tall glass. He said, 'You did your work very well, very neatly. They are quite satisfied with you. You'll be able to take a long holiday now.' He was fat, he was vulgar, he was false, but he gave an impression of great power as he sat there with the cream dripping from his mouth. He was prosperity, he was one of those who possessed things, but Raven possessed nothing but the contents of the wallet, the clothes he stood up in, the hare-lip, the automatic he should have left behind. He said, 'I'll be moving.'

'Good-bye, my man, good-bye,' Mr Cholmondeley said, sucking through a straw.

Raven rose and went. Dark and thin and made for destruction, he wasn't at ease among the little tables, among the bright fruit drinks. He went out into the Circus and up Shaftesbury Avenue. The shop windows were full of tinsel and hard red Christmas berries. It maddened him, the sentiment of it. His hands clenched in his pockets. He leant his face against

9

a modiste's window and jeered silently through the glass. A girl with a neat curved figure bent over a dummy. He fed his eyes contemptuously on her legs and hips; so much flesh, he thought, on sale in the Christmas window.

A kind of subdued cruelty drove him into the shop. He let his hare-lip loose on the girl when she came towards him with the same pleasure that he might have felt in turning a machine-gun on a picture gallery. He said, 'That dress in the window. How much?'

She said, 'Five guineas.' She wouldn't 'sir' him. His lip was like a badge of class. It revealed the poverty of parents who couldn't afford a clever surgeon.

He said, 'It's pretty, isn't it?'

She lisped at him genteelly, 'It's been vewwy much admired.'

'Soft. Thin. You'd have to take care of a dress like that, eh? Do for someone pretty and well off?'

She lied without interest, 'It's a model.' She was a woman, she knew all about it, she knew how cheap and vulgar the little shop really was.

'It's got class, eh?'

'Oh yes,' she said, catching the eye of a dago in a purple suit through the pane, 'it's got class.'

'All right,' he said. 'I'll give you five pounds for it.' He took a note from Mr Cholmondeley's wallet.

'Shall I pack it up?'

'No,' he said. 'The girl'll fetch it.' He grinned at her with his raw lip. 'You see, she's class. This the best dress you have?' and when she nodded and took the note away he said, 'It'll just suit Alice then.'

And so out into the Avenue with a little of his scorn expressed, out into Frith Street and round the corner into the German café where he kept a room. A shock awaited him there, a little fir tree in a tub hung with coloured glass, a crib. He said to the old man who owned the café, 'You believe in this? This junk?'

'Is there going to be war again?' the old man said. 'It's terrible what you read.'

'All this business of no room in the inn. They used to give us

10

plum pudding. A decree from Caesar Augustus. You see I know the stuff, I'm educated. They used to read it us once a year.'

'I have seen one war.'

'I hate the sentiment.'

'Well,' the old man said, 'it's good for business.'

Raven picked up the bambino. The cradle came with it all of a piece: cheap painted plaster. 'They put him on the spot, eh? You see I know the whole story. I'm educated.'

He went upstairs to his room. It hadn't been seen to: there was still dirty water in the basin and the ewer was empty. He remembered the fat man saying, 'Chumley, my man, Chumley. It's pronounced Chumley,' flashing his emerald ring. He called furiously, 'Alice,' over the banisters.

She came out of the next room, a slattern, one shoulder too high, with wisps of fair bleached hair over her face. She said, 'You needn't shout.'

He said, 'It's a pigsty in there. You can't treat me like that. Go in and clean it.' He hit her on the side of the head and she cringed away from him, not daring to say anything but, 'Who do you think you are?'

'Get on,' he said, 'you humpbacked bitch.' He began to laugh at her when she crouched over the bed. 'I've bought you a Christmas dress, Alice. Here's the receipt. Go and fetch it. It's a lovely dress. It'll suit you.'

'You think you're funny,' she said.

'I've paid a fiver for this joke. Hurry, Alice, or the shop'll be shut.' But she got her own back calling up the stairs, 'I won't look worse than what you do with that split lip.' Everyone in the house could hear her, the old man in the café, his wife in the parlour, the customers at the counter. He imagined their smiles. 'Go it, Alice, what an ugly pair you are.' He didn't really suffer; he had been fed the poison from boyhood drop by drop: he hardly noticed its bitterness now.

He went to the window and opened it and scratched on the sill. The kitten came to him, making little rushes along the drain pipe, feinting at his hand. 'You little bitch,' he said, 'you little bitch.' He took a small twopenny carton of cream out of

11

his overcoat pocket and spilt it in his soap-dish. She stopped playing and rushed at him with a tiny cry. He picked her up by the scruff and put her on top of his chest of drawers with the cream. She wriggled from his hand, she was no larger than the rat he'd trained in the home, but softer. He scratched her behind the ear and she struck back at him in a preoccupied way. Her tongue quivered on the surface of the milk.

Dinner-time, he told himself. With all that money he could go anywhere. He could have a slap-up meal at Simpson's with the business men; cut off the joint and any number of veg.

When he got by the public call-box in the dark corner below the stairs he caught his name 'Raven'. The old man said, 'He always has a room here. He's been away.'

'You,' a strange voice said, 'what's your name – Alice – show me his room. Keep an eye on the door, Saunders.'

Raven went on his knees inside the telephone-box. He left the door ajar because he never liked to be shut in. He couldn't see out, but he had no need to see the owner of the voice to recognize: police, plain clothes, the Yard accent. The man was so near that the floor of the box vibrated to his tread. Then he came down again. 'There's no one there. He's taken his hat and coat. He must have gone out.'

'He might have,' the old man said. 'He's a soft-walking sort of fellow.'

The stranger began to question them. 'What's he like?'

The old man and the girl both said in a breath, 'A hare-lip.'

'That's useful,' the detective said. 'Don't touch his room. I'll be sending a man round to take his fingerprints. What sort of a fellow is he?'

Raven could hear every word. He couldn't imagine what they were after. He knew he'd left no clues; he wasn't a man who imagined things; he knew. He carried the picture of that room and flat in his brain as clearly as if he had the photographs. They had nothing against him. It had been against orders to keep the automatic, but he could feel it now safe under his armpit. Besides, if they had picked up any clue they'd have stopped him at Dover. He listened to the voices with a dull anger; he wanted his dinner; he hadn't had a square meal for twenty-four hours, and now with two hundred pounds in his pocket he could buy anything, anything.

'I can believe it,' the old man said. 'Why, tonight he even made fun of my poor wife's crib.'

'A bloody bully,' the girl said. '*I* shan't be sorry when you've locked him up.'

He told himself with surprise: they hate me.

She said, 'He's ugly through and through. That lip of his. It gives you the creeps.'

'An ugly customer all right.'

'I wouldn't have him in the house,' the old man said. 'But he pays. You can't turn away someone who pays. Not in these days.'

'Has he friends?'

'You make me laugh,' Alice said. 'Him friends. What would he do with friends?'

He began to laugh quietly to himself on the floor of the little dark box: that's me they're talking about, me: staring up at the pane of glass with his hand on his automatic.

'You seem kind of bitter? What's he been doing to you? He was going to give you a dress, wasn't he?'

'Just his dirty joke.'

'You were going to take it, though.'

'You bet I wasn't. Do you think I'd take a present from him? I was going to sell it back to them and show him the money, and wasn't I going to laugh?'

He thought again with bitter interest: they hate me. If they open this door, I'll shoot the lot.

'I'd like to take a swipe at that lip of his. I'd laugh. I'd say I'd laugh.'

'I'll put a man,' the strange voice said, 'across the road. Tip him the wink if our man comes in.' The café door closed.

'Oh,' the old man said, 'I wish my wife was here. She would not miss this for ten shillings.'

'I'll give her a ring,' Alice said. 'She'll be chatting at Mason's. She can come right over and bring Mrs Mason too.

13

Let 'em all join in the fun. It was only a week ago Mrs Mason said she didn't want to see his ugly face in her shop again.'

'Yes, be a good girl, Alice. Give her a ring.'

Raven reached up his hand and took the bulb out of the fitment; he stood up and flattened himself against the wall of the box. Alice opened the door and shut herself in with him. He put his hand over her mouth before she had time to cry. He said, 'Don't you put the pennies in the box. I'll shoot if you do. I'll shoot if you call out. Do what I say.' He whispered in her ear. They were as close together as if they were in a single bed. He could feel her crooked shoulder pressed against his chest. He said, 'Lift the receiver. Pretend you're talking to the old woman. Go on. I don't care a damn if I shoot you. Say, hello, Frau Groener.'

'Hello, Frau Groener.'

'Spill the whole story.'

'They are after Raven.'

'Why?'

'That five-pound note. They were waiting at the shop.'

'What do you mean?'

'They'd got its number. It was stolen.'

He'd been double-crossed. His mind worked with mechanical accuracy like a ready-reckoner. You only had to supply it with the figures and it gave you the answer. He was possessed by a deep sullen rage. If Mr Cholmondeley had been in the box with him, he would have shot him: he wouldn't have cared a damn.

'Stolen from where?'

'You ought to know that.'

'Don't give me any lip. Where from?'

He didn't even know who Cholmondeley's employers were. It was obvious what had happened: they hadn't trusted him. They had arranged this so that he might be put away. A newsboy went by outside calling, 'Ultimatum. Ultimatum.' His mind registered the fact, but no more: it seemed to have nothing to do with him. He repeated. 'Where from?'

'I don't know. I don't remember.'

With the automatic stuck against her back he even tried to

14

plead with her. 'Remember, can't you? It's important. I didn't do it.'

'I bet you didn't,' she said bitterly into the unconnected 'phone.

'Give me a break. All I want you to do is remember.'

She said, 'On your life I won't.'

'I gave you that dress, didn't I?'

'You didn't. You tried to plant your money, that's all. You didn't know they'd circulated the numbers to every shop in town. We've even got them in the café.'

'If I'd done it, why should I want to know where they came from?'

'It'll be a bigger laugh than ever if you get jugged for something you didn't do.'

'Alice,' the old man called from the café, 'is she coming?'

'I'll give you ten pounds.'

'Phoney notes. No thank you, Mr Generosity.'

'Alice,' the old man called again; they could hear him coming along the passage.

'Justice,' he said bitterly, jabbing her between the ribs with the automatic.

'You don't need to talk about justice,' she said. 'Driving me like I was in prison. Hitting me when you feel like it. Spilling ash all over the floor. I've got enough to do with your slops. Milk in the soap-dish. Don't talk about justice.'

Pressed against him in the tiny dark box she suddenly came alive to him. He was so astonished that he forgot the old man till he had the door of the box open. He whispered passionately out of the dark, 'Don't say a word or I'll plug you.' He had them both out of the box in front of him. He said, 'Understand this. They aren't going to get me. I'm not going to prison. I don't care a damn if I plug one of you. I don't care if I hang. My father hanged ... what's good enough for him ... Get along in front of me up to my room. There's hell coming to somebody for this.'

When he had them there he locked the door. A customer was ringing the café bell over and over again. He turned on them. 'I've got a good mind to plug you. Telling them about

15

my hare-lip. Why can't you play fair?' He went to the window; he knew there was an easy way down – that was why he had chosen the room. The kitten caught his eye, prowling like a toy tiger in a cage up and down the edge of the chest of drawers, afraid to jump. He lifted her up and threw her on his bed; she tried to bite his finger as she went; then he got through on to the leads. The clouds were massing up across the moon, and the earth seemed to move with them, an icy barren globe, through the vast darkness.

4

Anne Crowder walked up and down the small room in her heavy tweed coat; she didn't want to waste a shilling on the gas meter, because she wouldn't get her shilling's worth before morning. She told herself, I'm lucky to have got that job. I'm glad to be going off to work again, but she wasn't convinced. It was eight now; they would have four hours together till midnight. She would have to deceive him and tell him she was catching the nine o'clock, not the five o'clock train, or he would be sending her back to bed early. He was like that. No romance. She smiled with tenderness and blew on her fingers.

The telephone at the bottom of the house was ringing. She thought it was the doorbell and ran to the mirror in the wardrobe. There wasn't enough light from the dull globe to tell her if her make-up would stand the brilliance of the Astoria Dance Hall. She began making up all over again; if she was pale he would take her home early.

The landlady stuck her head in at the door and said, 'It's your gentleman. On the 'phone.'

'On the 'phone?'

'Yes,' the landlady said, sidling in for a good chat, 'he sounded all of a jump. Impatient, I should say. Half barked my head off when I wished him good evening.'

'Oh,' she said despairingly, 'it's only his way. You mustn't mind him.'

'He's going to call off the evening, I suppose,' the landlady said. 'It's always the same. You girls who go travelling round never get a square deal. You said *Dick Whittington*, didn't you?'

'No, no, *Aladdin*.'

She pelted down the stairs. She didn't care a damn who saw her hurry. She said, 'Is that you, darling?' There was always something wrong with their telephone. She could hear his voice so hoarsely vibrating against her ear she could hardly realize it was his. He said, 'You've been ages. This is a public call-box. I've put in my last pennies. Listen, Anne, I can't be with you. I'm sorry. It's work. We're on to the man in that safe robbery I told you about. I shall be out all night on it. We've traced one of the notes.' His voice beat excitedly against her ear.

She said, 'Oh, that's fine, darling. I know you wanted . . .' but she couldn't keep it up. 'Jimmy,' she said, 'I shan't be seeing you again. For weeks.'

He said, 'It's tough, I know. I'd been thinking . . . Listen. You'd better not catch that early train, what's the point? There isn't a nine o'clock. I've been looking them up.'

'I know. I just said . . .'

'You'd better go to-night. Then you can get a rest before rehearsals. Midnight from Euston.'

'But I haven't packed . . .'

He took no notice. It was his favourite occupation planning things, making decisions. He said, 'If I'm near the station, I'll try . . .'

'Your two minutes up.'

He said, 'Oh hell, I've no coppers. Darling, I love you.'

She struggled to bring it out herself, but his name stood in the way, impeded her tongue. She could never bring it out without hesitation – 'Ji –' The line went dead on her. She thought bitterly: he oughtn't to go out without coppers. She thought: it's not right, cutting off a detective like that. Then she went back up the stairs; she wasn't crying; it was just as if somebody had died and left her alone and scared, scared of the new faces and the new job, the harsh provincial jokes, the fellows who were fresh, scared of herself, scared of not being able to remember clearly how good it was to be loved.

The landlady said, 'I just thought so. Why not come down and have a cup of tea and a good chat? It does you good to talk. Really good. A doctor said to me once it clears the lungs. Stands to reason, don't it? You can't help getting dust up and a good talk blows it out. I wouldn't bother to pack yet. There's hours and hours. My old man would never of died if he'd talked more. Stands to reason. It was something poisonous in his throat cut him off in his prime. If he'd talked more he'd have blown it out. It's better than spitting.'

5

The crime reporter couldn't make himself heard. He kept on trying to say to the chief reporter, 'I've got some stuff on that safe robbery.'

The chief reporter had had too much to drink. They'd all had too much to drink. He said, 'You can go home and read *The Decline and Fall* . . .'

The crime reporter was a young earnest man who didn't drink and didn't smoke; it shocked him when someone was sick in one of the telephone-boxes. He shouted at the top of his voice: 'They've traced one of the notes.'

'Write it down, write it down, old boy,' the chief reporter said, 'and then smoke it.'

'The man escaped – held up a girl – it's a terribly good story,' the earnest young man said. He had an Oxford accent; that was why they had made him crime reporter; it was the news-editor's joke.

'Go home and read Gibbon.'

The earnest young man caught hold of someone's sleeve. 'What's the matter? Are you all crazy? Isn't there going to be any paper or what?'

'War in forty-eight hours,' somebody bellowed at him.

'But this is a wonderful story I've got. He held up a girl and an old man, climbed out of a window . . .'

'Go home. There won't be any room for it.'

'They've killed the annual report of the Kensington Kitten Club.'

'No Round the Shops.'

'They've made the Limehouse Fire a News in Brief.'

'Go home and read Gibbon.'

'He got clean away with a policeman watching the front door. The Flying Squad's out. He's armed. The police are taking revolvers. It's a lovely story.'

The chief reporter said, 'Armed! Go away and put your head in a glass of milk. We'll all be armed in a day or two. They've published their evidence. It's clear as daylight a Serb shot him. Italy's supporting the ultimatum. They've got forty-eight hours to climb down. If you want to buy armament shares hurry and make your fortune.'

'You'll be in the army this day week,' somebody said.

'Oh no,' the young man said, 'no, I won't be that. You see I'm a pacifist.'

The man who was sick in the telephone-box said, 'I'm going home. There wouldn't be any room in the paper if the Bank of England was blown up.'

A little thin piping voice said, '*My* copy's going in.'

'I tell you there isn't any room.'

'There'll be room for mine. Gas Masks for All. Special Air Raid Practices for Civilians in every town of more than fifty thousand inhabitants.' He giggled.

'The funny thing is – it's – it's – ' but nobody ever heard what it was: a boy opened the door and flung them in a pull of the middle page: damp letters on a damp grey sheet; the headlines came off on the hands: 'Yugoslavia Asks for Time. Adriatic Fleet at War Stations. Paris Rioters Break into Italian Embassy.' Everyone was suddenly quite quiet as an aeroplane went by; driving low overhead through the dark, heading south, a scarlet tail-lamp, pale transparent wings in the moonlight. They watched it through the great glass ceiling, and suddenly nobody wanted to have another drink.

The chief reporter said, 'I'm tired. I'm going to bed.'

'Shall I follow up this story?' the crime reporter asked.

'If it'll make you happy, but *That's* the only news from now on.'

They stared up at the glass ceiling, the moon, the empty sky.

6

The station clock marked three minutes to midnight. The ticket collector at the barrier said, 'There's room in the front.'

'A friend's seeing me off,' Anne Crowder said. 'Can't I get in at this end and go up front when we start?'

'They've locked the doors.'

She looked desperately past him. They were turning out the lights in the buffet; no more trains from that platform.

'You'll have to hurry, miss.'

The poster of an evening paper caught her eye and as she ran down the train, looking back as often as she was able, she couldn't help remembering that war might be declared before they met again. He would go to it; he always did what other people did, she told herself with irritation, although she knew it was his reliability she loved. She wouldn't have loved him if he'd been eccentric, had his own opinions about things; she lived too closely to thwarted genius, to second touring company actresses who thought they ought to be Cochran stars, to admire difference. She wanted her man to be ordinary, she wanted to be able to know what he'd say next.

A line of lamp-struck faces went by her; the train was full, so full that in the first-class carriages you saw strange shy awkward people who were not at ease in the deep seats, who feared the ticket-collector would turn them out. She gave up the search for a third-class carriage, opened a door, dropped her *Woman and Beauty* on the only seat and struggled back to the window over legs and protruding suitcases. The engine was getting up steam, the smoke blew back up the platform, it was difficult to see as far as the barrier.

A hand pulled at her sleeve. 'Excuse me,' a fat man said, 'if you've quite finished with that window. I want to buy some chocolate.'

She said, 'Just one moment, please. Somebody's seeing me off.'

'He's not here. It's too late. You can't monopolize the window like that. I must have some chocolate.' He swept her on one side and waved an emerald ring under the light. She tried to look over his shoulder to the barrier; he almost filled the window. He called 'Boy, Boy!' waving the emerald ring. He said, 'What chocolate have you got? No, not Motorist's, not Mexican. Something sweet.'

Suddenly through a crack she saw Mather. He was past the barrier, he was coming down the train looking for her, looking in all the third-class carriages, running past the first-class. She implored the fat man: 'Please, please do let me come. I can see my friend.'

'In a moment. In a moment. Have you Nestlé? Give me a shilling packet.'

'Please let me.'

'Haven't you anything smaller,' the boy said, 'than a ten-shilling note?'

Mather went by, running past the first-class. She hammered on the window, but he didn't hear her, among the whistles and the beat of trolley wheels, the last packing cases rolling into the van. Doors slammed, a whistle blew, the train began to move.

'Please. Please.'

'I must get my change,' the fat man said, and the boy ran beside the carriage counting the shillings into his palm. When she got to the window and leant out they were past the platform, she could only see a small figure on a wedge of asphalt who couldn't see her. An elderly woman said, 'You oughtn't to lean out like that. It's dangerous.'

She trod on their toes getting back to her seat, she felt unpopularity well up all around her, everyone was thinking, 'She oughtn't to be in the carriage. What's the good of our paying first-class fares when . . .' But she wouldn't cry; she was fortified by all the conventional remarks which came automatically to her mind about spilt milk and it will be all the same in fifty years. Nevertheless she noted with deep dislike on the label dangling from the fat man's suitcase his destination, which was the same as hers, Nottwich. He sat opposite her with the *Passing*

Show and the *Evening News* and the *Financial Times* on his lap eating sweet milk chocolate.

Chapter 2

1

RAVEN walked with his handkerchief over his lip across Soho Square, Oxford Street, up Charlotte Street. It was dangerous but not so dangerous as showing his hare-lip. He turned to the left and then to the right into a narrow street where big-breasted women in aprons called across to each other and a few solemn children scouted up the gutter. He stopped by a door with a brass plate, Dr Alfred Yogel on the second floor, on the first floor the North American Dental Company. He went upstairs and rang the bell. There was a smell of greens from below and somebody had drawn a naked torso in pencil on the wall.

A woman in nurse's uniform opened the door, a woman with a mean lined face and untidy grey hair. Her uniform needed washing; it was spotted with grease-marks and what might have been blood or iodine. She brought with her a harsh smell of chemicals and disinfectants. When she saw Raven holding his handkerchief over his mouth she said, 'The dentist's on the floor below.'

'I want to see Dr Yogel.'

She looked him over closely, suspiciously, running her eyes down his dark coat. 'He's busy.'

'I can wait.'

One naked globe swung behind her head in the dingy passage. 'He doesn't generally see people as late as this.'

'I'll pay for the trouble,' Raven said. She judged him with just the same appraising stare as the doorkeeper at a shady nightclub. She said, 'You can come in.' He followed her into a waiting-room: the same bare globe, a chair, a round oak table splashed with dark paint. She shut him in and he heard her voice start in the next room. It went on and on. He picked up the only magazine, *Good Housekeeping* of eighteen months

22

back, and began mechanically to read: 'Bare walls are very popular today, perhaps one picture to give the necessary point of colour . . .'

The nurse opened the door and jerked her hand. 'He'll see you.' Dr Yogel was washing his hands in a fixed basin behind his long yellow desk and swivel chair. There was no other furniture in the room except a kitchen chair, a cabinet and a long couch. His hair was jet-black; it looked as if it had been dyed, and there was not much of it; it was plastered in thin strands across the scalp. When he turned he showed a plump hard bonhomous face, a thick sensual mouth. He said, 'And what can we do for you?' You felt he was more accustomed to deal with women than with men. The nurse stood harshly behind waiting.

Raven lowered his handkerchief. He said, 'Can you do anything about this lip quickly?'

Dr Yogel came up and prodded it with a little fat forefinger. 'I'm not a surgeon.'

Raven said, 'I can pay.'

Dr Yogel said, 'It's a job for a surgeon. It's not in my line at all.'

'I know that,' Raven said, and caught the quick flicker of glances between the nurse and Dr Yogel. Dr Yogel lifted up the lip on each side; his fingernails were not quite clean. He watched Raven carefully and said, 'If you come back tomorrow at ten . . .' His breath smelt faintly of brandy.

'No,' Raven said. 'I want it done now at once.'

'Ten pounds,' Dr Yogel said quickly.

'All right.'

'In cash.'

'I've got it with me.'

Dr Yogel sat down at his desk. 'And now if you'll give me your name . . .'

'You don't need to know my name.'

Dr Yogel said gently: 'Any name . . .'

'Chumley, then.'

'CHOLMO . . .'

'No. Spell it CHUMLEY.'

23

Dr Yogel filled up a slip of paper and handed it to the nurse. She went outside and closed the door behind her. Dr Yogel went to the cabinet and brought out a tray of knives. Raven said, 'The light's bad.'

'I'm used to it,' Dr Yogel said. 'I've a good eye.' But as he held up a knife to the light his hand very slightly trembled. He said softly, 'Lie down on the couch, old man.'

Raven lay down. He said, 'I knew a girl who came to you. Name of Page. She said you did her trick fine.'

Dr Yogel said, 'She oughtn't to talk about it.'

'Oh,' Raven said, 'you are safe with me. I don't go back on a fellow who treats me right.' Dr Yogel took a case like a portable gramophone out of his cabinet and carried it over to the couch. He produced a long tube and a mask. He smiled gently and said, 'We don't run to anaesthetists here, old man.'

'Stop,' Raven said, 'you're not going to give me gas.'

'It would hurt without it, old man,' Dr Yogel said, approaching with the mask, 'it would hurt like hell.'

Raven sat up and pushed the mask aside. 'I won't have it,' he said, 'not gas. I've never had gas. I've never passed out yet. I like to see what's going on.'

Dr Yogel laughed gently and pulled at Raven's lip in a playful way. 'Better get used to it, old man. We'll all be gassed in a day or two.'

'What do you mean?'

'Well, it looks like war, doesn't it?' Dr Yogel said, talking rapidly and unwinding more tube, turning screws in a soft, shaking, inexorable way. 'The Serbs can't shoot a Minister of War like that and get away with it. Italy's ready to come in. And the French are warming up. We'll be in it ourselves inside a week.'

Raven said, 'All that because an old man . . .' He explained, 'I haven't read the papers.'

'I wish I'd known beforehand,' Dr Yogel said, making conversation, fixing his cylinder. 'I'd have made a fortune in munition shares. They've gone up to the sky, old man. Now lean back. It won't take a moment.' He again approached the mask. He said, 'You've only got to breathe deep, old man.'

Raven said, 'I told you I wouldn't have gas. Get that straight. You can cut me about as much as you like, but I won't have gas.'

'It's very silly of you, old man,' Dr Yogel said. 'It's going to hurt.' He went back to the cabinet and again picked up a knife, but his hand shook more than ever. He was frightened of something. And then Raven heard from outside the tiny tinkle a telephone makes when the receiver is lifted. He jumped up from the couch; it was bitterly cold, but Dr Yogel was sweating; he stood by the cabinet holding his surgical knife, unable to say a word. Raven said, 'Keep quiet. Don't speak.' He flung the door suddenly open and there was the nurse in the little dim hall with the telephone at her ear. Raven stood sideways so that he could keep his eye on both of them. 'Put back that receiver,' he said. She put it back, watching him with her little mean conscienceless eyes. He said furiously, 'You double-crossing – ' He said, 'I've got a mind to shoot you both.'

'Old man,' Dr Yogel said, 'old man. You've got it all wrong,' but the nurse said nothing. She had all the guts in their partnership, she was toughened by a long career of illegalities, by not a few deaths. Raven said, 'Get away from that 'phone.' He took the knife out of Dr Yogel's hand and hacked and sawed at the telephone wire. He was touched by something he had never felt before: a sense of injustice stammered on his tongue. These people were of his own kind; they didn't belong inside the legal borders; for the second time in one day he had been betrayed by the lawless. He had always been alone, but never so alone as this. The telephone wire gave. He wouldn't speak another word for fear his temper might master him and he might shoot. This wasn't the time for shooting. He went downstairs in a dark loneliness of spirit, his handkerchief over his face, and from the little wireless shop at the street corner heard, 'We have received the following notice . . .' The same voice followed him down the street from the open windows of the little impoverished homes, the suave expressionless voice from every house: 'New Scotland Yard. Wanted. James Raven. Aged about twenty-eight. Easily recognizable from his hare-lip. A little above the middle height. Last seen wearing a dark overcoat and a black felt hat. Any information leading to the arrest ...' Raven walked away from the voice, out into the traffic of Oxford Street, bearing south.

There were too many things he didn't understand: this war they were talking of, why he had been double-crossed. He wanted to find Cholmondeley. Cholmondeley was of no account, he was acting under orders, but if he found Cholmondeley he could squeeze out of him ... He was harassed, hunted, lonely, he bore with him a sense of great injustice and a curious pride. Going down the Charing Cross Road, past the music shops and the rubber goods shops, he swelled with it: after all it needed a man to start a war as he was doing.

He had no idea where Cholmondeley lived; the only clue he had was an accommodation address. It occurred to him there was a faint chance that if he watched the small shop to which Cholmondeley's letters were sent he might see him: a very faint chance, but it was strengthened by the fact of his escape. Already the news was on the air, it would be in the evening papers, Cholmondeley might want to clear out of the way for a while, and there was just a possibility that before he went he would call for letters. But that depended on whether he used that address for other letters besides Raven's. Raven wouldn't have believed there was one chance in a thousand if it were not that Cholmondeley was a fool. You didn't have to eat many ices with him to learn that.

The shop was in a side street opposite a theatre. It was a tiny one-roomed place in which was sold nothing above the level of *Film Fun* and *Breezy Stories*. There were postcards from Paris in sealed envelopes, American and French magazines, and books on flagellation in paper jackets for which the pimply youth or his sister, whoever was in the shop, charged twenty shillings, fifteen shillings back if you returned the book.

It wasn't an easy shop to watch. A woman policeman kept an eye on the tarts at the corner and opposite there was just the long blank theatre wall, the gallery door. Against the wall you were as exposed as a fly against wall-paper, unless, he thought, waiting for the lights to flash green and let him pass, unless – the play was popular.

And it was popular. Although the doors wouldn't open for another hour, there was quite a long queue for the gallery. Raven hired a camp stool with almost his last small change and sat down. The shop was only just across the way. The youth wasn't in charge, but his sister. She sat there just inside the door in an old green dress that might have been stripped from one of the billiard tables in the pub next door. She had a square face that could never have looked young, a squint that her heavy steel spectacles did nothing to disguise. She might have been any age from twenty to forty, a parody of a woman, dirty and depraved, crouched under the most lovely figures, the most beautiful vacant faces the smut photographers could hire.

Raven watched: with a handkerchief over his mouth, one of sixty in the gallery queue, he watched. He saw a young man stop and eye *Plaisirs de Paris* furtively and hurry on; he saw an old man go into the shop and come out again with a brown-paper parcel. Somebody from the queue went across and bought cigarettes.

An elderly woman in pince-nez sat beside him. She said over her shoulder, 'That's why I always liked Galsworthy. He was a gentleman. You knew where you were, if you know what I mean.'

'It always seems to be the Balkans.'

'I liked *Loyalties*.'

'He was such a humane man.'

A man stood between Raven and the shop holding up a little square of paper. He put it in his mouth and held up another square. A tart ambled by on the other side of the road and said something to the girl in the shop. The man put the second piece of paper in his mouth.

'They say the fleet . . .'

'He makes you *think*. That's what I like.'

Raven thought: if he doesn't come before the queue begins to move I'll have to go.

'Anything in the papers?'

27

'Nothing new.'

The man in the road took the papers out of his mouth and began to tear them and fold them and tear them. Then he opened them out and it was a paper St George's Cross, blowing flimsily in the cold wind.

'He used to subscribe heavily to the Anti-Vivisection Society. Mrs Milbanke told me. She showed me one of his cheques with his signature.'

'He was really humane.'

'And a *really* great writer.'

A girl and a boy who looked happy applauded the man with the paper flag and he took off his cap and began to come down the queue collecting coppers. A taxi drew up at the end of the street and a man got out. It was Cholmondeley. He went into the bookshop and the girl got up and followed him. Raven counted his money. He had two and sixpence and a hundred and ninety-five pounds in stolen notes he could do nothing with. He sank his face deeper in his handkerchief and got up hurriedly like a man taken ill. The paper-tearer reached him, held out his cap, and Raven saw with envy the odd dozen pennies, a sixpence, a threepenny bit. He would have given a hundred pounds for the contents of that cap. He pushed the man roughly and walked away.

At the other end of the road there was a taxi rank. He stood there bowed against the wall, a sick man, until Cholmondeley came out.

He said, 'Follow that taxi,' and sank back with a sense of relief, moving back up Charing Cross Road, Tottenham Court Road, the Euston Road where all the bicycles had been taken in for the night and the second-hand car dealers from that end of Great Portland Street were having a quick one, before they bore their old school ties and their tired tarnished bonhomie back to their lodgings. He wasn't used to being hunted; this was better: to hunt.

Nor did the meter fail him. He had a shilling to spare when Mr Cholmondeley led the way in by the Euston war memorial to the great smoky entrance and rashly he gave it to the driver: rashly because there was a long wait ahead of him with noth-

28

ing but his hundred and ninety-five pounds to buy a sandwich with. For Mr Cholmondeley led the way with two porters behind him to the left-luggage counter, depositing there three suitcases, a portable typewriter, a bag of golf clubs, a small attaché case and a hat-box. Raven heard him ask from which platform the midnight train went.

Raven sat down in the great hall beside a model of Stephenson's 'Rocket'. He had to think. There was only one midnight train. If Cholmondeley was going to report, his employers were somewhere in the smoky industrial north; for there wasn't a stop before Nottwich. But again he was faced with his wealthy poverty; the numbers of the notes had been circulated everywhere; the booking clerks would almost certainly have them. The trail for a moment seemed to stop at the barrier to Number 3 platform.

But slowly a plan did form in Raven's mind as he sat under the 'Rocket' among the bundles and crumbs of sandwich-eaters. He *had* a chance, for it was possible that the ticket-collectors on the trains had not been given the numbers. It was the kind of loophole the authorities might forget. There remained, of course, this objection: that the note would eventually give away his presence on the north-bound train. He would have to take a ticket to the limit of the journey and it would be easy enough to trace him to the town where he alighted. The hunt would follow him, but there might be a time lag of half a day in which his own hunt could get nearer to *his* prey. Raven could never realize other people; they didn't seem to him to live in the same way as he lived; and though he bore a grudge against Mr Cholmondeley, hated him enough to kill him, he couldn't imagine Mr Cholmondeley's own fears and motives. He was the greyhound and Mr Cholmondeley only the mechanical hare; but in this case the greyhound was chased in its turn by another mechanical hare.

He was hungry, but he couldn't risk changing a note; he hadn't even a copper to pass him into the lavatory. After a while he got up and walked the station to keep warm among the frozen smuts, the icy turbulence. At eleven-thirty he saw from behind a chocolate machine Mr Cholmondeley fetch his luggage, followed him at a distance until he passed through the barrier and down the length of the lit train. The Christmas crowds had begun; they were different from the ordinary crowd, you had a sense of people going home. Raven stood back in the shadow of an indicator and heard their laughter and calls, saw smiling faces raised under the great lamps; the pillars of the station had been decorated to look like enormous crackers. The suitcases were full of presents, a girl had a sprig of holly in her coat, high up under the roof dangled a bough of mistletoe lit by flood-lamps. When Raven moved he could feel the automatic rubbing beneath his arm.

At two minutes to twelve Raven ran forward, the engine smoke was blowing back along the platform, the doors were slammed. He said to the collector at the barrier: 'I haven't time to get a ticket. I'll pay on the train.'

He tried the first carriages. They were full and locked. A porter shouted to him to go up front, and he ran on. He was only just in time. He couldn't find a seat, but stood in the corridor with his face pressed against the pane to hide his hare-lip, watching London recede from him: a lit signal box and inside a saucepan of cocoa heating on the stove, a signal going green, a long line of blackened houses standing rigid against the cold-starred sky; watching because there was nothing else to do to keep his lip hidden, but like a man watching something he loves slide back from him out of his reach.

2

Mather walked back up the platform. He was sorry to have missed Anne, but it wasn't important. He would be seeing her again in a few weeks. It was not that his love was any less than hers but that his mind was more firmly anchored. He was on a job; if he pulled it off, he might be promoted; they could marry. Without any difficulty at all he wiped his mind clear of her.

Saunders was waiting on the other side of the barrier. Mather said, 'We'll be off.'

'Where next?'

'Charlie's.'

They sat in the back seat of a car and dived back into the narrow dirty streets behind the station. A prostitute put her tongue out at them. Saunders said, 'What about J-J-J-Joe's?'

'I don't think so, but we'll try it.'

The car drew up two doors away from a fried-fish shop. A man sitting beside the driver got down and waited for orders. 'Round to the back, Frost,' Mather said. He gave him two minutes and then hammered on the door of the fish shop. A light went on inside and Mather could see through the window the long counter, the stock of old newspapers, the dead grill. The door opened a crack. He put his foot in and pushed it wide. He said, ''Evening, Charlie,' looking round.

'Mr Mather,' Charlie said. He was as fat as an eastern eunuch and swayed his great hips coyly when he walked like a street woman.

'I want to talk to you,' Mather said.

'Oh, I'm delighted,' Charlie said. 'Step this way, Mr Mather. I was just off to bed.'

'I bet you were,' Mather said. 'Got a full house down there tonight?'

'Oh, Mr Mather. What a wag you are. Just one or two Oxford boys.'

'Listen. I'm looking for a fellow with a hare-lip. About twenty-eight years old.'

'He's not here.'

'Dark coat, black hat.'

'I don't know him, Mr Mather.'

'I'd like to take a look over your basement.'

'Of course, Mr Mather. There are just one or two Oxford boys. Do you mind if I go down first? Just to introduce you, Mr Mather.' He led the way down the stone stairs. 'It's safer.'

'I can look after myself,' Mather said. 'Saunders, stay in the shop.'

Charlie opened a door. 'Now, boys, don't be scared. Mr Mather's a friend of mine.' They faced him in an ominous line at the end of the room, the Oxford boys, with their broken noses and their cauliflower ears, the dregs of pugilism.

''Evening,' Mather said. The tables had been swept clear of drink and cards. He plodded down the last steps into the stone-floored room. Charlie said, 'Now, boys, you don't need to get scared.'

'Why don't you get a few Cambridge boys into this club?' Mather said.

'Oh, what a wag you are, Mr Mather.'

They followed him with their eyes as he crossed the floor; they wouldn't speak to him; he was the Enemy. They didn't have to be diplomats like Charlie, they could show their hatred. They watched every move he made. Mather said, 'What are you keeping in that cupboard?' Their eyes followed him as he went towards the cupboard door.

Charlie said, 'Give the boys a chance, Mr Mather. They don't mean any harm. This is one of the best-run clubs – ' Mather pulled open the door of the cupboard. Four women fell into the room. They were like toys turned from the same mould with their bright brittle hair. Mather laughed. He said, 'The joke's on me. That's a thing I never expected in one of your clubs, Charlie. Good night all.' The girls got up and dusted themselves. None of the men spoke.

'Really, Mr Mather,' Charlie said, blushing all the way up-stairs. 'I do wish this hadn't happened in my club. I don't know what you'll think. But the boys didn't mean any harm. Only you know how it is. They don't like to leave their sisters alone.'

'What's that?' Saunders said at the top of the stairs.

'So I said they could bring their sisters and the dear girls sit around . . .'

'What's that?' Saunders said. 'G-g-g-girls?'

'Don't forget, Charlie,' Mather said. 'Fellow with a hare-lip. You'd better let me know if he turns up here. You don't want your club closed.'

'Is there a reward?'

'There'd be a reward for you all right.'

They got back into the car. 'Pick up Frost,' Mather said.

'Then Joe's.' He took his notebook out and crossed off another name. 'And after Joe's six more – '

'We shan't be f-f-finished till three,' Saunders said.

'Routine. He's out of town by now. But sooner or later he'll cash another note.'

'Finger-prints?'

'Plenty. There was enough on his soap-dish to stock an album. Must be a clean sort of fellow. Oh, he doesn't stand a chance. It's just a question of time.'

The lights of Tottenham Court Road flashed across their faces. The windows of the big shops were still lit up. 'That's a nice bedroom suite,' Mather said.

'It's a lot of f-fuss, isn't it,' Saunders said. 'About a few notes, I mean. When there may be a w-w-w-w . . .'

Mather said, 'If those fellows over there had our efficiency there mightn't be a war. We'd have caught the murderer by now. Then all the world could see whether the Serbs . . . Oh,' he said softly, as Heal's went by, a glow of soft colour, a gleam of steel, allowing himself about the furthest limits of his fancy, 'I'd like to be tackling a job like that. A murderer with all the world watching.'

'Just a few n-notes,' Saunders complained.

'No, you are wrong,' Mather said, 'it's the routine which counts. Five-pound notes today. It may be something better next time. But it's the routine which matters. That's how I see it,' he said, letting his anchored mind stretch the cable as far as it could go as they drove round St Giles's Circus and on towards Seven Dials, stopping every hole the thief might take one by one. 'It doesn't matter to me if there is a war. When it's over I'll still want to be going on with this job. It's the organization I like. I always want to be on the side that organizes. On the other you get your geniuses, of course, but you get all your shabby tricksters, you get all the cruelty and the selfishness and the pride.'

You got it all, except the pride, in Joe's where they looked up from their bare tables and let him run the place through, the extra aces back in the sleeve, the watered spirit out of sight, facing him each with his individual mark of cruelty and

33

egotism. Even pride was perhaps there in a corner, bent over a sheet of paper, playing an endless game of double noughts and crosses against himself because there was no one else in that club he deigned to play with.

Mather again crossed off a name and drove south-west towards Kennington. All over London there were other cars doing the same: he was part of an organization. He did not want to be a leader, he did not even wish to give himself up to some God-sent fanatic of a leader, he liked to feel that he was one of thousands more or less equal working for a concrete end – not equality of opportunity, not government by the people or by the richest or by the best, but simply to do away with crime which meant uncertainty. He liked to be certain, to feel that one day quite inevitably he would marry Anne Crowder.

The loudspeaker in the car said: 'Police cars proceed back to the King's Cross area for intensified search. Raven driven to Euston Station about seven p.m. May not have left by train.' Mather leant across to the driver, 'Right about and back to Euston.' They were by Vauxhall. Another police car came past them through the Vauxhall tunnel. Mather raised his hand. They followed it back over the river. The flood-lit clock on the Shell-Mex building showed half-past one. The light was on in the clock tower at Westminster: Parliament was having an all-night sitting as the opposition fought their losing fight against mobilization.

It was six o'clock in the morning when they drove back towards the Embankment. Saunders was asleep. He said, 'That's fine.' He was dreaming that he had no impediment in his speech; he had an independent income; he was drinking champagne with a girl; everything was fine. Mather totted things up on his notebook; he said to Saunders, 'He got on a train for sure. I'd bet you – ' Then he saw that Saunders was asleep and slipped a rug across his knees and began to consider again. They turned in at the gates of New Scotland Yard.

Mather saw a light in the chief inspector's room and went up.

'Anything to report?' Cusack asked.

34

'Nothing. He must have caught a train, sir.'

'We've got a little to go on at this end. Raven followed somebody to Euston. We are trying to find the driver of the first car. And another thing, he went to a doctor called Yogel to try and get his lip altered. Offered some more of those notes. Still handy too with that automatic. We've got him taped. As a kid he was sent to an industrial school. He's been smart enough to keep out of our way since. I can't think why he's broken out like this. A smart fellow like that. He's blazing a trail.'

'Has he much money besides the notes?'

'We don't think so. Got an idea, Mather?'

Colour was coming into the sky above the city. Cusack switched off his table-lamp and left the room grey. 'I think I'll go to bed.'

'I suppose,' Mather said, 'that all the booking offices have the numbers of those notes?'

'Every one.'

'It looks to me,' Mather said, 'that if you had nothing but phoney notes and wanted to catch an express – '

'How do we know it was an express?'

'Yes, I don't know why I said that, sir. Or perhaps – if it was a slow train with plenty of stops near London, surely someone would have reported by this time – '

'You may be right.'

'Well, if I wanted to catch an express, I'd wait till the last minute and pay on the train. I don't suppose the ticket collectors carry the numbers.'

'I think you're right. Are you tired, Mather?'

'No.'

'Well, I am. Would you stay here and ring up Euston and King's Cross and St Pancras, all of them? Make a list of all the outgoing expresses after seven. Ask them to telephone up the line to all stations to check up on any man travelling without a ticket who paid on the train. We'll soon find out where he stepped off. Good night, Mather.'

'Good morning, sir.' He liked to be accurate.

There was no dawn that day in Nottwich. Fog lay over the city like a night sky with no stars. The air in the streets was clear. You have only to imagine that it was night. The first tram crawled out of its shed and took the steel track down towards the market. An old piece of newspaper blew up against the door of the Royal Theatre and flattened out. In the streets on the outskirts of Nottwich nearest the pits an old man plodded by with a pole tapping at the windows. The stationer's window in the High Street was full of Prayer Books and Bibles: a printed card remained among them, a relic of Armistice Day, like the old drab wreath of Haig poppies by the War Memorial: 'Look up, and swear by the slain of the war that you'll never forget.' Along the line a signal lamp winked green in the dark day and the lit carriages drew slowly in past the cemetery, the glue factory, over the wide tidy cement-lined river. A bell began to ring from the Roman Catholic cathedral. A whistle blew.

The packed train moved slowly into another morning: smuts were thick on all the faces, everyone had slept in his clothes. Mr Cholmondeley had eaten too many sweets; his teeth needed cleaning; his breath was sweet and stuffy. He put his head into the corridor and Raven at once turned his back and stared out at the sidings, the trucks heaped with local coal; a smell of bad fish came in from the glue factory. Mr Cholmondeley dived back across the carriage to the other side trying to make out at which platform the train was drawing in. He said: 'Excuse me,' trampling on the feet; Anne smiled softly to herself and hacked his ankle. Mr Cholmondeley glared at her. She said: 'I'm sorry,' and began to mend her face with her tissues and her powder, to bring it up to standard, so that she could bear the thought of the Royal Theatre, the little dressing-rooms and the oil-heating, the rivalry and the scandals.

'If you'll let me by,' Mr Cholmondeley said fiercely, 'I'm getting down here.'

Raven saw his ghost in the window-pane getting down. But

he didn't dare follow him closely. It was almost as if a voice blown over many foggy miles, over the long swelling fields of the hunting counties, the villa'd suburbs creeping up to town, had spoken to him: 'any man travelling without a ticket,' he thought, with the slip of white paper the collector had given him in his hand. He opened the door and watched the passengers flow by him to the barrier. He needed time, and the paper in his hand would so quickly identify him. He needed time, and he realized now that he wouldn't have even so much as a twelve-hour start. They would visit every boarding house, every lodging in Nottwich; there was nowhere for him to stay.

Then it was that the idea struck him, by the slot machine on No. 2 arrival platform, which thrust him finally into other people's lives, broke the world in which he walked alone.

Most of the passengers had gone now, but one girl waited for a returning porter by the buffet door. He went up to her and said, 'Can I help and carry your bags?'

'Oh, if you would,' she said. He stood with his head a little bent, so that she mightn't see his lip.

'What about a sandwich?' he said. 'It's been a hard journey.'

'Is it open,' she said, 'this early?'

He tried the door. 'Yes, it's open.'

'Is it an invitation?' she said. 'You're standing treat?'

He gazed at her with faint astonishment: her smile, the small neat face with the eyes rather too wide apart; he was more used to the absent-minded routine endearments of prostitutes than to this natural friendliness, this sense of rather lost and desperate amusement. He said, 'Oh yes. It's on me.' He carried the bags inside and hammered on the counter. 'What'll you have?' he said. In the pale light of the electric globe he kept his back to her; he didn't want to scare her yet.

'There's a rich choice,' she said. 'Bath buns, penny buns, last year's biscuits, ham sandwiches. I'd like a ham sandwich and a cup of coffee. Or will that leave you broke? If so, leave out the coffee.'

He waited till the girl behind the counter had gone again, till the other's mouth was full of sandwich so that she couldn't have screamed if she'd tried. Then he turned his face on her. He was disconcerted when she showed no repulsion, but smiled as well as she could with her mouth full. He said, 'I want your ticket. The police are after me. I'll do anything to get your ticket.'

She swallowed the bread in her mouth and began to cough. She said, 'For God's sake, hit me on the back.' He nearly obeyed her; she'd got him rattled; he wasn't used to normal life and it upset his nerve. He said, 'I've got a gun,' and added lamely, 'I'll give you this in return.' He laid the paper on the counter and she read it with interest between the coughs. 'First class. All the way to – Why, I'll be able to get a refund on this. I call that a fine exchange, but why the gun?'

He said: 'The ticket.'

'Here.'

'Now,' he said, 'you are going out of the station with me. I'm not taking any chances.'

'Why not eat your ham sandwich first?'

'Be quiet,' he said. 'I haven't the time to listen to your jokes.'

She said, 'I like he-men. My name's Anne. What's yours?' The train outside whistled, the carriages began to move, a long line of light going back into the fog, the steam blew along the platform. Raven's eyes left her for a moment; she raised her cup and dashed the hot coffee at his face. The pain drove him backwards with his hands to his eyes; he moaned like an animal; this was pain. This was what the old War Minister had felt, the woman secretary, his father when the trap sprang and the neck took the weight. His right hand felt for the automatic, his back was against the door; people were driving him to do things, to lose his head. He checked himself; with an effort he conquered the agony of the burns, the agony which drove him to kill. He said, 'I've got you covered. Pick up those cases. Go out in front of me with that paper.'

She obeyed him, staggering under the weight. The ticket collector said: 'Changed your mind? This would have taken you to Edinburgh. Do you want to break the journey?'

'Yes,' she said, 'yes. That's it.' He took out a pencil and

began to write on the paper. An idea came to Anne: she wanted him to remember her and the ticket. There might be inquiries. 'No,' she said, 'I'll give it up. I don't think I'll be going on. I'll stay here,' and she went out through the barrier, thinking: he won't forget that in a hurry.

The long street ran down between the small dusty houses. A milk float clattered round a corner out of sight. She said, 'Well, can I go now?'

'You think me a fool,' he said bitterly. 'Keep on walking.'

'You might take one of these bags.' She dropped one in the road and went on; he had to pick it up. It was heavy, he carried it in his left hand, he needed his right for the automatic.

She said, 'This isn't taking us into Nottwich. We ought to have turned right at the corner.'

'I know where I'm going.'

'I wish I did.'

The little houses went endlessly on under the fog. It was very early. A woman came to the door and took in the milk. Through a window Anne saw a man shaving. She wanted to scream to him, but he might have been in another world; she could imagine his stupid stare, the slow working of the brain before he realized anything was wrong. On they went, Raven a step behind. She wondered if he were bluffing her; he must be wanted for something very serious if he was really ready to shoot.

She spoke her thoughts aloud, 'Is it murder?' and the lapse of her flippancy, the whispered fear, came to Raven like something familiar, friendly: he was used to fear. It had lived inside him for twenty years. It was normality he couldn't cope with. He answered her without strain, 'No, I'm not wanted for that.'

She challenged him, 'Then you wouldn't dare to shoot,' but he had the answer pat, the answer which never failed to convince because it was the truth. 'I'm not going to prison. I'd rather hang. My father hanged.'

She asked again, 'Where are we going?' watching all the time for her chance. He didn't answer.

39

'Do you know this place?' but he had said his say. And suddenly the chance was there: outside a little stationer's where the morning posters leaned, looking in the window filled with cheap notepaper, pens and ink bottles – a policeman. She felt Raven come up behind her, it was all too quick, she hadn't time to make up her mind, they were past the policeman and on down the mean road. It was too late to scream now; he was twenty yards away; there'd be no rescue. She said in a low voice, 'It *must* be murder.'

The repetition stung him into speech. 'That's justice for you. Always thinking the worst. They've pinned a robbery on to me, and I don't even know where the notes were stolen.' A man came out of a public-house and began to wipe the steps with a wet cloth; they could smell frying bacon; the suitcases weighed on their arms. Raven couldn't change his hands for fear of leaving hold of the automatic. He said, 'If a man's born ugly, he doesn't stand a chance. It begins at school. It begins before that.'

'What's wrong with your face?' she asked with bitter amusement. There seemed hope while he talked. It must be harder to murder anyone with whom you'd had any kind of relationship.

'My lip, of course.'

'What's up with your lip?'

He said with astonishment, 'Do you mean you haven't noticed – ?'

'Oh,' Anne said, 'I suppose you mean your hare-lip. I've seen worse things than that.' They had left the little dirty houses behind them. She read the name of the new street: Shakespeare Avenue. Bright-red bricks and tudor gables and half timbering, doors with stained glass, names like Restholme. These houses represented something worse than the meanness of poverty, the meanness of the spirit. They were on the very edge of Nottwich now, where the speculative builders were running up their hire-purchase houses. It occurred to Anne that he had brought her here to kill her in the scarred fields behind the housing estate, where the grass had been trampled into the clay and the stumps of trees showed where an old wood had been. Plodding on they passed a house with an open door which at any hour of the day visitors could enter and inspect, from the small square parlour to the small square bedroom and the bathroom and water closet off the landing. A big placard said: 'Come in and Inspect A Cozyholme. Ten Pounds Down and a House Is Yours.'

'Are you going to buy a house?' she said with desperate humour.

He said, 'I've got a hundred and ninety pounds in my pocket and I couldn't buy a box of matches with them. I tell you, I was double-crossed. I never stole these notes. A bastard gave them me.'

'That was generous.'

He hesitated outside 'Sleepy Nuik'. It was so new that the builder's paint had not been removed from the panes. He said, 'It was for a piece of work I did. I did the work well. He ought to have paid me properly. I followed him here. A bastard called Chol-mon-deley.'

He pushed her through the gate of 'Sleepy Nuik', up the unmade path and round to the back door. They were at the edge of the fog here: it was as if they were at the boundary between night and day; it faded out in long streamers into the grey winter sky. He put his shoulder against the back door and the little doll's house lock snapped at once out of the cheap rotten wood. They stood in the kitchen, a place of wires waiting for bulbs, of tubes waiting for the gas cooker. 'Get over to the wall,' he said, 'where I can watch you.'

He sat down on the floor with the pistol in his hand. He said, 'I'm tired. All night standing in that train. I can't think properly. I don't know what to do with you.'

Anne said, 'I've got a job here. I haven't a penny if I lose it. I'll give you my word I'll say nothing if you'll let me go.' She added hopelessly, 'But you wouldn't believe me.'

'People don't trouble to keep their word to me,' Raven said. He brooded darkly in his dusty corner by the sink. He said, 'I'm safe here for a while as long as you are here too.' He put his hand to his face and winced at the soreness of the

41

burns. Anne made a movement. He said, 'Don't move. I'll shoot if you move.'

'Can't I sit down?' she said. 'I'm tired too. I've got to be on my feet all the afternoon.' But while she spoke she saw herself, bundled into a cupboard with the blood still wet. She added, 'Dressed up as a Chink. Singing.' But he wasn't listening to her; he was making his own plans in his own darkness. She tried to keep her courage up with the first song that came into her head, humming it because it reminded her of Mather, the long ride home, the 'see you tomorrow'.

> 'It's only Kew
> To you,
> But to me
> It's Paradise.'

He said, 'I've heard that tune.' He couldn't remember where: he remembered a dark night and a cold wind and hunger and the scratch of a needle. It was as if something sharp and cold were breaking in his heart with great pain. He sat there under the sink with the automatic in his hand and began to cry. He made no sound, the tears seemed to run like flies of their own will from the corners of his eyes. Anne didn't notice for a while, humming the song. *'They say that's a snow-flower a man brought from Greenland.'* Then she saw. She said, 'What's the matter?'

Raven said, 'Keep back against that wall or I'll shoot.'

'You're all in.'

'That doesn't matter to you.'

'Well, I suppose I'm human,' Anne said. 'You haven't done me any harm yet.'

He said, 'This doesn't mean anything. I'm just tired.' He looked along the bare dusty boards of the unfinished kitchen. He tried to swagger. 'I'm tired of living in hotels. I'd like to fix up this kitchen. I learned to be an electrician once. I'm educated.' He said: '"Sleepy Nuik". It's a good name when you are tired. But they've gone and spelt "Nook" wrong.'

'Let me go,' Anne said. 'You can trust me. I'll not say a thing. I don't even know who you are.'

He laughed miserably. 'Trust you. I'd say I can. When you get into the town you'll see my name in the papers and my description, what I'm wearing, how old I am. I never stole the notes, but *I* can't put a description in of the man I want: name of Chol-mon-deley, profession double-crosser, fat, wears an emerald ring . . .'

'Why,' she said, 'I believe I travelled down with a man like that. I wouldn't have thought he'd have the nerve . . .'

'Oh, he's only the agent,' Raven said, 'but if I could find him I'd squeeze the names . . .'

'Why don't you give yourself up? Tell the police what happened?'

'That's a great idea, that is. Tell them it was Cholmondeley's friends got the old Czech killed. You're a bright girl.'

'The old Czech?' she exclaimed. A little more light came into the kitchen as the fog lifted over the housing estate, the wounded fields. She said, 'You don't mean what the papers are so full of?'

'That's it,' he said with gloomy pride.

'You know the man who shot him?'

'As well as myself.'

'And Cholmondeley's mixed up in it . . . Doesn't that mean – that everyone's all wrong?'

'They don't know a thing about it, these papers. They can't give credit where credit's due.'

'And you know and Cholmondeley. Then there won't be a war at all if you find Cholmondeley.'

'I don't care a damn whether there's a war or not. I only want to know who it is who double-crossed me. I want to get even,' he explained, looking up at her across the floor, with his hand over his mouth, hiding his lip, noticing that she was young and flushed and lovely with no more personal interest than a mangy wolf will show from the cage in the groomed well-fed bitch beyond the bars. 'A war won't do people any harm,' he said. 'It'll show them what's what, it'll give them a taste of their own medicine. I know. There's always been a war for me.' He touched the automatic. 'All that worries me is what to do with you to keep you quiet for twenty-four hours.'

She said under her breath, 'You wouldn't kill me, would you?'

'If it's the only way,' he said. 'Let me think a bit.'

'But I'd be on your side,' she implored him, looking this way and that for anything to throw, for a chance of safety.

'Nobody's on my side,' Raven said. 'I've learned that. Even a crook doctor ... You see – I'm ugly. I don't pretend to be one of your handsome fellows. But I'm educated. I've thought things out.' He said quickly, 'I'm wasting time. I ought to get started.'

'What are you going to do?' she asked, scrambling to her feet.

'Oh,' he said in a tone of disappointment, 'you are scared again. You were fine when you weren't scared.' He faced her across the kitchen with the automatic pointed at her breast. He pleaded with her. 'There's no need to be scared. This lip – '

'I don't mind your lip,' she said desperately. You aren't bad-looking. You ought to have a girl. She'd stop you worrying about that lip.'

He shook his head. 'You're talking that way because you are scared. You can't get round me that way. But it's hard luck on you, my picking on you. You shouldn't be so afraid of death. We've all got to die. If there's a war, you'll die anyway. It's sudden and quick: it doesn't hurt,' he said, remembering the smashed skull of the old man – death was like that: no more difficult than breaking an egg.

She whispered, 'Are you going to shoot me?'

'Oh no, no,' he said, trying to calm her, 'turn your back and go over to that door. We'll find a room where I can lock you up for a few hours.' He fixed his eyes on her back; he wanted to shoot her clean: he didn't want to hurt her.

She said, 'You aren't so bad. We might have been friends if we hadn't met like this. If this was the stage-door. Do you meet girls at stage-doors?'

'Me,' he said, 'no. They wouldn't look at me.'

'You aren't ugly,' she said. 'I'd rather you had that lip than

44

a cauliflower ear like all those fellows who think they are tough. The girls go crazy on them when they are in shorts. But they look silly in a dinner jacket.' Raven thought: if I shoot her here anyone may see her through a window; I'll shoot her upstairs in the bathroom. He said, 'Go on. Walk.'

She said, 'Let me go this afternoon. Please. I'll lose my job if I'm not at the theatre.'

They came out into the little glossy hall, which smelt of paint. She said, 'I'll give you a seat for the show.'

'Go on,' he said, 'up the stairs.'

'It's worth seeing. Alfred Bleek as the Widow Twankey.' There were only three doors on the little landing: one had ground-glass panes. 'Open the door,' he said, 'and go in there.' He decided that he would shoot her in the back as soon as she was over the threshold; then he would only have to close the door and she would be out of sight. A small aged voice whispered agonizingly in his memory through a closed door. Memories had never troubled him. He didn't mind death; it was foolish to be scared of death in this bare wintry world. He said hoarsely, 'Are you happy? I mean, you like your job?'

'Oh, not the job,' she said. 'But the job won't go on for ever. Don't you think someone might marry me? I'm hoping.'

He whispered, 'Go in. Look through that window,' his finger touching the trigger. She went obediently forward; he brought the automatic up, his hand didn't tremble, he told himself that she would feel nothing. Death wasn't a thing she need be scared about. She had taken her handbag from under her arm; he noticed the odd sophisticated shape; a circle of twisted glass on the side and within it chromium initials, A.C.; she was going to make her face up.

A door closed and a voice said, 'You'll excuse me bringing you here this early, but I have to be at the office till late . . .'

'That's all right, that's all right, Mr Graves. Now don't you call this a snug little house?'

He lowered the pistol as Anne turned. She whispered breathlessly, 'Come in here quick.' He obeyed her, he didn't understand, he was still ready to shoot her if she screamed.

45

She saw the automatic and said, 'Put it away. You'll only get into trouble with that.'

Raven said, 'Your bags are in the kitchen.'

'I know. They've come in by the front door.'

'Gas and electric,' a voice said, 'laid on. Ten pounds down and you sign along the dotted line and move in the furniture.'

A precise voice which went with pince-nez and a high collar and thin flaxen hair said, 'Of course, I shall have to think it over.'

'Come and look upstairs, Mr Graves.'

They could hear them cross the hall and climb the stairs, the agent talking all the time. Raven said, 'I'll shoot if you – '

'Be quiet,' Anne said. 'Don't talk. Listen. Have you those notes? Give me two of them.' When he hesitated she whispered urgently, 'We've got to take a risk.' The agent and Mr Graves were in the best bedroom now. 'Just think of it, Mr Graves,' the agent was saying, 'with flowered chintz.'

'Are the walls sound-proof?'

'By a special process. Shut the door,' the door closed and the agent's voice went thinly, distinctly on, 'and in the passage you couldn't hear a thing. These houses were specially made for family men.'

'And now,' Mr Graves said, 'I should like to see the bathroom.'

'Don't move,' Raven threatened her.

'Oh, put it away,' Anne said, 'and be yourself.' She closed the bathroom door behind her and walked to the door of the bedroom. It opened and the agent said with the immediate gallantry of a man known in all the Nottwich bars, 'Well, well, what have we here?'

'I was passing,' Anne said, 'and saw the door open. I'd been meaning to come and see you, but I didn't think you'd be up this early.'

'Always on the spot for a young lady,' the agent said.

'I want to buy this house.'

'Now look here,' Mr Graves said, a young-old man in a black suit who carried about with him in his pale face and irascible air the idea of babies in small sour rooms, of insufficient sleep. 'You can't do that. I'm looking over this house.'

'My husband sent me here to buy it.'

'I'm here first.'

'Have you bought it?'

'I've got to look it over first, haven't I?'

'Here,' Anne said, showing two five-pound notes. 'Now all I have to do . . .'

'Is sign along the dotted line,' the agent said.

'Give me time,' Mr Graves said. 'I like this house.' He went to the window. 'I like the view.' His pale face stared out at the damaged fields stretching under the fading fog to where the slag-heaps rose along the horizon. 'It's quiet country,' Mr Graves said. 'It'll be good for the children and the wife.'

'I'm sorry,' Anne said, 'but you see I'm ready to pay and sign.'

'References?' the agent said.

'I'll bring them this afternoon.'

'Let me show you another house, Mr Graves.' The agent belched slightly and apologized. 'I'm not used to business before breakfast.'

'No,' Mr Graves said, 'if I can't have this I won't have any.' Pallid and aggrieved he planted himself in the best bedroom of 'Sleepy Nuik' and presented his challenge to fate, a challenge which he knew from long and bitter experience was always accepted.

'Well,' the agent said, 'you can't have this. First come, first served.'

Mr Graves said, 'Good morning,' carried his pitiful, narrow-chested pride downstairs; at least he could claim that, if he had been always too late for what he really wanted, he had never accepted substitutes.

'I'll come with you to the office,' Anne said, 'straight away,' taking the agent's arm, turning her back on the bathroom where the dark pinched man stood waiting with his pistol, going downstairs into the cold overcast day which smelt to her as sweet as summer because she was safe again.

47

> 'What did Aladdin say
> When he came to Pekin?'

Obediently the long shuffling row of them repeated with tired vivacity, bending forward, clapping their knees, *'Chin Chin.'* They had been rehearsing for five hours.

'It won't do. It hasn't got any sparkle. Start again, please.'

> 'What did Aladdin say ...'

'How many of you have they killed so far?' Anne said under her breath. *'Chin Chin.'*

'Oh, half a dozen.'

'I'm glad I got in at the last minute. A fortnight of this! No thank you.'

'Can't you put some Art into it?' the producer implored them. 'Have some pride. This isn't just any panto.'

'What did Aladdin say ...'

'You look washed out,' Anne said.

'You don't look too good yourself.'

'Things happen quick in this place.'

'Once more, girls, and then we'll go on to Miss Maydew's scene.'

> 'What did Aladdin say
> When he came to Pekin?'

'You won't think that when you've been here a week.'

Miss Maydew sat sideways in the front row with her feet up on the next stall. She was in tweeds and had a golf-and-grouse-moor air. Her real name was Binns, and her father was Lord Fordhaven. She said in a voice of penetrating gentility to Alfred Bleek, 'I said I won't be presented.'

'Who's the fellow at the back of the stalls?' Anne whispered. He was only a shadow to her.

'I don't know. Hasn't been here before. One of the men who put up the money, I expect, waiting to get an eyeful.' She began to mimic an imaginary man. 'Won't you introduce me to the girls, Mr Collier? I want to thank them for working so hard to make this panto a success. What about a little dinner, missy?'

'Stop talking, Ruby, and make it snappy,' said Mr Collier.

> 'What did Aladdin say
> When he came to Pekin?'

'All right. That'll do.'

'Please, Mr Collier,' Ruby said, 'may I ask you a question?'

'Now, Miss Maydew, your scene with Mr Bleek. Well, what is it you want to know?'

'What *did* Aladdin say?'

'I want discipline,' Mr Collier said, 'and I'm going to have discipline.' He was rather under-sized with a fierce eye and straw-coloured hair and a receding chin. He was continually glancing over his shoulder in fear that somebody was getting at him from behind. He wasn't a good director; his appointment was due to more 'wheels within wheels' than you could count. Somebody owed money to somebody else who had a nephew ... but Mr Collier was not the nephew: the chain of causes went much further before you reached Mr Collier. Somewhere it included Miss Maydew, but the chain was so long you couldn't follow it. You got a confused idea that Mr Collier must owe his position to merit. Miss Maydew didn't claim that for herself. She was always writing little articles in the cheap women's papers on: 'Hard Work the only Key to Success on the Stage.' She lit a new cigarette and said, 'Are you talking to *me*?' She said to Alfred Bleek, who was in a dinner-jacket with a red knitted shawl round his shoulders, 'It was to get away from all that ... royal garden parties.'

Mr Collier said, 'Nobody's going to leave this theatre.' He looked nervously over his shoulder at the stout gentleman emerging into the light from the back of the stalls, one of the innumerable 'wheels within wheels' that had spun Mr Collier into Nottwich, into this exposed position at the front of the stage, into this fear that nobody would obey him.

'Won't you introduce me to the girls, Mr Collier?' the

stout gentleman said. 'If you are finishing. I don't want to interrupt.'

'Of course,' Mr Collier said. He said, 'Girls, this is Mr Davenant, one of our chief backers.'

'Davis, not Davenant,' the fat man said. 'I bought out Davenant.' He waved his hand; the emerald ring on his little finger flashed and caught Anne's eye. He said, 'I want to have the pleasure of taking every one of you girls out to dinner while this show lasts. Just to tell you how I appreciate the way you are working to make the panto a success. Whom shall I begin with?' He had an air of desperate jollity. He was like a man who suddenly finds he has nothing to think about and somehow must fill the vacuum.

'Miss Maydew,' he said half-heartedly, as if to show to the chorus the honesty of his intentions by inviting the principal boy.

'Sorry,' Miss Maydew said, 'I'm dining with Bleek.'

Anne walked out on them; she didn't want to high-hat Davis, but his presence there shocked her. She believed in Fate and God and Vice and Virtue, Christ in the stable, all the Christmas stuff; she believed in unseen powers that arranged meetings, drove people along ways they didn't mean to go; but she was quite determined she wouldn't help. She wouldn't play God or the Devil's game; she had evaded Raven, leaving him there in the bathroom of the little empty house, and Raven's affairs no longer concerned her. She wouldn't give him away; she was not yet on the side of the big organized battalions; but she wouldn't help him either. It was a strictly neutral course she steered out of the changing-room, out of the theatre door, into Nottwich High Street.

But what she saw there made her pause. The street was full of people; they stretched along the southern pavement, past the theatre entrance, as far as the market. They were watching the electric bulbs above Wallace's, the big drapers, spelling out the night's news. She had seen nothing like it since the last election, but this was different, because there were no cheers. They were reading of the troop movements over Europe, of the precautions against gas raids. Anne was not old enough to

50

remember how the last war began, but she had read of the crowds outside the Palace, the enthusiasm, the queues at the recruiting offices, and that was how she had pictured every war beginning. She had feared it only for herself and Mather. She had thought of it as a personal tragedy played out against a background of cheers and flags. But this was different; this silent crowd wasn't jubilant, it was afraid. The white faces were turned towards the sky with a kind of secular entreaty; they weren't praying to any God; they were just willing that the electric bulbs would tell a different story. They were caught there, on the way back from work, with tools and attaché cases, by the rows of bulbs, spelling out complications they simply didn't understand.

Anne thought: can it be true that that fat fool ... that the boy with the hare-lip *knows* ... Well, she told herself, I believe in Fate, I suppose I can't just walk out and leave them. I'm in it up to the neck. If only Jimmy were here. But Jimmy, she remembered with pain, was on the other side; he was among those hunting Raven down. And Raven must be given the chance to finish *his* hunt first. She went back into the theatre.

Mr Davenant – Davis – Cholmondeley, whatever his name was, was telling a story. Miss Maydew and Alfred Bleek had gone. Most of the girls had gone too to change. Mr Collier watched and listened nervously; he was trying to remember who Mr Davis was; Mr Davenant had been silk stockings and had known Callitrope, who was the nephew of the man Dreid owed money to. Mr Collier had been quite safe with Mr Davenant, but he wasn't certain about Davis ... This panto wouldn't last for ever and it was as fatal to get *in* with the wrong people as to get *out* with the right. It was possible that Davis was the man Cohen had quarrelled with, or he might be the uncle of the man Cohen had quarrelled with. The echoes of that quarrel were still faintly reverberating through the narrow back-stage passages of provincial theatres in the second-class touring towns. Soon they would reach the third companies and everyone would either move up one or move down one, except those who couldn't move down any lower.

Mr Collier laughed nervously and glared in a miserable attempt to be in and out simultaneously.

'I thought somebody breathed the word dinner,' Anne said. 'I'm hungry.'

'First come, first served,' Mr Davis–Cholmondeley said cheerily. 'Tell the girls I'll be seeing them. Where shall it be, Miss?'

'Anne.'

'That's fine,' Mr Davis–Cholmondeley said. 'I'm Willie.'

'I bet you know this town well,' Anne said. 'I'm new.' She came close to the floodlights and deliberately showed herself to him; she wanted to see whether he recognized her; but Mr Davis never looked at a face. He looked past you. His large square face didn't need to show its force by any eye-to-eye business. Its power lay in its existence at all; you couldn't help wondering, as you wondered with an outsize mastiff, how much sheer weight of food had daily to be consumed to keep him fit.

Mr Davis winked at Mr Collier, and said, 'Oh yes, I know this town. In a manner of speaking I made this town.' He said, 'There isn't much choice. There's the Grand or the Metropole. The Metropole's more intimate.'

'Let's go to the Metropole.'

'They have the best sundaes too in Nottwich.'

The street was no longer crowded, just the usual number of people looking in the windows, strolling home, going into the Imperial Cinema. Anne thought, where is Raven now? How can I find Raven?

'It's not worth taking a taxi,' Mr Davis said, 'the Metropole's only just round the corner. You'll like the Metropole,' he repeated. 'It's more intimate than the Grand,' but it wasn't the kind of hotel you associated with intimacy. It came in sight at once all along one side of the market place, as big as a railway station, of red and yellow stone with a clock-face in a pointed tower.

'Kind of Hôtel de Ville, eh?' Mr Davis said. You could tell how proud he was of Nottwich.

There were sculptured figures in between every pair of

windows; all the historic worthies of Nottwich stood in stiff neo-Gothic attitudes, from Robin Hood up to the Mayor of Nottwich in 1864. 'People come a long way to see this,' Mr Davis said.

'And the Grand? What's the Grand like?'

'Oh, the Grand,' Mr Davis said, 'the Grand's gaudy.'

He pushed her in ahead of him through the swing doors, and Anne saw how the porter recognized him. It wasn't going to be hard, she thought, to trace Mr Davis in Nottwich; but how to find Raven?

The restaurant had enough room for the passengers of a liner; the roof was supported on pillars painted in stripes of sage-green and gold. The curved ceiling was blue scattered with gold stars arranged in their proper constellations. 'It's one of the sights of Nottwich,' Mr Davis said. 'I always keep a table under Venus.' He laughed nervously, settling in his seat, and Anne noticed that they weren't under Venus at all but under Jupiter.

'You ought to be under the Great Bear,' she said.

'Ha, ha, that's good,' Mr Davis said. 'I must remember that.' He bent over the wine-list. 'I know you ladies always like a sweet wine.' He confessed, 'I've a sweet tooth myself.' He sat there studying the card, lost to everything; he wasn't interested in her; he seemed interested at that moment in nothing but a series of tastes, beginning with the lobster he had ordered. This was his chosen home: the huge stuffy palace of food; this was his idea of intimacy, one table set among two hundred tables.

Anne thought he had brought her there for a flirtation. She had imagined that it would be easy to get on terms with Mr Davis, even though the ritual a little scared her. Five years of provincial theatres had not made her adept at knowing how far she could go without arousing in the other more excitement than she could easily cope with. Her retreats were always sudden and dangerous. Over the lobster she thought of Mather, of security, of loving one man. Then she put out her knee and touched Mr Davis's. Mr Davis took no notice, cracking his way through a claw. He might just as well have been alone. It made her uneasy, to be so neglected. It didn't seem natural. She touched his knee again and said, 'Anything on your mind, Willie?'

The eyes he raised were like the lenses of a powerful microscope focused on an unmounted slide. He said, 'What's that? This lobster all right, eh?' He stared past her over the wide rather empty restaurant, all the tables decorated with holly and mistletoe. He called, 'Waiter, I want an evening paper,' and set to again at his claw. When the paper was brought he turned first of all to the financial page. He seemed satisfied; what he read there was as good as a lollipop.

Anne said, 'Would you excuse me a moment, Willie?' She took three coppers out of her bag and went to the ladies' lavatory. She stared at herself in the glass over the wash basin; there didn't seem to be anything wrong. She said to the old woman there, 'Do I look all right to you?'

The woman grinned. 'Perhaps he doesn't like so much lipstick.'

'Oh no,' Anne said, 'he's the lipstick type. A change from home. Hubbie on the razzle.' She said, 'Who is he? He calls himself Davis. He says he made this town.'

'Excuse me, dear, but your stocking's laddered.'

'It's not his doing, anyway. Who is he?'

'I've never heard of him, dear. Ask the porter.'

'I think I will.'

She went to the front door. 'That restaurant's so hot,' she said. 'I had to get a bit of air.' It was a peaceful moment for the porter of the Metropole. Nobody came in; nobody went out. He said, 'It's cold enough outside.' A man with one leg stood on the kerb and sold matches; the trams went by; little lighted homes full of smoke and talk and friendliness. A clock struck half-past eight and you could hear from one of the streets outside the square the shrill voices of children singing a tuneless carol. Anne said, 'Well, I must be getting back to Mr Davis.' She said, 'Who *is* Mr Davis?'

'He's got plenty,' the porter said.

'He says he made this town.'

'That's boasting,' the porter said. 'It's Midland Steel made

54

this town. You'll see their offices in the Tanneries. But they're ruining the town now. They *did* employ fifty thousand. Now they don't have ten thousand. I was a doorkeeper there once myself. But they even cut down the doorkeepers.'

'It must have been cruel,' Anne said.

'It was worse for him,' the porter said, nodding through the door at the one-legged man. 'He had twenty years with them. Then he lost his leg and the court brought it in wilful negligence, so they didn't give him a tanner. They economized there too, you see. It was negligence, all right; he fell asleep. If you tried watching a machine do the same thing once every second for eight hours, you'd feel sleepy yourself.'

'But Mr Davis?'

'Oh, I don't know anything about Mr Davis. He may have something to do with the boot factory. Or he may be one of the directors of Wallace's. They've got money to burn.' A woman came through the door carrying a Pekinese; she wore a heavy fur coat. She asked: 'Has Mr Alfred Piker been in here?'

'No, ma'am.'

'There. It's just what his uncle was always doing. Disappearing.' She said, 'Keep hold of the dog,' and rolled away across the square.

'That's the Mayoress,' the porter said.

Anne went back. But something had happened. The bottle of wine was almost empty and the paper lay on the floor at Mr Davis's feet. Two sundaes had been laid in place, but Mr Davis hadn't touched his. It wasn't politeness; something had put him out. He growled at her, 'Where have you been?' She tried to see what he had been reading; it wasn't the financial page any more, but she could make out only the main head-lines: 'Decree *Nisi* for Lady —' the name was too complicated to read upside down; 'Manslaughter Verdict on Motorist'. Mr Davis said, 'I don't know what's wrong with the place. They've put salt or something in the sundaes.' He turned his furious dewlapped face at the passing waiter. 'Call this a Knickerbocker Glory?'

'I'll bring you another, sir.'

'You won't. My bill.'

'So we call it a day,' Anne said.

Mr Davis looked up from the bill with something very like fear. 'No, no,' he said, 'I didn't mean that. You won't go and leave me flat now?'

'Well, what do you want to do, the flickers?'

'I thought,' Mr Davis said, 'you might come back with me to my place and have a tune on the radio and a glass of something good. We might foot it together a bit, eh?' He wasn't looking at her; he was hardly thinking of what he was saying. He didn't look dangerous. Anne thought she knew his type, you could pass them off with a kiss or two, and when they were drunk tell them a sentimental story until they began to think you were their sister. This would be the last: soon she would be Mather's; she would be safe. But first she was going to learn where Mr Davis lived.

As they came out into the square the carol singers broke on them, six small boys without an idea of a tune between them. They wore wool gloves and mufflers and they stood across Mr Davis's path chanting: *'Mark my footsteps well, my page.'*

'Taxi, sir?' the porter asked.

'No.' Mr Davis explained to Anne, 'It saves threepence to take one from the rank in the Tanneries.' But the boys got in his way, holding out their caps for money. 'Get out of the way,' Mr Davis said. With the intuition of children they recognized his uneasiness and baited him, pursuing him along the kerb, singing: *'Follow in them boldly.'* The loungers outside the Crown turned to look. Somebody clapped. Mr Davis suddenly rounded and seized the hair of the boy nearest him; he pulled it till the boy screamed; pulled it till a tuft came out between his fingers. He said, 'That will teach you,' and sinking back a moment later in the taxi from the rank in the Tanneries, he said with pleasure, 'They can't play with me.' His mouth was open and his lip was wet with saliva; he brooded over his victory in the same way as he had brooded over the lobster; he didn't look to Anne as safe as she had thought. She reminded herself that he was only an agent. He *knew* the murderer, Raven said; he hadn't committed it himself.

'What's that building?' she asked, seeing a great black glass-front stand out from the Victorian street of sober offices where once the leather-workers had tanned their skins.

'Midland Steel,' Mr Davis said.

'Do you work there?'

Mr Davis for the first time returned look for look. 'What made you think that?'

'I don't know,' Anne said and recognized with uneasiness that Mr Davis was only simple when the wind stood one way.

'Do you think you could like me?' Mr Davis said, fingering her knee.

'I dare say I might.'

The taxi had left the Tanneries. It heaved over a net of tram-lines and came out into the Station Approach. 'Do you live out of town?'

'Just at the edge,' Mr Davis said.

'They ought to spend more on lighting in this place.'

'You're a cute little girl,' Mr Davis said. 'I bet you know what's what.'

'It's no good looking for eggshell if that's what you mean,' Anne said, as they drove under the great steel bridge that carried the line on to York. There were only two lamps on the whole of the long steep gradient to the station. Over a wooden fence you could see the shunted trucks on the side line, the stacked coal ready for entrainment. An old taxi and a bus waited for passengers outside the small dingy station entrance. Built in 1860 it hadn't kept pace with Nottwich.

'You've got a long way to go to work,' Anne said.

'We are nearly there.'

The taxi turned to the left. Anne read the name of the road: Khyber Avenue, a long row of mean villas showing apart-ment cards. The taxi stopped at the end of the road. Anne said, 'You don't mean you live *here*?' Mr Davis was paying off the driver. 'Number sixty-one,' he said (Anne noticed there was no card in this window between the pane and the thick lace curtains). He smiled in a soft ingratiating way and said, 'It's really nice inside, dear.' He put a key in the lock and thrust her firmly forward into a little dimly lit hall with a

57

hatstand. He hung up his hat and walked softly towards the stairs on his toes. There was a smell of gas and greens. A blue fan of flame lit up a dusty plant.

'We'll turn on the wireless,' Mr Davis said, 'and have a tune.'

A door opened in the passage and a woman's voice said, 'Who's that?'

'Just Mr Cholmondeley.'

'Don't forget to pay before you go up.'

'The first floor,' Mr Davis said. 'The room straight ahead of you. I won't be a moment,' and he waited on the stairs till she passed him. The coins clinked in his pocket as his hand groped for them.

There *was* a wireless in the room, standing on a marble washstand, but there was certainly no space to dance in, for the big double bed filled the room. There was nothing to show the place was ever lived in: there was dust on the wardrobe mirror and the ewer beside the loud speaker was dry. Anne looked out of the window behind the bedposts on a little dark yard. Her hand trembled against the sash: this was more than she had bargained for. Mr Davis opened the door.

She was badly frightened. It made her take the offensive. She said at once, 'So you call yourself Mr Cholmondeley?'

He blinked at her, closing the door softly behind him: 'What if I do?'

'And you said you were taking me home. This isn't your home.'

Mr Davis sat down on the bed and took off his shoes. He said, 'We mustn't make a noise, dear. The old woman doesn't like it.' He opened the door of the washstand and took out a cardboard box; it spilt soft icing sugar out of its cracks all over the bed and the floor as he came towards her. 'Have a piece of Turkish Delight.'

'This isn't your home,' she persisted.

Mr Davis, with his fingers half-way to his mouth, said, 'Of course it isn't. You don't think I'd take you to my home, do you? You aren't as green as that. I'm not going to lose my reputation.' He said, 'We'll have a tune, shall we, first?' And turning the dials he set the instrument squealing and moaning. 'Lot of atmospherics about,' Mr Davis said, twisting and turning the dials until very far away you could hear a dance band playing, a dreamy rhythm underneath the shrieking in the air; you could just discern the tune: *'Night light, Love light.'* 'It's our own Nottwich programme,' Mr Davis said. 'There isn't a better band on the Midland Regional. From the Grand. Let's do a step or two,' and grasping her round the waist he began to shake up and down between the bed and the wall.

'I've known better floors,' Anne said, trying to keep up her spirits with her own hopeless form of humour, 'but I've never known a worse crush,' and Mr Davis said, 'That's good. I'll remember that.' Quite suddenly, blowing off relics of icing sugar which clung round his mouth, he grew passionate. He fastened his lips on her neck. She pushed him away and laughed at him at the same time. She had to keep her head. 'Now I know what a rock feels like,' she said, 'when the sea amen – anem – damn, I can never say that word.'

'That's good,' Mr Davis said mechanically, driving her back.

She began to talk rapidly about anything which came into her head. She said, 'I wonder what this gas practice will be like. Wasn't it terrible the way they shot the old woman through her eyes?'

He loosed her at that, though she hadn't really meant anything by it. He said, 'Why do you bring that up?'

'I was just reading about it,' Anne said. 'The man must have made a proper mess in that flat.'

Mr Davis implored her, 'Stop. Please stop.' He explained weakly, leaning back for support against the bedpost, 'I've got a weak stomach. I don't like horrors.'

'I like thrillers,' Anne said. 'There was one I read the other day . . .'

'I've got a very vivid imagination,' Mr Davis said.

'I remember once when I cut my finger . . .'

'Don't. Please don't.'

Success made her reckless. She said, 'I've got a vivid imagination too. I thought someone was watching this house.'

'What do you mean?' He was scared all right. But she went too far. She said, 'There was a dark fellow watching the door. He had a hare-lip.'

Mr Davis went to the door and locked it. He turned the wireless low. He said, 'There's no lamp within twenty yards. You couldn't have seen his lip.'

'I just thought . . .'

'I wonder how much he told you,' Mr Davis said. He sat down on the bed and looked at his hands. 'You wanted to know where I lived, whether I worked . . .' He cut his sentence short and looked up at her with horror. But she could tell from his manner that he was no longer afraid of her; it was something else that scared him. He said, 'They'd never believe you.'

'Who wouldn't?'

'The police. It's a wild story.' To her amazement he began to sniffle, sitting on the bed nursing his great hairy hands. 'There must be some way out. I don't want to hurt you. I don't want to hurt anyone. I've got a weak stomach.'

Anne said, 'I don't know a thing. Please open the door.'

Mr Davis said in a low furious voice, 'Be quiet. You've brought it on yourself.'

She said again, 'I don't know anything.'

'I'm only an agent,' Mr Davis said. 'I'm not responsible.' He explained gently, sitting there in his stockinged feet with tears in his deep selfish eyes, 'It's always been our policy to take no risks. It's not my fault that fellow got away. I did my best. I've always done my best. But he won't forgive me again.'

'I'll scream if you don't open that door.'

'Scream away. You'll only make the old woman cross.'

'What are you going to do?'

'There's more than half a million at stake,' Mr Davis said. 'I've got to make sure this time.' He got up and came towards her with his hands out; she screamed and shook the door, then fled from it because there was no reply and ran round the bed. He just let her run; there was no escape in the tiny cramped room. He stood there muttering to himself,

60

'Horrible. Horrible.' You could tell he was on the verge of sickness, but the fear of somebody else drove him on.

Anne implored him, 'I'll promise anything.'

He shook his head, 'He'd never forgive me,' and sprawled across the bed and caught her wrist. He said thickly, 'Don't struggle. I won't hurt you if you don't struggle,' pulling her to him across the bed, feeling with his other hand for the pillow. She told herself even then: it isn't me. It's other people who are murdered. Not me. The urge to life which made her disbelieve that this could possibly be the end of everything for her, for the loving enjoying I, comforted her even when the pillow was across her mouth; never allowed her to realize the full horror, as she fought against his hands, strong and soft and sticky with icing sugar.

5

The rain blew up along the River Weevil from the east; it turned to ice in the bitter night and stung the asphalt walks, pitted the paint on the wooden seats. A constable came quietly by in his heavy raincoat gleaming like wet macadam, moving his lantern here and there in the dark spaces between the lamps. He said, 'Good night' to Raven without another glance. It was couples he expected to find, even in December under the hail, the signs of poor cooped provincial passion.

Raven buttoned to the neck went on, looking for any shelter. He wanted to keep his mind on Cholmondeley, on how to find the man in Nottwich. But continually he found himself thinking instead of the girl he had threatened that morning. He remembered the kitten he had left behind in the Soho café. He had loved that kitten.

It had been sublimely unconscious of his ugliness. 'My name's Anne.' 'You aren't ugly.' She never knew, he thought, that he had meant to kill her; she had been as innocent of his intention as a cat he had once been forced to drown; and he remembered with astonishment that she had not betrayed him, although he had told her that the police were after him. It was even possible that she had believed him.

61

These thoughts were colder and more uncomfortable than the hail. He wasn't used to any taste that wasn't bitter on the tongue. He had been made by hatred; it had constructed him into this thin smoky murderous figure in the rain, hunted and ugly. His mother had borne him when his father was in gaol, and six years later when his father was hanged for another crime, she had cut her own throat with a kitchen knife; afterwards there had been the home. He had never felt the least tenderness for anyone; he was made in this image and he had his own odd pride in the result; he didn't want to be unmade. He had a sudden terrified conviction that he must be himself now as never before if he was to escape. It was not tenderness that made you quick on the draw.

Somebody in one of the larger houses on the river-front had left his garage gate ajar; it was obviously not used for a car, but only to house a pram, a child's playground and a few dusty dolls and bricks. Raven took shelter there; he was cold through and through except in the one spot that had lain frozen all his life. That dagger of ice was melting with great pain. He pushed the garage gate a little further open; he had no wish to appear furtively hiding if anyone passed along the river beat; anyone might be excused for sheltering in a stranger's garage from *this* storm, except, of course, a man wanted by the police with a hare-lip.

These houses were only semi-detached. They were joined by their garages. Raven was closely hemmed in by the red-brick walls. He could hear the wireless playing in both houses. In the one house it switched and changed as a restless finger turned the screw and beat up the wavelengths, bringing a snatch of rhetoric from Berlin, of opera from Stockholm. On the National Programme from the other house an elderly critic was reading verse. Raven couldn't help but hear, standing in the cold garage by the baby's pram, staring out at the black hail:

> 'A shadow flits before me,
> Not thou, but like to thee;
> Ah Christ, that it were possible

> For one short hour to see
> The souls we loved, that they might tell us
> What and where they be.'

He dug his nails into his hands, remembering his father who had been hanged and his mother who had killed herself in the basement kitchen, all the long parade of those who had done him down. The elderly cultured Civil Service voice read on:

> 'And I loathe the squares and streets,
> and the faces that one meets,
> Hearts with no love for me ...'

He thought: give her time and she too will go to the police. That's what always happens in the end with a skirt,

> – 'My whole soul out to thee' –

trying to freeze again, as hard and safe as ever, the icy fragment.

'That was Mr Druce Winton, reading a selection from *Maud* by Lord Tennyson. This ends the National Programme. Good night, everybody.'

Chapter 3

1

MATHER'S train got in at eleven that night and with Saunders he drove straight through the almost empty streets to the police station. Nottwich went to bed early; the cinemas closed at ten-thirty and a quarter of an hour later everyone had left the middle of Nottwich by tram or bus. Nottwich's only tart hung round the market place, cold and blue under her umbrella, and one or two business men were having a last cigar in the hall of the Metropole. The car slid on the icy road. Just before the police station Mather noticed the posters of *Aladdin* outside the Royal Theatre. He said to Saunders, 'My girl's in that show.' He felt proud and happy.

The Chief Constable had come down to the police station to meet Mather. The fact that Raven was known to be armed and desperate gave the chase a more serious air than it would

63

otherwise have had. The Chief Constable was fat and excited. He had made a lot of money as a tradesman and during the war had been given a commission and the job of presiding over the local military tribunal. He prided himself on having been a terror to pacifists. It atoned a little for his own home life and a wife who despised him. That was why he had come down to the station to meet Mather: it would be something to boast about at home.

Mather said, 'Of course, sir, we don't *know* he's here. But he was on the train all right, and his ticket was given up. By a woman.'

'Got an accomplice, eh?' the Chief Constable asked.

'Perhaps. Find the woman and we may have Raven.'

The Chief Constable belched behind his hand. He had been drinking bottled beer before he came out and it always repeated itself. The superintendent said, 'Directly we heard from the Yard we circulated the number of the notes to all shops, hotels and boarding houses.'

'That a map, sir,' Mather asked, 'with your beats marked?'

They walked over to the wall and the superintendent pointed out the main points in Nottwich with a pencil: the railway station, the river, the police station.

'And the Royal Theatre,' Mather said, 'will be about there?'

'That's right.'

'What's brought 'im to Nottwich?' the Chief Constable asked.

'I wish we knew, sir. Now these streets round the station, are they hotels?'

'A few boarding houses. But the worst of it is,' the superintendent said, absent-mindedly turning his back on the Chief Constable, 'a lot of these houses take occasional boarders.'

'Better circulate them all.'

'Some of them wouldn't take much notice of a police request. Houses of call, you know. Quick ten minutes and the door always open.'

'Nonsense,' the Chief Constable said, 'we don't have that kind of place in Nottwich.'

'If you wouldn't mind my suggesting it, sir, it wouldn't be a bad thing to double the constables on any beats of that kind. Send the sharpest men you've got. I suppose you've had his description in the evening papers? He seems to be a pretty smart safebreaker.'

'There doesn't seem to be much more we can do tonight,' the superintendent said. 'I'm sorry for the poor devil if he's found nowhere to sleep.'

'Keep a bottle of whisky here, super?' the Chief Constable asked. 'Do us all good to 'ave a drink. Had too much beer. It returns. Whisky's better, but the wife doesn't like the smell.' He leant back in his chair with his fat thighs crossed and watched the inspector with a kind of child-like happiness; he seemed to be saying, what a spree this is, drinking again with the boys. Only the superintendent knew what an old devil he was with anyone weaker than himself. 'Just a splash, super.' He said over his glass, 'You caught that old bastard Baines out nicely,' and explained to Mather. 'Street betting. He's been a worry for months.'

'He was straight enough. I don't believe in harrying people. Just because he was taking money out of Macpherson's pocket.'

'Ah,' the Chief Constable said, 'but that's legal. Macpherson's got an office and a telephone. He's got expenses to carry. Cheerio, boys. To the ladies.' He drained his glass. 'Just another two fingers, super.' He blew out his chest. 'What about some more coal on the fire? Let's be snug. There's no work we can do tonight.'

Mather was uneasy. It was quite true there wasn't much one could do, but he hated inaction. He stayed by the map. It wasn't such a large place, Nottwich. They ought not to take long to find Raven, but here he was a stranger. He didn't know what dives to raid, what clubs and dance halls. He said, 'We think he's followed someone here. I'd suggest, sir, that first thing in the morning we interview the ticket collector again. See how many local people he can remember leaving the train. We might be lucky.'

'Do you know that story about the Archbishop of York?'

the Chief Constable asked. 'Yes, yes. We'll do that. But there's no hurry. Make yourself at 'ome, man, and take some Scotch. You're in the Midlands now. The slow Midlands (eh, super?). We don't 'ustle, but we get there just the same.'

Of course, he was right. There *was* no hurry, and there wasn't anything anyone could do at this hour, but as Mather stood beside the map, it was just as if someone were calling him, 'Hurry. Hurry. Hurry. Or you may be too late.' He traced the main streets with his finger; he wanted to be as familiar with them as he was with central London. Here was the G.P.O., the market, the Metropole, the High Street; what was this? the Tanneries. 'What's this big block in the Tanneries, sir?' he asked.

'That'll be Midland Steel,' the superintendent said and turning to the Chief Constable he went on patiently, 'No, sir. I hadn't heard that one. That's a good one, sir.'

'The mayor told me that,' the Chief Constable said. 'He's a sport, old Piker. Do you know what he said when we had that committee on the gas practice? He said, "This'll give us a chance to get into a strange bed." He meant the women couldn't tell who was who in a gas mask. You see?'

'Very witty man, Mr Piker, sir.'

'Yes, super, but I was too smart for him there. I was on the spot that day. Do you know what I said?'

'No, sir.'

'I said, "*You* won't be able to find a strange bed, Piker." Catch me meaning? He's a dog, old Piker.'

'What are your arrangements for the gas practice, sir?' Mather asked with his finger jabbed on the Town Hall.

'You can't expect people to buy gas masks at twenty-five bob a time, but we're having a raid the day after tomorrow with smoke bombs from Hanlow aerodrome, and anyone found in the street without a mask will be carted off by ambulance to the General Hospital. So anyone who's too busy to stop indoors will have to buy a mask. Midland Steel are supplying all their people with masks, so it'll be business as usual there.'

'Kind of blackmail,' the superintendent said. 'Stay in or buy a mask. The transport companies have spent a pretty penny on masks.'

'What hours, sir?'

'We don't tell them that. Sirens hoot. You know the idea. Boy Scouts on bicycles. They've been lent masks. But of course *we* know it'll be all over before noon.'

Mather looked back at the map. 'These coal yards,' he said, 'round the station. You've got them well covered?'

'We are keeping an eye on those,' the superintendent said. 'I saw to that as soon as the Yard rang through.'

'Smart work, boys, smart work,' the Chief Constable said, swallowing the last of his whisky. 'I'll be off home. Busy day before us all tomorrow. You'd like a conference with me in the morning, I dare say, super?'

'Oh, I don't think we'll trouble you that early, sir.'

'Well, if you do need any advice, I'm always at the end of the 'phone. Good night, boys.'

'Good night, sir. Good night.'

'The old boy's right about one thing.' The superintendent put the whisky away in his cupboard. 'We can't do anything more tonight.'

'I won't keep you up, sir,' Mather said. 'You mustn't think I'm fussy. Saunders will tell you I'm as ready to knock off as any man, but there's something about this case ... I can't leave it alone. It's a queer case. I was looking at this map, sir, and trying to think where I'd hide. What about these dotted lines out here on the east?'

'It's a new housing estate.'

'Half-built houses?'

'I've put two men on special beat out there.'

'You've got everything taped pretty well, sir. You don't really need us.'

'You mustn't judge us by *him*.'

'I'm not quite easy in my mind. He's followed someone here. He's a smart lad. We've never had anything on him before, and yet for the last twenty-four hours he's done nothing but make mistakes. The chief said he's blazing a trail, and it's true. It strikes me that he's desperate to get someone.'

The superintendent glanced at the clock.

'I'm off, sir,' Mather said. 'See you in the morning. Good night, Saunders. I'm just going to take a stroll around a bit before I come to the hotel. I want to get this place clear.'

He walked out into the High Street. The rain had stopped and was freezing in the gutters. He slipped on the pavement and had to push his hand on the lamp standard. They turned the lights very low in Nottwich after eleven. Over the way, fifty yards down towards the market, he could see the portico of the Royal Theatre. No lights at all to be seen there. He found himself humming, *'But to me it's Paradise,'* and thought: it's good to love, to have a centre, a certainty, not just to be *in* love floating around. He wanted that too to be organized as soon as possible: he wanted love stamped and sealed and signed and the licence paid for. He was filled with a dumb tenderness he would never be able to express outside marriage. He wasn't a lover; he was already like a married man, but a married man with years of happiness and confidence to be grateful for.

He did the maddest thing he'd done since he had known her: he went and took a look at her lodgings. He had the address. She'd given it him over the 'phone, and it fitted in with his work to find his way to All Saints Road. He learnt quite a lot of things on the way, keeping his eyes open: it wasn't really a waste of time. He learnt, for instance, the name and address of the local papers: the *Nottwich Journal* and the *Nottwich Guardian*, two rival papers facing each other across Chatton Street, one of them next a great gaudy cinema. From their posters he could even judge their publics: the *Journal* was popular, the *Guardian* was 'class'. He learnt too where the best fish-and-chip shops were and the public-houses where the pitmen went; he discovered the park, a place of dull wilted trees and palings and gravel paths for perambulators. Any of these facts might be of use and they humanized the map of Nottwich so that he could think of it in terms of people, just as he thought of London, when he was on a job, in terms of Charlies and Joes.

All Saints Road was two rows of small neo-Gothic houses

lined up as carefully as a company on parade. He stopped outside No. 14 and wondered if she were awake. She'd get a surprise in the morning; he had posted a card at Euston telling her he was putting up at the Crown, the commercial 'house'. There was a light on in the basement: the landlady was still awake. He wished he could have sent a quicker message than that card; he knew the dreariness of new lodgings, of waking to the black tea and the unfriendly face. It seemed to him that life couldn't treat her well enough.

The wind froze him, but he lingered there on the opposite pavement, wondering whether she had enough blankets on her bed, whether she had any shillings for the gas meter. Encouraged by the light in the basement he nearly rang the bell to ask the landlady whether Anne had all she needed. But he made his way instead towards the Crown. He wasn't going to look silly; he wasn't even going to tell her that he'd been and had a look at where she slept.

2

A knock on the door woke him. It was barely seven. A woman's voice said, 'You're wanted on the 'phone,' and he could hear her trailing away downstairs, knocking a broom handle against the banisters. It was going to be a fine day.

Mather went downstairs to the telephone, which was behind the bar in the empty saloon. He said, 'Mather. Who's that?' and heard the station sergeant's voice, 'We've got some news for you. He slept last night in St Mark's, the Roman Catholic Cathedral. And someone reports he was down by the river earlier.'

But by the time he was dressed and at the station more evidence had come in. The agent of a housing estate had read in the local paper about the stolen notes and brought to the station two notes he had received from a girl who said she wanted to buy a house. He'd thought it odd because she had never turned up to sign the papers.

'That'll be the girl who gave up his ticket,' the superintendent said. 'They are working together on this.'

'And the cathedral?' Mather asked.

'A woman saw him come out early this morning. Then when she got home (she was on the way to chapel) and read the paper, she told a constable on point duty. We'll have to have the churches locked.'

'No, watched,' Mather said. He warmed his hand over the iron stove. 'Let me talk to this house agent.'

The man came breezily in in plus fours from the outer room. 'Name of Green,' he said.

'Could you tell me, Mr Green, what this girl looked like?'

'A nice little thing,' Mr Green said.

'Short? Below five-feet four?'

'No, I wouldn't say that.'

'You said little?'

'Oh,' Mr Green said, 'term of affection, you know. Easy to get on with.'

'Fair? Dark?'

'Oh, I couldn't say that. Don't look at their hair. Good legs.'

'Anything strange in her manner?'

'No, I wouldn't say that. Nicely spoken. She could take a joke.'

'Then you wouldn't have noticed the colour of her eyes?'

'Well, as a matter of fact, I did. I always look at a girl's eyes. They like it. "Drink to me only", you know. A bit of poetry. That's my gambit. Kind of spiritual, you know.'

'And what colour were they?'

'Green with a spot of gold.'

'What was she wearing? Did you notice that?'

'Of course I did,' Mr Green said. He moved his hands in the air. 'It was something dark and soft. You know what I mean.'

'And the hat? Straw?'

'No. It wasn't straw.'

'Felt?'

'It might have been a kind of felt. That was dark too. I noticed that.'

'Would you know her again if you saw her?'

'Of course I would,' Mr Green said. 'Never forget a face.'

'Right,' Mather said, 'you can go. We may want you later to identify the girl. We'll keep these notes.'

'But I say,' Mr Green said, 'those are good notes. They belong to the company.'

'You can consider the house is still for sale.'

'I've had the ticket collector here,' the superintendent said. 'Of course he doesn't remember a thing that helps. In these stories you read people always remember *something*, but in real life they just say she was wearing something dark or something light.'

'You've sent someone up to look at the house? Is this the man's story? It's odd. She must have gone there straight from the station. Why? And why pretend to buy the house and pay him with stolen notes?'

'It looks as if she was desperate to keep the other man from buying. As if she'd got something hidden there.'

'Your man had better go through the house with a comb, sir. But of course they won't find much. If there was still anything to find she'd have turned up to sign the papers.'

'No, she'd have been afraid,' the superintendent said, 'in case he'd found out they were stolen notes.'

'You know,' Mather said, 'I wasn't much interested in this case. It seemed sort of petty. Chasing down a small thief when the whole world will soon be fighting because of a murderer those fools in Europe couldn't catch. But now it's getting me. There's something odd about it. I told you what my chief said about Raven? He said he was blazing a trail. But he's managed so far to keep just ahead of us. Could I see the ticket collector's statement?'

'There's nothing in it.'

'I don't agree with you, sir,' Mather said, while the superintendent turned it up from the file of papers on his desk, 'the books are right. People generally do remember something. If they remembered nothing at all, it would look very queer. It's only spooks that don't leave any impression. Even that agent remembered the colour of her eyes.'

'Probably wrong,' the superintendent said. 'Here you are.

All he remembers is that she carried two suitcases. It's something, of course, but it's not worth much.'

'Oh, one could make guesses from that,' Mather said. 'Don't you think so?' He didn't believe in making himself too clever in front of the provincial police; he needed their co-operation. 'She was coming for a long stay (a woman can get a lot in one suitcase) or else, if she was carrying his case too, he was the dominant one. Believes in treating her rough and making her do all the physical labour. That fits in with Raven's character. As for the girl – '

'In these gangster stories,' the superintendent said, 'they call her a moll.'

'Well, this moll,' Mather said, 'is one of those girls who like being treated rough. Sort of clinging and avaricious, I picture her. If she had more spirit he'd carry one of the suitcases or else she'd split on him.'

'I thought this Raven was about as ugly as they are made.'

'That fits too,' Mather said. 'Perhaps she likes 'em ugly. Perhaps it gives her a thrill.'

The superintendent laughed. 'You've got a lot out of those suitcases. Read the report and you'll be giving me her photograph. Here you are. But he doesn't remember a thing about her, not even what she was wearing.'

Mather read it. He read it slowly. He said nothing, but something in his manner of shock and incredulity was conveyed to the superintendent. He said, 'Is anything wrong? There's nothing *there*, surely?'

'You said I'd be giving you her photograph,' Mather said. He took a slip of newspaper from the back of his watch. 'There it is, sir. You'd better circulate that to all stations in the city and to the Press.'

'But there's nothing in the report,' the superintendent said.

'Everybody remembers something. It wasn't anything you could have spotted. I seem to have private information about this crime, but I didn't know it till now.'

The superintendent said, 'He doesn't remember a thing. Except the suitcases.'

'Thank God for those,' Mather said. 'It may mean . . . You see he says here that one of the reasons he remembers her – he calls it remembering her – is that she was the only woman who got out of the train at Nottwich. And this girl I happen to know was travelling by it. She'd got an engagement at the theatre here.'

The superintendent said bluntly – he didn't realize the full extent of the shock, 'And is she of the type you said? Likes 'em ugly?'

'I thought she liked them plain,' Mather said, staring out through the window at a world going to work through the cold early day.

'Sort of clinging and avaricious?'

'No, damn it.'

'But if she'd had more spirit – ' the superintendent mocked; he thought Mather was disturbed because his guesses were wrong.

'She had all the spirit there was,' Mather said. He turned back from the window. He forgot the superintendent was his superior officer; he forgot you had to be tactful to these provincial police officers; he said, 'God damn it, don't you see? He didn't carry his suitcase because he had to keep her covered. He *made* her walk out to the housing estate.' He said, 'I've got to go out there. He meant to murder her.'

'No, no,' the superintendent said. 'You are forgetting: she paid the money to Green and walked out of the house with him alone. He saw her off the estate.'

'But I'd swear,' Mather said, 'she isn't in this. It's absurd. It doesn't make sense.' He said, 'We're engaged to be married.'

'That's tough,' the superintendent said. He hesitated, picked up a dead match and cleaned a nail, then he pushed the photograph back. 'Put it away,' he said. 'We'll go about this differently.'

'No,' Mather said. 'I'm on this case. Have it printed. It's a bad smudged photo.' He wouldn't look at it. 'It doesn't do her justice. But I'll wire home for a better likeness. I've got a whole strip of Photomatons at home. Her face from every angle. You couldn't have a better lot of photos for newspaper purposes.'

'I'm sorry, Mather,' the superintendent said. 'Hadn't I better speak to the Yard? Get another man sent?'

'You couldn't have a better on the case,' Mather said. 'I know her. If she's to be found, I'll find her. I'm going out to the house now. You see, your man may miss something. I *know* her.'

'There may be an explanation,' the superintendent said.

'Don't you see,' Mather said, 'that if there's an explanation it means – why, that she's in danger, she may even be – '

'We'd have found her body.'

'We haven't even found a living man,' Mather said. 'Would you ask Saunders to follow me out? What's the address?' He wrote it carefully down; he always noted facts; he didn't trust his brain for more than theories, guesses.

It was a long drive out to the housing estate. He had time to think of many possibilities. She might have fallen asleep and been carried on to York. She might not have taken the train . . . and there was nothing in the little hideous house to contradict him. He found a plainclothes man in what would one day be the best front room; in its flashy fireplace, its dark brown picture rail and the cheap oak of its wainscoting, it bore already the suggestion of heavy unused furniture, dark curtains and Gosse china. 'There's nothing,' the detective said, 'nothing at all. You can see, of course, that someone's been here. The dust has been disturbed. But there wasn't enough dust to make a footprint. There's nothing to be got here.'

'There's always something,' Mather said. 'Where did you find traces? All the rooms?'

'No, not all of them. But that's not evidence. There was no sign in this room, but the dust isn't as thick here. Maybe the builders swept up better. You can't say no one was in here.'

'How did she get in?'

'The lock of the back door's busted.'

'Could a girl do that?'

'A cat could do it. A determined cat.'

'Green says he came in at the front. Just opened the door of

74

this room and then took the other fellow straight upstairs, into the best bedroom. The girl joined them there just as he was going to show the rest of the house. Then they all went straight down and out of the house except the girl went into the kitchen and picked up her suitcases. He'd left the front door open and thought she'd followed them in.'

'She was in the kitchen all right. And in the bathroom.'

'Where's that?'

'Up the stairs and round to the left.'

The two men, they were both large, nearly filled the cramped bathroom. 'Looks as if she heard them coming,' the detective said, 'and hid in here.'

'What brought her up? If she was in the kitchen she had only to slip out at the back.' Mather stood in the tiny room between the bath and the lavatory seat and thought: *she* was here yesterday. It was incredible. It didn't fit in at any point with what he knew of her. They had been engaged for six months; she couldn't have disguised herself so completely: on the bus ride from Kew that evening, humming the song – what was it? – something about a snowflower; the night they sat two programmes round at the cinema because he'd spent his week's pay and hadn't been able to give her dinner. She never complained as the hard mechanized voices began all over again, 'A wise guy, huh?' 'Baby, you're swell.' 'Siddown, won't you?' 'Thenks', at the edge of their consciousness. She was straight, she was loyal, he could swear that; but the alternative was a danger he hardly dared contemplate. Raven was desperate. He heard himself saying with harsh conviction, 'Raven was here. He drove her up at the point of his pistol. He was going to shut her in here – or maybe shoot her. Then he heard voices. He gave her the notes and told her to get rid of the other fellows. If she tried anything on, he'd have shot her. Damn it, isn't it plain?' but the detective only repeated the substance of the superintendent's criticism, 'She walked right out of the place alone with Green. There was nothing to prevent her going to the police station.'

'He may have followed at a distance.'

'It looks to me,' the detective said, 'as if you are taking the most *unlikely* theory,' and Mather could tell from his manner how puzzled he was at the Yard man's attitude: these Londoners were a little too ingenious: he believed in good sound Midland common sense. It angered Mather in his professional pride; he even felt a small chill of hatred against Anne for putting him in a position where his affection warped his judgement. He said, 'We've no proof that she didn't try to tell the police,' and he wondered: do I want her dead and innocent or alive and guilty? He began to examine the bathroom with meticulous care. He even pushed his finger up the taps in case . . . He had a wild idea that if it were really Anne who had stood here, she would have wanted to leave a message. He straightened himself impatiently. 'There's nothing here.' He remembered there was a test: she might have missed her train. 'I want a telephone,' he said.

'There'll be one down the road at the agent's.'

Mather rang up the theatre. There was no one there except a caretaker, but as it happened she could tell him that no one had been absent from rehearsal. The producer, Mr Collier, always posted absentees on the board inside the stage door. He was great on discipline, Mr Collier. Yes, and she remembered that there *was* a new girl. She happened to see her going out with a man at dinner-time after the rehearsal just as she came back to the theatre to tidy up a bit and thought: 'that's a new face'. She didn't know who the man was. He might be one of the backers. 'Wait a moment, wait a moment,' Mather said; he had to think what to do next; she *was* the girl who gave the agent the stolen notes; he had to forget that she was Anne who had so wildly wished that they could marry before Christmas, who had hated the promiscuity of her job, who had promised him that night on the bus from Kew that she would keep out of the way of all rich business backers and stage-door loungers. He said: 'Mr Collier? Where can I find him?'

'He'll be at the theatre tonight. There's a rehearsal at eight.'

'I want to see him at once.'

'You can't. He's gone up to York with Mr Bleek.'

'Where can I find any of the girls who were at the rehearsal?'

'I dunno. I don't have the address book. They'll be all over town.'

'There must be *someone* who was there last night – '

'You could find Miss Maydew, of course.'

'Where?'

'I don't know where she's staying. But you've only got to look at the posters of the jumble.'

'The jumble? What do you mean?'

'She's opening the jumble up at St Luke's at two.'

Through the window of the agent's office Mather saw Saunders coming up the frozen mud of the track between the Cozyholmes. He rang off and intercepted him. 'Any news come in?'

'Yes,' Saunders said. The superintendent had told him everything, and he was deeply distressed. He liked Mather. He owed everything to Mather; it was Mather who had brought him up every stage of promotion in the police force, who had persuaded the authorities that a man who stammered could be as good a policeman as the champion reciter at police concerts. But he would have loved him anyway for a quality of idealism, for believing so implicitly in what he did.

'Well? Let's have it.'

'It's about your g-girl. She's disappeared.' He took the news at a run, getting it out in one breath. 'Her landlady rang up the station, said she was out all night and never came back.'

'Run away,' Mather said.

Saunders said, 'D-don't you believe it. You t-t-t-told her to take that train. She wasn't going till the m-m-m-m-morning.'

'You're right,' Mather said. 'I'd forgotten that. Meeting him must have been an accident. But it's a miserable choice, Saunders. She may be dead now.'

'Why should he do that? We've only got a theft on him. What are you going to do next?'

'Back to the station. And then at two,' he smiled miserably, 'a jumble sale.'

The vicar was worried. He wouldn't listen to what Mather had to say; he had too much to think about himself. It was the curate, the new bright broad-minded curate from a London east-end parish, who had suggested inviting Miss Maydew to open the jumble sale. He thought it would be a draw, but as the vicar explained to Mather, holding him pinned there in the pitch-pine ante-room of St Luke's Hall, a jumble was always a draw. There was a queue fifty yards long of women with baskets waiting for the door to open; they hadn't come to see Miss Maydew; they had come for bargains. St Luke's jumble sales were famous all over Nottwich.

A dry perky woman with a cameo brooch put her head in at the door. 'Henry,' she said, 'the committee are rifling the stalls again. Can't you *do* something about it? There'll be nothing left when the sale starts.'

'Where's Mander? It's *his* business,' the vicar said.

'Mr Mander, of course, is off fetching Miss Maydew.' The perky woman blew her nose and crying 'Constance, Constance!' disappeared into the hall.

'You can't really do anything about it,' the vicar said. 'It happens every year. These good women give their time voluntarily. The Altar Society would be in a very bad way without them. They *expect* to have first choice of everything that's sent in. Of course the trouble is: *they* fix the prices.'

'Henry,' the perky woman said, appearing again in the doorway, 'you *must* interfere. Mrs Penny has priced that very good hat Lady Cundifer sent at eighteen pence and bought it herself.'

'My dear, how can I say anything? They'd never volunteer again. You must remember they've given time and trouble . . .' but he was addressing a closed door. 'What worries me,' he said to Mather, 'is that this young lady will expect an ovation. She won't understand that nobody's interested in *who* opens a jumble sale. Things are so different in London.'

'She's late,' Mather said.

'They are quite capable of storming the doors,' the vicar said with a nervous glance through the window at the lengthening queue. 'I must confess to a little stratagem. After all she is our guest. She is giving time and trouble.' Time and trouble were the gifts of which the vicar was always most conscious. They were given more readily than coppers in the collection. He went on, 'Did you see any young boys outside?'

'Only women,' Mather said.

'Oh dear, oh dear. I *told* Troop Leader Lance. You see, I thought if one or two Scouts, in plain clothes, of course, brought up autograph books, it would please Miss Maydew, seem to show we appreciated ... the time and trouble.' He said miserably, 'The St Luke's troop is always the least trustworthy ...'

A grey-haired man with a carpet bag put his head in at the door. He said, 'Mrs 'Arris said as there was something wrong with the toilet.'

'Ah, Mr Bacon,' the vicar said, 'so kind of you. Step into the hall. You'll find Mrs Harris there. A little stoppage, so I understand.'

Mather looked at his watch. He said, 'I must speak to Miss Maydew directly – ' A young man entered at a rush; he said to the vicar, 'Excuse me, Mr Harris, but will Miss Maydew be speaking?'

'I hope not. I profoundly hope not,' the vicar said. 'It's hard enough as it is to keep the women from the stalls till after I've said a prayer. Where's my prayer book? Who's seen my prayer book?'

'Because I'm covering it for the *Journal*, and if she's not, you see, I can get away – '

Mather wanted to say: Listen to me. Your damned jumble is of no importance. My girl's in danger. She may be dead. He wanted to do things to people, but he stood there heavy, immobile, patient, even his private passion and fear subdued by his training. One didn't give way to anger, one plodded on calmly, adding fact to fact; if one's girl was killed, one had the satisfaction of knowing one had done one's best according to the standards of the best police force in the world. He wondered bitterly, as he watched the vicar search for his prayer book, whether that would be any comfort.

Mr Bacon came back and said, 'She'll pull now,' and disappeared with a clank of metal. A boisterous voice said, 'Upstage a little, upstage, Miss Maydew,' and the curate entered. He wore suede shoes, he had a shiny face and plastered hair and he carried an umbrella under his arm like a cricket bat; he might have been returning to the pavilion after scoring a duck in a friendly, taking his failure noisily as a good sportsman should. 'Here is my C.O., Miss Maydew, on the O.P. side.' He said to the vicar, 'I've been telling Miss Maydew about our dramatics.'

Mather said, 'May I speak to you a moment privately, Miss Maydew?'

But the vicar swept her away. 'A moment, a moment, first our little ceremony. Constance! Constance!' and almost immediately the ante-room was empty except for Mather and the journalist, who sat on the table swinging his legs, biting his nails. An extraordinary noise came from the next room: it was like the trampling of a herd of animals, a trampling suddenly brought to a standstill at a fence; in the sudden silence one could hear the vicar hastily finishing off the Lord's Prayer, and then Miss Maydew's clear immature principal boy's voice saying, 'I declare this jumble well and truly – ' and then the trampling again. She had got her words wrong – it had always been foundation stones her mother laid; but no one noticed. Everyone was relieved because she hadn't made a speech. Mather went to the door; half a dozen boys were queued up in front of Miss Maydew with autograph albums; the St Luke's troop hadn't failed after all. A hard astute woman in a toque said to Mather, 'This stall will interest *you*. It's a Man's Stall,' and Mather looked down at a dingy array of pen-wipers and pipe-cleaners and hand-embroidered tobacco pouches. Somebody had even presented a lot of old pipes. He lied quickly, 'I don't smoke.'

The astute woman said, 'You've come here to spend money, haven't you, as a duty? You may as well take *some*thing that will be of use. You won't find anything on any of the other stalls,' and between the women's shoulders, as he craned to follow the movements of Miss Maydew and the St Luke's troop, he caught a few grim glimpses of discarded vases, chipped fruit stands, yellowing piles of babies' napkins. 'I've got several pairs of braces. You may just as well take a pair of braces.'

Mather, to his own astonishment and distress, said, 'She may be dead.'

The woman said, 'Who dead?' and bristled over a pair of mauve suspenders.

'I'm sorry,' Mather said. 'I wasn't thinking.' He was horrified with himself for losing grip. He thought: I ought to have let them exchange me. It's going to be too much. He said, 'Excuse me,' seeing the last Scout shut his album.

He led Miss Maydew into the ante-room. The journalist had gone. He said, 'I'm trying to trace a girl in your company called Anne Crowder.'

'Don't know her,' Miss Maydew said.

'She only joined the cast yesterday.'

'They all look alike,' Miss Maydew said, 'like Chinamen. I never can learn their names.'

'This one's fair. Green eyes. She has a good voice.'

'Not in *this* company,' Miss Maydew said, 'not in *this* company. I can't listen to them. It sets my teeth on edge.'

'You don't remember her going out last night with a man, at the end of rehearsal?'

'Why should I? Don't be so sordid.'

'He invited you out too.'

'The fat fool,' Miss Maydew said.

'Who was he?'

'I don't know. Davenant, I think Collier said, or did he say Davis? Never saw him before. I suppose he's the man Cohen quarrelled with. Though somebody said something about Callitrope.'

'This is important, Miss Maydew. The girl's disappeared.'

'It's always happening on these tours. If you go into their dressing-rooms it's always *Men* they are talking about. How can they ever hope to act? So sordid.'

'You can't help me at all? You've no idea where I can find this man Davenant?'

'Collier will know. He'll be back tonight. Or perhaps he won't. I don't think he knew him from Adam. It's coming back to me now. Collier called him Davis and he said, No, he was Davenant. He'd bought out Davis.'

Mather went sadly away. Some instinct that always made him go where people were, because clues were more likely to be found among a crowd of strangers than in empty rooms or deserted streets, drove him through the hall. You wouldn't have known among these avid women that England was on the edge of war. 'I said to Mrs 'Opkinson, if you are addressing me, I said.' 'That'll look tasty on Dora.' A very old woman said across a pile of artificial silk knickers, ''E lay for five hours with 'is knees drawn up.' A girl giggled and said in a hoarse whisper, 'Awful. I'd say so. 'E put 'is fingers right down.' Why should these people worry about war? They moved from stall to stall in an air thick with their own deaths and sicknesses and loves. A woman with a hard driven face touched Mather's arm; she must have been about sixty years old; she had a way of ducking her head when she spoke as if she expected a blow, but up her head would come again with a sour unconquerable malice. He had watched her, without really knowing it, as he walked down the stalls. Now she plucked at him; he could smell fish on her fingers. 'Reach me that bit of stuff, dear,' she said. 'You've got long arms. No, not that. The pink,' and began to fumble for money – in Anne's bag.

4

Mather's brother had committed suicide. More than Mather he had needed to be part of an organization, to be trained and disciplined and given orders, but unlike Mather he hadn't found his organization. When things went wrong he killed himself, and Mather was called to the mortuary to identify the body. He had hoped it was a stranger until they had exposed the pale drowned lost face. All day he had been trying to find

82

his brother, hurrying from address to address, and the first feeling he had when he saw him there was not grief. He thought: I needn't hurry, I can sit down. He went out to an A.B.C. and ordered a pot of tea. He only began to feel his grief after the second cup.

It was the same now. He thought: I needn't have hurried, I needn't have made a fool of myself before that woman with the braces. She must be dead. I needn't have felt so rushed.

The old woman said, 'Thank you, dear,' and thrust the little piece of pink material away. He couldn't feel any doubt whatever about the bag. He had given it her himself; it was an expensive bag, not a kind you would expect to find in Nottwich, and to make it quite conclusive, you could still see, within a little circle of twisted glass, the place where two initials had been removed. It was all over for ever; he hadn't got to hurry any more; a pain was on its way worse than he had felt in the A.B.C. (a man at the next table had been eating fried plaice and now, he didn't know why, he associated a certain kind of pain with the smell of fish). But first it was a perfectly cold calculating satisfaction he felt, that he had the devils in his hands already. Someone was going to die for this. The old woman had picked up a small bra and was testing the elastic with a malicious grin because it was meant for someone young and pretty with breasts worth preserving. 'The silly things they wear,' she said.

He could have arrested her at once, but already he had decided that wouldn't do; there were more in it than the old woman; he'd get them all, and the longer the chase lasted the better; he wouldn't have to begin thinking of the future till it was over. He was thankful now that Raven was armed because he himself was forced to carry a gun, and who could say whether chance might not allow him to use it?

He looked up and there on the other side of the stall, with his eyes fixed on Anne's bag, was the dark bitter figure he had been seeking, the hare-lip imperfectly hidden by a few days' growth of moustache.

Chapter 4

1

RAVEN had been on his feet all the morning. He had to keep moving; he couldn't use the little change he had on food, because he did not dare to stay still, to give anyone the chance to study his face. He bought a paper outside the post office and saw his own description there, printed in black type inside a frame. He was angry because it was on a back page: the situation in Europe filled the front page. By midday, moving here and moving there with his eyes always open for Cholmondeley, he was dog-tired. He stood for a moment and stared at his own face in a barber's window; ever since his flight from the café he had remained unshaven; a moustache would hide his scar, but he knew from experience how his hair grew in patches, strong on the chin, weak on the lip, and not at all on either side of the red deformity. Now the scrubby growth on his chin was making him conspicuous and he didn't dare go into the barber's for a shave. He passed a chocolate machine, but it would take only sixpenny or shilling pieces, and his pocket held nothing but half-crowns, florins, half-pennies. If it had not been for his bitter hatred he would have given himself up; they couldn't give him more than five years, but the death of the old minister lay, now that he was so tired and harried, like an albatross round his neck. It was hard to realize that he was wanted only for theft.

He was afraid to haunt alleys, to linger in culs-de-sac because if a policeman passed and he was the only man in sight he felt conspicuous; the man might give him a second glance, and so he walked all the time in the most crowded streets and took the risk of innumerable recognitions. It was a dull cold day, but at least it wasn't raining. The shops were full of Christmas gifts, all the absurd useless junk which had lain on back shelves all the year was brought out to fill the windows; foxhead brooches, book-rests in the shape of the Cenotaph, woollen cosies for boiled eggs, innumerable games with

84

counters and dice and absurd patent variations on darts or bagatelle, 'Cats on a Wall', the old shooting game, and 'Fishing for Gold Fish'. In a religious shop by the Catholic Cathedral he found himself facing again the images that angered him in the Soho café; the plaster mother and child, the wise men and the shepherds. They were arranged in a cavern of brown paper among the books of devotion, the little pious scraps of St Theresa. 'The Holy Family': he pressed his face against the glass with a kind of horrified anger that that tale still went on. 'Because there was no room for them in the inn'; he remembered how they had sat in rows on the benches waiting for Christmas dinner, while the thin precise voice read on about Caesar Augustus and how everyone went up to his own city to be taxed. Nobody was beaten on Christmas Day: all punishments were saved for Boxing Day. Love, Charity, Patience, Humility – he was educated; he knew all about those virtues; he'd seen what they were worth. They twisted everything; even that story in there, it was historical, it had happened, but they twisted it to their own purposes. They made him a God because they could feel fine about it all, they didn't have to consider themselves responsible for the raw deal they'd given him. He'd consented, hadn't he? That was the argument, because he could have called down 'a legion of angels' if he'd wanted to escape hanging there. On your life he could, he thought with bitter lack of faith, just as easily as his own father taking the drop at Wandsworth could have saved himself when the trap opened. He stood there with his face against the glass waiting for somebody to deny *that* reasoning, staring at the swaddled child with a horrified tenderness, 'the little bastard', because he was educated and knew what the child was in for, the double-crossing Judas and only one man to draw a knife on his side when the Roman soldiers came for him in the garden.

A policeman came up the street, as Raven stared into the window, and passed without a glance. It occurred to him to wonder how much they knew. Had the girl told them her story? He supposed she had by this time. It would be in the paper, and he looked. There was not a word about her there.

It shook him. He'd nearly killed her and she hadn't gone to them: that meant she had believed what he'd told her. He was momentarily back in the garage again beside the Weevil in the rain and dark with the dreadful sense of desolation, of having missed something valuable, of having made an irretrievable mistake, but he could no longer comfort himself with any conviction with his old phrase: 'give her time ... it always happens with a skirt'. He wanted to find her, but he thought: what a chance, I can't even find Cholmondeley. He said bitterly to the tiny scrap of plaster in the plaster cradle: 'If you were a God, you'd know I wouldn't harm her: you'd give me a break, you'd let me turn and see her on the pavement,' and he turned with half a hope, but of course there was nothing there.

As he moved away he saw a sixpence in the gutter. He picked it up and went back the way he had come to the last chocolate slot machine he had passed. It was outside a sweet shop and next a church hall, where a queue of women waited along the pavement for some kind of sale to open. They were getting noisy and impatient; it was after the hour when the doors should have opened, and he thought what fine game they would be for a really expert bag-picker. They were pressed against each other and would never notice a little pressure on the clasp. There was nothing personal in the thought; he had never fallen quite so low, he believed, as picking women's bags. But it made him idly pay attention to them, as he walked along the line. One stood out from the others, carried by an old rather dirty woman, new, expensive, sophisticated, of a kind he had seen before; he remembered at once the occasion, the little bathroom, the raised pistol, the compact she had taken from the bag.

The door was opened and the women pushed in; almost at once he was alone on the pavement beside the slot machine and the jumble-sale poster: 'Entrance 6d.' It couldn't be her bag, he told himself, there must be hundreds like it, but nevertheless he pursued it through the pitch-pine door. 'And lead us not into temptation,' the vicar was saying from a dais at one end of the hall above the old hats and the chipped vases and the stacks of women's underwear. When the prayer was finished he was flung by the pressure of the crowd against a stall of fancy goods: little framed amateur water-colours of lakeland scenery, gaudy cigarette boxes from Italian holidays, brass ashtrays and a row of discarded novels. Then the crowd lifted him and pushed on towards the favourite stall. There was nothing he could do about it. He couldn't seek for any individual in the crowd, but that didn't matter, for he found himself pressed against a stall, on the other side of which the old woman stood. He leant across and stared at the bag; he remembered how the girl had said, 'My name's Anne,' and there, impressed on the leather, was a faint initial A, where a chromium letter had been removed. He looked up, he didn't notice that there was another man beside the stall, his eyes were filled with the image of a dusty wicked face.

He was shocked by it just as he had been shocked by Mr Cholmondeley's duplicity. He felt no guilt about the old War Minister, he was one of the great ones of the world, one of those who 'sat', he knew all the right words, he was educated, 'in the chief seats at the synagogues', and if he was sometimes a little worried by the memory of the secretary's whisper through the imperfectly shut door, he could always tell himself that he had shot her in self-defence. But this was evil: that people of the same class should prey on each other. He thrust himself along the edge of the stall until he was by her side. He bent down. He whispered, 'How did you get that bag?' but an arrowhead of predatory women forced themselves between; she couldn't even have seen who had whispered to her. As far as she knew it might have been a woman mistaking it for a bargain on one of the stalls, but nevertheless the question had scared her. He saw her elbowing her way to the door and he fought to follow her.

When he got out of the hall she was just in sight, trailing her long old-fashioned skirt round a corner. He walked fast. He didn't notice in his hurry that he in his turn was followed by a man whose clothes he would immediately have recognized, the soft hat and overcoat worn like a uniform. Very soon he began to remember the road they took; he had been

87

this way with the girl. It was like retracing in mind an old experience. A newspaper shop would come in sight next moment, a policeman had stood just there, he had intended to kill her, to take her out somewhere beyond the houses and shoot her quite painlessly in the back. The wrinkled deep malice in the face he had seen across the stall seemed to nod at him: 'You needn't worry, we have seen to all that for you.'

It was incredible how quickly the old woman scuttled. She held the bag in one hand, lifted the absurd long skirt with the other; she was like a female Rip Van Winkle who had emerged from her sleep in the clothes of fifty years ago. He thought: they've done something to her, but who are 'they'? She hadn't been to the police; she'd believed his story; it was only to Cholmondeley's advantage that she should disappear. For the first time since his mother died he was afraid for someone else, because he knew too well that Cholmondeley had no scruples.

Past the station she turned to the left up Khyber Avenue, a line of dingy apartment houses. Coarse grey lace quite hid the interior of little rooms save when a plant in a jardinière pressed glossy green palms against the glass between the lace. There were no bright geraniums lapping up the air behind closed panes: those scarlet flowers belong to a poorer class than the occupants of Khyber Avenue, to the exploited. In Khyber Avenue they had progressed to the aspidistra of the small exploiters. They were all Cholmondeleys on a tiny scale. Outside No. 61 the old woman had to wait and fumble for her key; it gave Raven time to catch her up. He put his foot against the closing door and said, 'I want to ask you some questions.'

'Get out,' the old woman said. 'We don't 'ave anything to do with your sort.'

He pressed the door steadily open. 'You'd better listen,' he said. 'It'd be good for you.' She stumbled backwards amongst the crowded litter of the little dark hall: he noted it all with hatred: the glass case with a stuffed pheasant, the moth-eaten head of a stag picked up at a country auction to act as a hatstand, the black metal umbrella-holder painted with gold

88

stars, the little pink glass shade over the gas-jet. He said, 'Where did you get that bag? Oh,' he said, 'it wouldn't take much to make me squeeze your old neck.'

'Acky!' the old woman screamed. 'Acky!'

'What do you do here, eh?' He opened one of the two doors at random off the hall and saw a long cheap couch with the ticking coming through the cover, a large gilt mirror, a picture of a naked girl knee-deep in the sea; the place reeked of scent and stale gas.

'Acky!' the old woman screamed again. 'Acky!'

He said, 'So that's it, eh? You old bawd,' and turned back into the hall. But she was supported now. She had Acky with her; he had come through to her side from the back of the house on rubber-soled shoes, making no sound. Tall and bald, with a shifty pious look, he faced Raven. 'What d'you want, my man?' He belonged to a different class altogether: a good school and a theological college had formed his accent; something else had broken his nose.

'What names!' the old woman said, turning on Raven from under Acky's protecting arm.

Raven said, 'I'm in a hurry. I don't want to break up this place. Tell me where you got that bag.'

'If you refer to my wife's reticule,' the bald man said, 'it was given her – was it not, Tiny? – by a lodger.'

'When?'

'A few nights ago.'

'Where is she now?'

'She only stayed one night.'

'Why did she give her bag to you?'

'We only pass this way once,' Acky said, 'and therefore – you know the quotation?'

'Was she alone?'

'Of course she wasn't alone,' the old woman said. Acky coughed, put his hand over her face and pushed her gently behind him. 'Her betrothed,' he said, 'was with her.' He advanced towards Raven. 'That face,' he said, 'is somehow familiar. Tiny, my dear, fetch me a copy of the *Journal*.'

'No need,' Raven said. 'It's me all right.' He said, 'You've

89

lied about that bag. If the girl was here, it was last night. I'm going to search this bawdy house of yours.'

'Tiny,' her husband said, 'go out at the back and call the police.' Raven's hand was on his gun, but he didn't move, he didn't draw it, his eyes were on the old woman as she trailed indeterminately through the kitchen door. 'Hurry, Tiny, my dear.'

Raven said, 'If I thought she was going, I'd shoot you straight, but she's not going to any police. You're more afraid of them than I am. She's in the kitchen now hiding in a corner.'

Acky said, 'Oh no, I assure you she's gone; I heard the door; you can see for yourself,' and as Raven passed him he raised his hand and struck with a knuckle-duster at a spot behind Raven's ear.

But Raven had expected that. He ducked his head and was safely through in the kitchen doorway with his gun out. 'Stay put,' he said. 'This gun doesn't make any noise. I'll plug you where you'll feel it if you move.' The old woman was where he had expected her to be, between the dresser and the door squeezed in a corner. She moaned, 'Oh, Acky, you ought to 'ave 'it 'im.'

Acky began to swear. The obscenity trickled out of his mouth effortlessly like dribble, but the tone, the accent never changed; it was still the good school, the theological college. There were a lot of Latin words Raven didn't understand. He said impatiently, 'Now where's the girl?' But Acky simply didn't hear; he stood there in a kind of nervous seizure with his pupils rolled up almost under the lids; he might have been praying; for all Raven knew some of the Latin words might be prayers: '*Saccus stercoris*', '*fauces*'. He said again: 'Where's the girl?'

'Leave 'im alone,' the old woman said. ''E can't 'ear you. Acky,' she moaned from her corner by the dresser, 'it's all right, love, you're at 'ome.' She said fiercely to Raven, 'The things they did to 'im.'

Suddenly the obscenity stopped. He moved and blocked the kitchen door. The hand with the knuckle-duster grasped the lapel of his coat. Acky said softly, 'After all, my Lord

Bishop, you too, I am sure – in your day – among the hay-cocks,' and tittered.

Raven said, 'Tell him to move. I'm going to search this house.' He kept his eye on both of them. The little stuffy house wore on his nerves, madness and wickedness moved in the kitchen. The old woman watched him with hatred from her corner. Raven said, 'My God, if you've killed her . . .' He said, 'Do you know what it feels like to have a bullet in your belly? You'll just lie there and bleed . . .' It seemed to him that it would be like shooting a spider. He suddenly shouted to her husband, 'Get out of my way.'

Acky said, 'Even St Augustine . . .' watching him with glazed eyes, barring the door. Raven struck him in the face, then backed out of reach of the flailing arm. He raised his pistol and the woman screamed at him, 'Stop! I'll get 'im out.' She said, 'Don't you dare to touch Acky. They've treated 'im bad enough in 'is day.' She took her husband's arm; she only came half-way to his shoulder, grey and soiled and miserably tender. 'Acky, dear,' she said, 'come into the par-lour.' She rubbed her old wicked wrinkled face against his sleeve. 'Acky, there's a letter from the bishop.'

His pupils moved down again like those of a doll. He was almost himself again. He said, 'Tut-tut! I gave way, I think, to a little temper.' He looked at Raven with half-recognition. 'That fellow's still here, Tiny.'

'Come into the parlour, Acky dear. I've got to talk to you.' He let her pull him away into the hall and Raven followed them and mounted the stairs. All the way up he heard them talking. They were planning something between them; as like as not when he was out of sight and round the corner they'd slip out and call the police. If the girl was really not here or if they had disposed of her, they had little to fear from the police. On the first-floor landing there was a tall cracked mirror; he came up the stairs into its reflection, unshaven chin, hare-lip and ugliness. His heart beat against his ribs; if he had been called on to fire now, quickly, in self-defence, his hand and eye would have failed him. He thought hopelessly: this is ruin. I'm losing grip, a skirt's got me down. He opened the first door to hand and came into what was obviously the best bedroom, a wide double-bed with a flowery eiderdown, veneered walnut furniture, a little embroidered bag for hair combings, a tumbler of Lysol on the washstand for someone's false teeth. He opened the big wardrobe door and a musty smell of old clothes and camphor balls came out at him. He went to the closed window and looked out at Khyber Avenue, and all the while he looked he could hear the whispers from the parlour: Acky and Tiny plotting together. His eye for a moment noted a large rather clumsy-looking man in a soft hat chatting to a woman at the house opposite; another man came up the road and they strolled together out of sight. He recognized the police at once. They mightn't, of course, have seen him there, they might be engaged on a purely routine inquiry. He went quickly out on to the landing and listened: Acky and Tiny were quite silent now. He thought at first they might have left the house, but when he listened carefully he could hear the faint whistling of the old woman's breath somewhere near the foot of the stairs.

There was another door on the landing. He tried the handle. It was locked. He wasn't going to waste any more time with the old people downstairs. He shot through the lock and crashed the door open. But there was no one there. The room was empty. It was a tiny room almost filled by its double-bed, its dead fireplace hidden by a smoked brass trap. He looked out of the window and saw nothing but a small stone yard, a dustbin, a high sooty wall keeping out neighbours, the grey waning afternoon light. On the washstand was a wireless set, and the wardrobe was empty. He had no doubt what this room was used for.

But something made him stay: some sense uneasily remaining in the room of someone's terror. He couldn't leave it, and there was the locked door to be accounted for. Why should they have locked up an empty room unless it held some clue, some danger to themselves? He turned over the pillows of the bed and wondered, his hand loose on the pistol, his brain stirring with another's agony. Oh, to know, to know. He felt the painful weakness of a man who had depended always on his gun. I'm educated, aren't I, the phrase came mockingly into his mind, but he knew that one of the police out there could discover in this room more than he. He knelt down and looked under the bed. Nothing there. The very tidiness of the room seemed unnatural, as if it had been tidied after a crime. Even the mats looked as if they had been shaken.

He asked himself whether he had been imagining things. Perhaps the girl had really given the old woman her bag? But he couldn't forget that they had lied about the night she'd stayed with them, had picked the initial off the bag. And they had locked this door. But people did lock doors – against burglars, but in that case surely they left the key on the outside. Oh, there was an explanation, he was only too aware of that, for everything; why should you leave another person's initials on a bag? When you had many lodgers, naturally you forgot which night ... There were explanations, but he couldn't get over the impression that something had happened here, that something had been tidied away, and it came over him with a sense of great desolation that only he could not call in the police to find this girl. Because he was an outlaw she had to be an outlaw too. *Ah, Christ! that it were possible*. The rain beating on the Weevil, the plaster child, the afternoon light draining from the little stone yard, the image of his own ugliness fading in the mirror, and from below stairs Tiny's whistling breath. *For one short hour to see ...*

He went back on to the landing, but something all the time pulled him back as if he were leaving a place which had been dear to him. It dragged on him as he went upstairs to the second floor and into every room in turn. There was nothing in any of them but beds and wardrobes and the stale smell of scent and toilet things and in one cupboard a broken cane. They were all of them more dusty, less tidy, more used than the room he'd left. He stood up there among the empty rooms listening; there wasn't a sound to be heard now; Tiny and her Acky were quite silent below him waiting for him to come down. He wondered again if he had made a fool of himself and risked everything. But if they had nothing to hide, why hadn't they tried to call the police? He had left them alone, they had nothing to fear while he was upstairs, but something kept them to the house just as something kept him tied to the room on the first floor.

It took him back to it. He was happier when he had closed the door behind him and stood again in the small cramped space between the big bed and the wall. The drag at his heart ceased. He was able to think again. He began to examine the room thoroughly inch by inch. He even moved the radio on the washstand. Then he heard the stairs creak and leaning his head against the door he listened to someone he supposed was Acky mounting the stairs step by step with clumsy caution; then he was crossing the landing and there he must be, just outside the door waiting and listening. It was impossible to believe that those old people had nothing to fear. Raven went along the walls, squeezing by the bed, touching the glossy flowery paper with his fingers; he had heard of people before now papering over a cavity. He reached the fireplace and un-hooked the brass trap.

Propped up inside the fireplace was a woman's body, the feet in the grate, the head out of sight in the chimney. The first thought he had was of revenge; if it's the girl, if she's dead, I'll shoot them both, I'll shoot them where it hurts most so that they die slow. Then he went down on his knees to ease the body out.

The hands and feet were roped, an old cotton vest had been tied between her teeth as a gag, the eyes were closed. He cut the gag away first; he couldn't tell whether she was alive or dead; he cursed her, 'Wake up, you bitch, wake up.' He leant over her, imploring her, 'Wake up.' He was afraid to leave her, there was no water in the ewer, he couldn't do a thing; when he had cut away the ropes he just sat on the floor beside her with his eyes on the door and one hand on his pistol and the other on her breast. When he could feel her breathing under his hand it was like beginning life over again.

She didn't know where she was. She said, 'Please. The sun. It's too strong.' There was no sun in the room; it would soon be too dark to read. He thought: what ages have they had her buried there, and held his hand over her eyes to shield them from the dim winter light of early evening. She said in a tired voice, 'I could go to sleep now. There's air.'

'No, no,' Raven said, 'we've got to get out of here,' but he wasn't prepared for her simple acquiescence. 'Yes, where to?'

He said, 'You don't remember who I am. I haven't anywhere. But I'll leave you some place where it's safe.'

She said, 'I've been finding out things.' He thought she meant things like fear and death, but as her voice strengthened she explained quite clearly, 'It was the man you said. Cholmondeley.'

'So you know me,' Raven said. But she took no notice. It was as if all the time in the dark she had been rehearsing what she had to say when she was discovered, at once, because there was no time to waste.

'I made a guess at somewhere where he worked. Some company. It scared him. He must work there. I don't remember the name. I've got to remember.'

'Don't worry,' Raven said. 'It'll come back. But how is it you aren't crazy ... Christ! you've got nerve.'

She said, 'I remembered till just now. I heard you looking for me in the room, and then you went away and I forgot everything.'

'Do you think you could walk now?'

'Of course I could walk. We've got to hurry.'

'Where to?'

'I had it all planned. It'll come back. I had plenty of time to think things out.'

'You sound as if you weren't scared at all.'

'I knew I'd be found all right. I was in a hurry. We haven't got much time. I thought about the war all the time.'

He said again admiringly, 'You've got nerve.'

She began to move her hands and feet up and down quite methodically as if she were following a programme she had drawn up for herself. 'I thought a lot about that war. I read somewhere, but I'd forgotten, about how babies can't wear gas masks because there's not enough air for them.' She knelt up with her hand on his shoulder. 'There wasn't much air there. It made things sort of vivid. I thought, we've got to stop

95

it. It seems silly, doesn't it, us two, but there's nobody else.' She said, 'My feet have got pins and needles bad. That means they are coming alive again.' She tried to stand up, but it wasn't any good.

Raven watched her. He said, 'What else did you think?'

She said, 'I thought about you. I wished I hadn't had to go away like that and leave you.'

'I thought you'd gone to the police.'

'I wouldn't do that.' She managed to stand up this time with her hand on his shoulder. 'I'm on your side.'

Raven said, 'We've got to get out of here. Can you walk?'

'Yes.'

'Then leave go of me. There's someone outside.' He stood by the door with his gun in his hand listening. They'd had plenty of time, those two, to think up a plan, longer than he. He pulled the door open. It was very nearly dark. He could see no one on the landing. He thought: the old devil's at the side waiting to get a hit at me with the poker. I'll take a run for it, and immediately tripped across the string they had tied across the doorway. He was on his knees with the gun on the floor; he couldn't get up in time and Acky's blow got him on the left shoulder. It staggered him, he couldn't move, he had just time to think: it'll be the head next time, I've gone soft, I ought to have thought of a string, when he heard Anne speak: 'Drop the poker.' He got painfully to his feet; the girl had snatched the gun as it fell and had Acky covered. He said with astonishment, 'You're fine.' At the bottom of the stairs the old woman cried out, 'Acky, where are you?'

'Give me the gun,' Raven said. 'Get down the stairs, you needn't be afraid of the old bitch.' He backed after her, keeping Acky covered, but the old couple had shot their bolt. He said regretfully, 'If he'd only rush I'd put a bullet in him.'

'It wouldn't upset *me*,' Anne said. 'I'd have done it myself.'

He said again, 'You're fine.' He nearly forgot the detectives he had seen in the street, but with his hand on the door he remembered. He said, 'I may have to make a bolt for it if the police are outside.' He hardly hesitated before he trusted her. 'I've found a hide-out for the night. In the goods yard. A

shed they don't use any longer. I'll be waiting by the wall tonight fifty yards down from the station.' He opened the door.
Nobody moved in the street; they walked out together and
down the middle of the road into a vacant dusk. Anne said,
'Did you see a man in the doorway opposite?'

'Yes,' Raven said. 'I saw him.'

'I thought it was like – but how could it – ?'

'There was another at the end of the street. They were
police all right, but they didn't know who I was. They'd have
tried to get me if they'd known.'

'And you'd have shot?'

'I'd have shot all right. But they didn't know it was me.' He
laughed with the night damp in his throat. 'I've fooled them
properly.' The lights went on in the city beyond the railway
bridge, but where they were it was just a grey dusk and the
sound of an engine shunting in the yard.

'I can't walk far,' Anne said. 'I'm sorry. I suppose I'm a bit
sick after all.'

'It's not far now,' Raven said. 'There's a loose plank. I got
it all fixed up for myself early this morning. Why, there's
even sacks, lots of sacks. It's going to be like home,' he said.

'Like home?' He didn't answer, feeling along the tarred
wall of the goods yard, remembering the kitchen in the basement and the first thing very nearly he could remember, his
mother bleeding across the table. She hadn't even troubled to
lock the door: that was all she cared about him. He'd done
some ugly things in his time, he told himself, but he'd never
been able to equal that ugliness. Some day he would. It would
be like beginning life over again: to have something else to
look back to when somebody spoke of death or blood or
wounds or home.

'A bit bare for a home,' Anne said.

'You needn't be scared of me,' Raven said. 'I won't keep
you. You can sit down a bit and tell me what he did to you,
what Cholmondeley did, and then you can be getting along
anywhere you want.'

'I couldn't go any farther if you paid me.' He had to put his
hands under her shoulders and hold her up against the tarred

97

wood, while he put more will into her from his own in-exhaustible reserve. He said, 'Hold on. We're nearly there.' He shivered in the cold, holding her with all his strength, try-ing in the dusk to see her face. He said, 'You can rest in the shed. There are plenty of sacks there.' He was like somebody describing with pride some place he lived in, that he'd bought with his own money or built with his own labour stone by stone.

2

Mather stood back in the shadow of the doorway. It was worse in a way than anything he'd feared. He put his hand on his revolver. He had only to go forward and arrest Raven – or stop a bullet in the attempt. He was a policeman; he couldn't shoot first. At the end of the street Saunders was waiting for him to move. Behind, a uniformed constable waited on them both. But he made no move. He let them go off down the road in the belief that they were alone. Then he followed as far as the corner and picked up Saunders. Saunders said, 'The d-d-devil.'

'Oh no,' Mather said, 'it's only Raven – and Anne.' He struck a match and held it to the cigarette which he had been holding between his lips for the last twenty minutes. They could hardly see the man and woman going off down the dark road by the goods-yard, but beyond them another match was struck. 'We've got them covered,' Mather said. 'They won't be able to get out of our sight now.'

'W-will you take them b-b-both?'

'We can't have shooting with a woman there,' Mather said. 'Can't you see what they'd make of it in the papers if a woman got hurt? It's not as if he was wanted for murder.'

'We've got to be careful of your girl,' Saunders brought out in a breath.

'Get moving again,' Mather said. 'We don't want to lose touch. I'm not thinking about *her* any more. I promise you that's over. She's led me up the garden properly. I'm just thinking of what's best with Raven – and any accomplice he's got in Nottwich. If we've got to shoot, we'll shoot.'

Saunders said, 'They've stopped.' He had sharper eyes than Mather. Mather said, 'Could you pick him off from here, if I rushed him?'

'No,' Saunders said. He began to move forward quickly. 'He's loosened a plank. They are getting through.'

'Don't worry,' Mather said. 'I'll follow. Bring up three more men and post one of them at the gap where I can find him. We've got all the gates into the yard picketed already. Bring the rest inside. But keep it quiet.' He could hear the slight shuffle of cinders where the two were walking; it wasn't so easy to follow them because of the sound his own feet made. They disappeared round a stationary truck and the light failed more and more. He caught a glimpse of their moving shadows and then an engine hooted and belched a grey plume of steam round him; for a moment it was like walking in a mountain fog. A warm dirty spray settled on his face; when he was clear he had lost them. He began to realize the difficulty of finding anyone in the yard at night. There were trucks everywhere; they could slip into one and lie down. He barked his shin and swore softly; then quite distinctly he heard Anne whisper, 'I can't make it.' There were only a few trucks between them; then the movements began again, heavier movements as if someone were carrying a weight. Mather climbed on to the truck and stared across a dark desolate waste of cinders and points, a tangle of lines and sheds and piles of coal and coke. It was like a No Man's Land full of torn iron across which one soldier picked his way with a wounded companion in his arms. Mather watched them with an odd sense of shame, as if he were a spy. The thin limping shadow became a human being who knew the girl he loved. There was a kind of relationship between them. He thought: how many years will he get for that robbery? He no longer wanted to shoot. He thought: poor devil, he must be pretty driven by now, he's probably looking for a place to sit down in, and there the place was, a small wooden workman's shed between the lines.

Mather struck a match again and presently Saunders was below him waiting for orders. 'They are in that shed,' Mather said. 'Get the men posted. If they try to get out, nab them quick. Otherwise wait for daylight. We don't want any accidents.'

'You aren't s-staying?'

'You'll be easier without me,' Mather said. 'I'll be at the station tonight.' He said gently: 'Don't think about me. Just go ahead. And look after yourself. Got your gun?'

'Of course.'

'I'll send the men along to you. It's going to be a cold watch, I'm afraid, but it's no good trying to rush that shed. He might shoot his way clear out.'

'It's t-t-t-tough on you,' Saunders said. The dark had quite come; it healed the desolation of the yard. Inside the shed there was no sign of life, no glimmer of light; soon Saunders couldn't have told that it existed, sitting there with his back to a truck out of the wind's way, hearing the breathing of the policeman nearest him and saying over to himself to pass the time (his mind's words free from any impediment) the line of a poem he had read at night-school about a dark tower: 'He must be wicked to deserve such pain.' It was a comforting line, he thought; those who followed his profession couldn't be taught a better; that's why he had remembered it.

3

'Who's coming to dinner, dear?' the Chief Constable asked, putting his head in at the bedroom door.

'Never you mind,' Mrs Calkin said, 'you'll change.'

The Chief Constable said: 'I was thinking, dear, as 'ow – '

'As how,' Mrs Calkin said firmly.

'The new maid. You might teach her that I'm *Major* Calkin.'

Mrs Calkin said, 'You'd better hurry.'

'It's not the Mayoress again, is it?' He trailed drearily out towards the bathroom, but on second thoughts nipped quietly downstairs to the dining-room. Must see about the drinks. But if it was the Mayoress there wouldn't be any. Piker never turned up; he didn't blame him. While there he might just as well take a nip; he took it neat for speed and cleaned the glass afterwards with a splash of soda and his handkerchief. He put the glass as an afterthought where the Mayoress would sit. Then he rang up the police station.

'Any news?' he asked hopelessly. He knew there was no real hope that they'd ask him down for a consultation.

The inspector's voice said, 'We know where he is. We've got him surrounded. We are just waiting till daylight.'

'Can I be of any use? Like me to come down, eh, and talk things over?'

'It's quite unnecessary, sir.'

He put the receiver down miserably, sniffed the Mayoress's glass (she'd never notice that) and went upstairs. Major Calkin, he thought wistfully, Major Calkin. The trouble is I'm a man's man. Looking out of the window of his dressing-room at the spread lights of Nottwich he remembered for some reason the war, the tribunal, the fun it had all been giving hell to the conchies. His uniform still hung there, next the tails he wore once a year at the Rotarian dinner when he was able to get among the boys. A faint smell of moth-balls came out at him. His spirits suddenly lifted. He thought: my God, in a week's time we may be at it again. Show the devils what we are made of. I wonder if the uniform will fit. He couldn't resist trying on the jacket over his evening trousers. It was a bit tight, he couldn't deny that, but the general effect in the glass was not too bad, a bit pinched; it would have to be let out. With his influence in the county he'd be back in uniform in a fortnight. With any luck he'd be busier than ever in this war.

'Joseph,' his wife said, 'whatever are you doing?' He saw her in the mirror placed statuesquely in the doorway in her new black and sequined evening dress like a shop-window model of an outsize matron. She said, 'Take it off at once. You'll smell of moth-balls now all dinner-time. The Mayoress is taking off her things and any moment Sir Marcus – '

'You might have told me,' the Chief Constable said. 'If I'd known Sir Marcus was coming . . . How did you snare the old boy?'

'He invited himself,' Mrs Calkin said proudly. 'So I rang up the Mayoress.'

'Isn't old Piker coming?'

'He hasn't been home all day.'

The Chief Constable slipped off his uniform jacket and put it away carefully. If the war had gone on another year they'd have made him a colonel: he had been getting on the very best terms with the regimental headquarters, supplying the mess with groceries at very little more than the cost price. In the next war he'd make the grade. The sound of Sir Marcus's car on the gravel brought him downstairs. The Lady Mayoress was looking under the sofa for her Pekinese, which had gone to ground defensively to escape strangers; she was on her knees with her head under the fringe saying, 'Chinky, Chinky,' ingratiatingly. Chinky growled out of sight. 'Well, well,' the Chief Constable said, trying to put a little warmth into his tones, 'and how's Alfred?'

'Alfred?' the Mayoress said, coming out from under the sofa, 'it's not Alfred, it's Chinky. Oh,' she said, talking very fast, for it was her habit to work towards another person's meaning while she talked, 'you mean how is he? Alfred? He's gone again.'

'Chinky?'

'No, Alfred.' One never got much further with the Mayoress.

Mrs Calkin came in. She said, 'Have you got him, dear?'

'No, he's gone again,' the Chief Constable said, 'if you mean Alfred.'

'He's under the sofa,' the Mayoress said. 'He won't come out.'

Mrs Calkin said, 'I ought to have warned you, dear. I thought of course you would know the story of how Sir Marcus hates the very sight of dogs. Of course, if he stays there quietly . . .'

'The poor dear,' Mrs Piker said, 'so sensitive, he could tell at once he wasn't wanted.'

The Chief Constable suddenly could bear it no longer. He said, 'Alfred Piker's my best friend. I won't have you say he wasn't wanted,' but no one took any notice of him. The maid had announced Sir Marcus.

Sir Marcus entered on the tips of his toes. He was a very

old, sick man with a little wisp of white beard on his chin resembling chicken fluff. He gave the effect of having withered inside his clothes like a kernel in a nut. He spoke with the faintest foreign accent and it was difficult to determine whether he was Jewish or of an ancient English family. He gave the impression that very many cities had rubbed him smooth. If there was a touch of Jerusalem, there was also a touch of St James's, if of some Central European capital, there were also marks of the most exclusive clubs in Cannes.

'So good of you, Mrs Calkin,' he said, 'to give me this opportunity . . .' It was difficult to hear what he said; he spoke in a whisper. His old scaley eyes took them all in. 'I have always been hoping to make the acquaintance . . .'

'May I introduce the Lady Mayoress, Sir Marcus?'

He bowed with the slightly servile grace of a man who might have been pawnbroker to the Pompadour. 'So famous a figure in the city of Nottwich.' There was no sarcasm or patronage in his manner. He was just old. Everyone was alike to him. He didn't trouble to differentiate.

'I thought you were on the Riviera, Sir Marcus,' the Chief Constable said breezily. 'Have a sherry. It's no good asking the ladies.'

'I don't drink, I'm afraid,' Sir Marcus whispered. The Chief Constable's face fell. 'I came back two days ago.'

'Rumours of war, eh? Dogs delight to bark . . .'

'Joseph,' Mrs Calkin said sharply, and glanced with meaning at the sofa.

The old eyes cleared a little. 'Yes. Yes,' Sir Marcus repeated. 'Rumours.'

'I see you've been taking on more men at Midland Steel, Sir Marcus.'

'So they tell me,' Sir Marcus whispered.

The maid announced dinner; the sound startled Chinky, who growled under the sofa, and there was an agonizing moment while they all watched Sir Marcus. But he had heard nothing, or perhaps the noise had faintly stirred his subconscious mind, for as he took Mrs Calkin in to the dining-room he whispered venomously, 'The dogs drove me away.'

'Some lemonade for Mrs Piker, Joseph,' Mrs Calkin said. The Chief Constable watched her drink with some nervousness. She seemed a little puzzled by the taste, she sipped and tried again. 'Really,' she said, 'what delicious lemonade. It has quite an aroma.'

Sir Marcus passed the soup; he passed the fish. When the entrée was served, he leant across the large silver-plated flower bowl inscribed 'To Joseph Calkin from the assistants in Calkin and Calkin's on the occasion . . .' (the inscription ran round the corner out of sight) and whispered, 'Might I have a dry biscuit and a little hot water?' He explained, 'My doctor won't allow me anything else at night.'

'Well, that's hard luck,' the Chief Constable said. 'Food and drink as a man gets older . . .' He glared at his empty glass: what a life, oh for a chance to get away for a bit among the boys, throw his weight about and know that he was a man.

The Lady Mayoress said suddenly, 'How Chinky would love these bones,' and choked.

'Who is Chinky?' Sir Marcus whispered.

Mrs Calkin said quickly, 'Mrs Piker has the most lovely cat.'

'I'm glad it isn't a dog,' Sir Marcus whispered. 'There is something about a dog,' the old hand gestured hopelessly with a piece of cheese biscuit, 'and of all dogs the Pekinese.' He said with extraordinary venom, 'Yap, yap, yap,' and sucked up some hot water. He was a man almost without pleasures; his most vivid emotion was venom, his main object defence: defence of his fortune, of the pale flicker of vitality he gained each year in the Cannes sun, of his life. He was quite content to eat cheese biscuits to the end of them if eating biscuits would extend his days.

The old boy couldn't have many left, the Chief Constable thought, watching Sir Marcus wash down the last dry crumb and then take a white tablet out of a little flat gold box in his waistcoat pocket. He had a heart; you could tell it in the way he spoke, from the special coaches he travelled in when he went by rail, the Bath chairs which propelled him softly down the long passages in Midland Steel. The Chief Constable had met him several times at civic receptions; after the General Strike Sir Marcus had given a fully equipped gymnasium to the police force in recognition of their services, but never before had Sir Marcus visited him at home.

Everyone knew a lot about Sir Marcus. The trouble was, all that they knew was contradictory. There were people who, because of his Christian name, believed that he was a Greek; others were quite as certain that he had been born in a ghetto. His business associates said that he was of an old English family; his nose was no evidence either way; you found plenty of noses like that in Cornwall and the west country. His name did not appear at all in *Who's Who*, and an enterprising journalist who once tried to write his life found extraordinary gaps in registers; it wasn't possible to follow any rumour to its source. There was even a gap in the legal records of Marseilles where one rumour said that Sir Marcus as a youth had been charged with theft from a visitor to a bawdy house. Now he sat there in the heavy Edwardian dining-room brushing biscuit crumbs from his waistcoat, one of the richest men in Europe.

No one even knew his age, unless perhaps his dentist; the Chief Constable had an idea that you could tell the age of a man by his teeth. But then they probably were *not* his teeth at his age: another gap in the records.

'Well, we shan't be leaving them to their drinks, shall we?' Mrs Calkin said in a sprightly way, rising from the table and fixing her husband with a warning glare, 'but I expect they have a lot to talk about together.'

When the door closed Sir Marcus said, 'I've seen that woman somewhere with a dog. I'm sure of it.'

'Would you mind if I gave myself a spot of port?' the Chief Constable said. 'I don't believe in lonely drinking, but if you really won't – Have a cigar?'

'No,' Sir Marcus whispered, 'I don't smoke.' He said, 'I wanted to see you – in confidence – about this fellow Raven. Davis is worried. The trouble is he caught a glimpse of the man. Quite by chance. At the time of the robbery at a friend's office in Victoria Street. This man called on some pretext. He has an idea that the wild fellow wants to put him out of the way. As a witness.'

'Tell him,' the Chief Constable said proudly, pouring himself out another glass of port, 'that he needn't worry. The man's as good as caught. We know where he is at this very moment. He's surrounded. We are only waiting till daylight, till he shows himself . . .'

'Why wait at all? Wouldn't it be better,' Sir Marcus whispered, 'if the silly desperate fellow were taken at once?'

'He's armed, you see. In the dark anything might happen. He might shoot his way clear. And there's another thing. He has a girl friend with him. It wouldn't do if he escaped and the girl got shot.'

Sir Marcus bowed his old head above the two hands that lay idly, with no dry biscuit or glass of warm water or white tablet to occupy them, on the table. He said gently, 'I want you to understand. In a way it is our responsibility. Because of Davis. If there were any trouble: if the girl was killed: all our money would be behind the police force. If there had to be an inquiry the best counsel . . . I have friends too, as you may suppose . . .'

'It would be better to wait till daylight, Sir Marcus. Trust me. I know how things stand. I've been a soldier, you know.'

'Yes, I understand that,' Sir Marcus said.

'Looks as if the old bulldog will have to bite again, eh? Thank God for a Government with guts.'

'Yes, yes,' Sir Marcus said. 'I should say it was almost certain now.' The scaley eyes shifted to the decanter. 'Don't let me stop you having your glass of port, Major.'

'Well, if you say so, Sir Marcus, I'll just have one more glass for a nightcap.'

Sir Marcus said, 'I'm very glad that you have such good news for me. It doesn't look well to have an armed ruffian loose in Nottwich. You mustn't risk any of your men's lives, Major. Better that this – waste product – should be dead than one of your fine fellows.' He suddenly leant back in his chair and gasped like a landed fish. He said, 'A tablet. Please. Quick.'

106

The Chief Constable picked the gold box from his pocket, but Sir Marcus had already recovered. He took the tablet himself. The Chief Constable said, 'Shall I order your car, Sir Marcus?'

'No, no,' Sir Marcus whispered, 'there's no danger. It's simply pain.' He stared with dazed old eyes down at the crumbs on his trousers. 'What were we saying? Fine fellows, yes, you mustn't risk *their* lives. The country will need them.'

'That's very true.'

Sir Marcus whispered with venom, 'To me this – ruffian – is a traitor. This is a time when every man is needed. I'd treat him like a traitor.'

'It's one way of looking at it.'

'Another glass of port, Major.'

'Yes, I think I will.'

'To think of the number of able-bodied men this fellow will take from their country's service even if he shoots no one. Warders. Police guards. Fed and lodged at his country's expense when other men . . .'

'Are dying. You're right, Sir Marcus.' The pathos of it all went deeply home. He remembered his uniform jacket in the cupboard: the buttons needed shining: the King's buttons. The smell of moth-balls lingered round him still. He said, 'Somewhere there's a corner of a foreign field that is for ever . . . Shakespeare knew. Old Gaunt when he said that – '

'It would be so much better, Major Calkin, if your men take no risks. If they shoot on sight. One must take up weeds – by the roots.'

'It would be better.'

'You're the father of your men.'

'That's what old Piker said to me once. God forgive him, he meant it differently. I wish you'd drink with me, Sir Marcus. You're an understanding man. You know how an officer feels. I was in the army once.'

'Perhaps in a week you will be in it again.'

'You know how a man feels. I don't want anything to come between us, Sir Marcus. There's one thing I'd like to tell you. It's on my conscience. There *was* a dog under the sofa.'

107

'A dog?'

'A Pekinese called Chinky. I didn't know as 'ow ...'

'She said it was a cat.'

'She didn't want you to know.'

Sir Marcus said, 'I don't like being deceived. I'll see to Piker at the elections.' He gave a small tired sigh as if there were too many things to be seen to, to be arranged, revenges to be taken, stretching into an endless vista of time, and so much time already covered – since the ghetto, the Marseilles brothel, if there had ever been a ghetto or a brothel. He whispered abruptly, 'So you'll telephone now to the station and tell them to shoot at sight? Say you'll take the responsibility. I'll look after you.'

'I don't see as 'ow, as how ...'

The old hands moved impatiently: so much to be arranged. 'Listen to me. I never promise anything I can't answer for. There's a training depot ten miles from here. I can arrange for you to have nominal charge of it, with the rank of colonel, directly war's declared.'

'Colonel Banks?'

'He'll be shifted.'

'You mean if I telephone?'

'No. I mean if you are successful.'

'And the man's dead?'

'He's not important. A young scoundrel. There's no reason to hesitate. Take another glass of port.'

The Chief Constable stretched out his hand for the decanter. He thought, with less relish than he would have expected, 'Colonel Calkin', but he couldn't help remembering other things. He was a sentimental man. He remembered his appointment: it had been 'worked', of course, no less than his appointment to the training depot would be worked, but there came vividly back to him his sense of pride at being head of one of the best police forces in the Midlands. 'I'd better not have any more port,' he said lamely. 'It's bad for my sleep and the wife ...'

Sir Marcus said, 'Well, Colonel,' blinking his old eyes, 'you'll be able to count on me for anything.'

'I'd like to do it,' the Chief Constable said imploringly. 'I'd like to please you, Sir Marcus. But I don't see as how . . . The police couldn't do that.'

'It would never be known.'

'I don't suppose they'd take my orders. Not on a thing like that.'

Sir Marcus whispered, 'Do you mean in your position – you haven't any *hold*?' He spoke with the astonishment of a man who had always been careful to secure his hold on the most junior of his subordinates.

'I'd like to please you.'

'There's the telephone,' Sir Marcus said. 'At any rate, you can use your influence. I never ask a man for more than he can do.'

The Chief Constable said: 'They are a good lot of boys. I've been down often to the station of an evening and had a drink or two. They're keen. You couldn't have keener men. They'll get him. You needn't be afraid, Sir Marcus.'

'You mean dead?'

'Alive or dead. They won't let him escape. They are good boys.'

'But he has got to be dead,' Sir Marcus said. He sneezed. The intake of breath seemed to have exhausted him. He lay back again, panting gently.

'I couldn't ask them, Sir Marcus, not like that. Why, it's like murder.'

'Nonsense.'

'Those evenings with the boys mean a lot to me. I wouldn't even be able to go down there again after doing that. I'd rather stay what I am. They'll give me a tribunal. As long as there's wars there'll be conchies.'

'There'd be no commission of any kind for you,' Sir Marcus said. 'I could see to that.' The smell of moth-balls came up from Calkin's evening shirt to mock him. 'I can arrange too that you shan't be Chief Constable much longer. You and Piker.' He gave a queer little whistle through the nose. He was too old to laugh, to use his lungs wastefully. 'Come. Have another glass.'

'No. I don't think I'd better. Listen, Sir Marcus, I'll put detectives at your office. I'll have Davis guarded.'

'I don't much mind about Davis,' Sir Marcus said. 'Will you get my chauffeur?'

'I'd like to do what you want, Sir Marcus. Won't you come back and see the ladies?'

'No, no,' Sir Marcus whispered, 'not with that dog there.' He had to be helped to his feet and handed his stick; a few dry crumbs lay in his beard. He said, 'If you change your mind tonight, you can ring me up. I shall be awake.' A man at his age, the Chief Constable thought charitably, would obviously think differently of death; it threatened him every moment on the slippery pavement, in a piece of soap at the bottom of a bath. It must seem quite a natural thing he was asking; great age was an abnormal condition: you had to make allowances. But watching Sir Marcus helped down the drive and into his deep wide car, he couldn't help saying over to himself, 'Colonel Calkin. Colonel Calkin.' After a moment he added, 'C.B.'.

The dog was yapping in the drawing-room. They must have lured it out. It was highly bred and nervous, and if a stranger spoke to it too suddenly or sharply, it would rush around in circles, foaming at the mouth, crying out in a horribly human way, its low fur sweeping the carpet like a vacuum cleaner. I might slip down, the Chief Constable thought, and have a drink with the boys. But the idea brought no lightening of his gloom and indecision. Was it possible that Sir Marcus could rob him of even that? But he had robbed him of it already. He couldn't face the superintendent or the inspector with this on his mind. He went into his study and sat down by the telephone. In five minutes Sir Marcus would be home. So much stolen from him already, surely there was little more he could lose by acquiescence. But he sat there doing nothing, a small plump bullying henpecked profiteer.

His wife put her head in at the door. 'Whatever are you doing, Joseph?' she said. 'Come at once and talk to Mrs Piker.'

110

Sir Marcus lived with his valet who was also a trained nurse at the top of the big building in the Tanneries. It was his only home. In London he stayed at Claridge's, in Cannes at the Carlton. His valet met him at the door of the building with his Bath chair and pushed him into the lift, then out along the passage to his study. The heat of the room had been turned up to the right degree, the tape-machine was gently ticking beside his desk. The curtains were not drawn and through the wide double-panes the night sky spread out over Nottwich striped by the searchlights from Hanlow aerodrome.

'You can go to bed, Mollison. I shan't be sleeping.'

Sir Marcus slept very little these days. In the little time left him to live a few hours of sleep made a distinct impression. And he didn't really need the sleep. No physical exertion demanded it. Now with the telephone within his reach he began to read first the memorandum on his desk, then the strips of tape. He read the arrangements for the gas drill in the morning. All the clerks on the ground floor who might happen to be needed for outside work were already supplied with gas masks. The sirens were expected to go almost immediately the rush hour was over and work in the offices had begun. Members of the transport staff, lorry drivers and special messengers would wear their masks immediately they started work. It was the only way to ensure that they wouldn't leave them behind somewhere and be caught unprotected during the hours of the practice and so waste in hospital the valuable hours of Midland Steel.

More valuable than they had ever been since November, 1918. Sir Marcus read the tape prices. Armament shares continued to rise, and with them steel. It made no difference at all that the British Government had stopped all export licences; the country itself was now absorbing more armaments than it had ever done since the peak year of Haig's assaults on the Hindenburg Line. Sir Marcus had many friends, in many countries; he wintered with them regularly at Cannes or in Soppelsa's yacht off Rhodes; he was the intimate friend of Mrs

Cranbeim. It was impossible now to export arms, but it was still possible to export nickel and most of the other metals which were necessary to the arming of nations. Even when war was declared, Mrs Cranbeim had been able to say quite definitely, that evening when the yacht pitched a little and Rosen was so distressingly sick over Mrs Ziffo's black satin, the British Government would not forbid the export of nickel to Switzerland or other neutral countries so long as the British requirements were first met. The future was very rosy indeed, for you could trust Mrs Cranbeim's word. She spoke directly from the horse's mouth, if you could so describe the elder statesman whose confidence she shared.

It seemed quite certain now; Sir Marcus read, in the tape messages, that the two governments chiefly concerned would not either amend or accept the terms of the ultimatum. Probably within five days, at least four countries would be at war and the consumption of munitions have risen to several million pounds a day.

And yet Sir Marcus was not quite happy. Davis had bungled things. When he had told Davis that a murderer ought not to be allowed to benefit from his crime, he had never expected all this silly business of the stolen notes. Now he must wait up all night for the telephone to ring. The old thin body made itself as comfortable as it could on the air-blown cushions: Sir Marcus was as painfully aware of his bones as a skeleton must be, wearing itself away against the leaden lining of its last suit. A clock struck midnight; he had lived one more whole day.

Chapter 5

1

RAVEN groped through the dark of the small shed till he had found the sacks. He piled them up, shaking them as one shakes a pillow. He whispered anxiously: 'You'll be able to rest there a bit?' Anne let his hand guide her to the corner. She said, 'It's freezing.'

'Lie down and I'll find more sacks.' He struck a match and the tiny flame went wandering through the close cold darkness. He brought the sacks and spread them over her, dropping the match.

'Can't we have a little light?' Anne asked.

'It's not safe. Anyway,' he said, 'it's a break for me. You can't see me in the dark. You can't see *this*.' He touched his lip secretly. He was listening at the door; he heard feet stumble on the tangle of metal and cinders and after a time a low voice spoke. He said, 'I've got to think. They know I'm here. Perhaps you'd better go. They've got nothing on you. If they come there's going to be shooting.'

'Do you think they know I'm here?'

'They must have followed us all the way.'

'Then I'll stay,' Anne said. 'There won't be any shooting while I'm here. They'll wait till morning, till you come out.'

'That's friendly of you,' he said with sour incredulity, all his suspicion of friendliness coming back.

'I've told you. I'm on your side.'

'I've got to think of a way,' he said.

'You may as well rest now. You've all the night to think in.'

'It *is* sort of – good in here,' Raven said, 'out of the way of the whole damned world of them. In the dark.' He wouldn't come near her, but sat down in the opposite corner with his automatic in his lap. He said suspiciously, 'What are you thinking about?' He was astonished and shocked by the sound of a laugh. 'Kind of homey,' Anne said.

'I don't take any stock in homes,' Raven said. 'I've been in one.'

'Tell me about it. What's your name?'

'You know my name. You've seen it in the papers.'

'I mean your Christian name.'

'Christian. That's a good joke, that one. Do you think anyone ever turns the other cheek these days?' He tapped the barrel of the automatic resentfully on the cinder floor. 'Not a chance.' He could hear her breathing there in the opposite corner, out of sight, out of reach, and he was afflicted by the odd sense that he had missed something. He said, 'I'm not

113

saying you aren't fine. I dare say you're Christian all right.'

'Search me,' Anne said.

'I took you out to that house to kill you . . .'

'To kill me?'

'What did you think it was for? I'm not a lover, am I? Girl's dream? Handsome as the day?'

'Why didn't you?'

'Those men turned up. That's all. I didn't fall for you. I don't fall for girls. I'm saved that. You won't find me ever going soft on a skirt.' He went desperately on, 'Why didn't you tell the police about me? Why don't you shout to them now?'

'Well,' she said, 'you've got a gun, haven't you?'

'I wouldn't shoot.'

'Why not?'

'I'm not all that crazy,' he said. 'If people go straight with me, I'll go straight with them. Go on. Shout. I won't do a thing.'

'Well,' Anne said, 'I don't have to ask your leave to be grateful, do I? You saved me tonight.'

'That lot wouldn't have killed you. They haven't the nerve to kill. It takes a man to kill.'

'Well, your friend Cholmondeley came pretty near it. He nearly throttled me when he guessed I was in with you.'

'In with me?'

'To find the man you're after.'

'The double-crossing bastard.' He brooded over his pistol, but his thoughts always disturbingly came back from hate to this dark safe corner; he wasn't used to that. He said, 'You've got sense all right. I like you.'

'Thanks for the compliment.'

'It's no compliment. You don't have to tell me. I've got something I'd like to trust you with, but I can't.'

'What's the dark secret?'

'It's not a secret. It's a cat I left back in my lodgings in London when they chased me out. You'd have looked after it.'

'You disappoint me, Mr Raven. I thought it was going to

114

be a few murders at least.' She exclaimed with sudden serious-ness, 'I've got it. The place where Davis works.'

'Davis?'

'The man you call Cholmondeley. I'm sure of it. Midland Steel. In a street near the Metropole. A big palace of a place.'

'I've got to get out of here,' Raven said, beating the auto-matic on the freezing ground.

'Can't you go to the police?'

'Me?' Raven said. 'Me go to the police?' He laughed. 'That'd be fine, wouldn't it? Hold out my hands for the cuffs . . .'

'I'll think of a way,' Anne said. When her voice ceased it was as if she had gone. He said sharply, 'Are you there?'

'Of course I'm here,' she said. 'What's worrying you?'

'It feels odd not to be alone.' The sour incredulity surged back. He struck a couple of matches and held them to his face, close to his disfigured mouth. 'Look,' he said, 'take a long look.' The small flames burnt steadily down. 'You aren't go-ing to help *me*, are you? Me?'

'You are all right,' she said. The flames touched his skin, but he held the two matches rigidly up and they burnt out against his fingers; the pain was like joy. But he rejected it; it had come too late; he sat in the dark feeling tears like heavy weights behind his eyes, but he couldn't weep. He had never known the particular trick that opened the right ducts at the right time. He crept a little way out of his corner towards her, feeling his way along the floor with the automatic. He said, 'Are you cold?'

'I've been in warmer places,' Anne said.

There were only his own sacks left. He pushed them over to her. 'Wrap 'em round,' he said.

'Have you got enough?'

'Of course I have. I can look after myself,' he said sharply, as if he hated her. His hands were so cold that he would have found it hard to use the automatic. 'I've got to get out of here.'

'We'll think of a way. Better have a sleep.'

'I can't sleep,' he said, 'I've been dreaming bad dreams lately.'

'We might tell each other stories? It's about the children's hour.'

'I don't know any stories.'

'Well, I'll tell you one. What kind? A funny one?'

'They never seem funny to me.'

'The three bears might be suitable.'

'I don't want anything financial. I don't want to hear anything about money.'

She could just see him now that he had come closer, a dark hunched shape that couldn't understand a word she was saying. She mocked him gently, secure in the knowledge that he would never realize she was mocking him. She said: 'I'll tell you about the fox and the cat. Well, this cat met a fox in a forest, and she'd always heard the fox cracked up for being wise. So she passed him the time of day politely and asked how he was getting along. But the fox was proud. He said, "How dare you ask me how I get along, you hungry mouse-hunter? What do you know about the world?" "Well, I do know one thing," the cat said. "What's that?" said the fox. "How to get away from the dogs," the cat said. "When they chase me, I jump into a tree." Then the fox went all high and mighty and said, "You've only one trick and I've a hundred. I've got a sack full of tricks. Come along with me and I'll show you." Just then a hunter ran quietly up with four hounds. The cat sprang into the tree and cried, "Open your sack, Mr Fox, open your sack." But the dogs held him with their teeth. So the cat laughed at him saying, "Mr Know-all, if you'd had just this one trick in your sack, you'd be safe up the tree with me now."' Anne stopped. She whispered to the dark shape beside her, 'Are you asleep?'

'No,' Raven said, 'I'm not asleep.'

'It's your turn now.'

'I don't know any stories,' Raven said, sullenly, miserably.

'No stories like that? You haven't been brought up properly.'

'I'm educated all right,' he protested, 'but I've got things on my mind. Plenty of them.'

'Cheer up. There's someone who's got more.'

116

'Who's that?'

'The fellow who began all this, who killed the old man, you know who I mean. Davis's friend.'

'What do you say?' he said furiously. 'Davis's friend?' He held his anger in. 'It's not the killing I mind; it's the double-crossing.'

'Well, of course,' Anne said cheerily, making conversation under the pile of sacks, 'I don't mind a little thing like killing myself.'

He looked up and tried to see her through the dark, hunting a hope. 'You don't mind that?'

'But there are killings *and* killings,' Anne said. 'If I had the man here who killed – what was the old man's name?'

'I don't remember.'

'Nor do I. We couldn't pronounce it anyway.'

'Go on. If he was here . . .'

'Why, I'd let you shoot him without raising a finger. And I'd say "Well done" to you afterwards.' She warmed to the subject. 'You remember what I told you, that they can't invent gas masks for babies to wear? That's the kind of thing he'll have on his mind. The mothers alive in their masks watching the babies cough up their insides.'

He said stubbornly, 'The poor ones'll be lucky. And what do I care about the rich? This isn't a world I'd bring children into.' She could just see his tense crouching figure. 'It's just their selfishness,' he said. 'They have a good time and what do they mind if someone's born ugly? Three minutes in bed or against a wall, and then a lifetime for the one that's born. Mother love,' he began to laugh, seeing quite clearly the kitchen table, the carving knife on the linoleum, the blood all over his mother's dress. He explained, 'You see I'm educated. In one of His Majesty's own homes. They call them that – homes. What do you think a home means?' But he didn't allow her time to speak. 'You are wrong. You think it means a husband in work, a nice gas cooker and a double-bed, carpet slippers and cradles and the rest. That's not a home. A home's solitary confinement for a kid that's caught talking in the chapel and the birch for almost anything you do. Bread and

117

water. A sergeant knocking you around if you try to lark a bit. That's a home.'

'Well, he was trying to alter all that, wasn't he? He was poor like we are.'

'Who are you talking about?'

'Old what's-his-name. Didn't you read about him in the papers? How he cut down all the army expenses to help clear the slums? There were photographs of him opening new flats, talking to the children. He wasn't one of the rich. He wouldn't have gone to war. That's why they shot him. You bet there are fellows making money now out of him being dead. And he'd done it all himself too, the obituaries said. His father was a thief and his mother committed – '

'Suicide?' Raven whispered. 'Did you read how she . . .'

'She drowned herself.'

'The things you read,' Raven said. 'It's enough to make a fellow think.'

'Well, I'd say the fellow who killed old what's-his-name had something to think about.'

'Maybe,' Raven said, 'he didn't know all the papers know. The men who paid him, they knew. Perhaps if we knew all there was to know, the kind of breaks the fellow had had, we'd see his point of view.'

'It'd take a lot of talking to make me see that. Anyway we'd better sleep now.'

'I've got to think,' Raven said.

'You'll think better after you've had a nap.'

But it was far too cold for him to sleep; he had no sacks to cover himself with, and his black tight overcoat was worn almost as thin as cotton. Under the door came a draught which might have travelled down the frosty rails from Scotland, a north-east wind, bringing icy fogs from the sea. He thought to himself: I didn't mean the old man any harm, there was nothing personal . . . 'I'd let you shoot him, and afterwards I'd say, "Well done".' He had a momentary crazy impulse to get up and go through the door with his automatic in his hand and let them shoot. 'Mr Know-all,' she could say then, 'if you'd only had this one trick in your sack, the dogs wouldn't . . .' But then it seemed to him that this knowledge he had gained of the old man was only one more count against Chol-mon-deley. Chol-mon-deley had known all this. There'd be one more bullet in his belly for this, and one more for Cholmondeley's master. But how was he to find the other man? He had only the memory of a photograph to guide him, a photograph which the old Minister had somehow connected with the letter of introduction Raven had borne, a young scarred boy's face which was probably an old man's now.

Anne said, 'Are you asleep?'

'No,' Raven said. 'What's troubling you?'

'I thought I heard someone moving.'

He listened. It was only the wind tapping a loose board outside. He said, 'You go to sleep. You needn't be scared. They won't come till it's light enough to see.' He thought: where would those two have met when they were so young? Surely not in the kind of home he'd known, the cold stone stairs, the cracked commanding bell, the tiny punishment cells. Quite suddenly he fell asleep and the old Minister was coming towards him saying, 'Shoot me. Shoot me in the eyes,' and Raven was a child with a catapult in his hands. He wept and wouldn't shoot and the old Minister said, 'Shoot, dear child. We'll go home together. Shoot.'

Raven woke again as suddenly. In his sleep his hand had gripped the automatic tight. It was pointed at the corner where Anne slept. He gazed with horror into the dark, hearing a whisper like the one he had heard through the door when the secretary tried to call out. He said, 'Are you asleep? What are you saying?'

Anne said: 'I'm awake.' She said defensively, 'I was just praying.'

'Do you believe in God?'

'I don't know,' Anne said. 'Sometimes maybe. It's a habit, praying. It doesn't do any harm. It's like crossing your fingers when you walk under a ladder. We all need any luck that's going.'

Raven said, 'We did a lot of praying in the home. Twice a day, and before meals too.'

'It doesn't prove anything.'

'No, it doesn't prove anything. Only you get sort of mad when everything reminds you of what's over and done with. Sometimes you want to begin fresh, and then someone praying, or a smell, or something you read in the paper, and it's all back again, the places and the people.' He came a little nearer in the cold shed for company; it made you feel more than usually alone to know that they were waiting for you outside, waiting for daylight so that they could take you without any risk of your escaping or of your firing first. He had a good mind to send her out directly it was day and stick where he was and shoot it out with them. But that meant leaving Chol-mon-deley and his employer free; it was just what would please them most. He said, 'I was reading once – I like reading – I'm educated, something about psicko – psicko – '

'Leave it at that,' Anne said. 'I know what you mean.'

'It seems your dreams mean things. I don't mean like tea-leaves or cards.'

'I knew someone once,' Anne said. 'She was so good with the cards it gave you the creeps. She used to have those cards with queer pictures on them. The Hanged Man . . .'

'It wasn't like that,' Raven said. 'It was – Oh, I don't know properly. I couldn't understand it all. But it seems if you told your dreams . . . It was like you carry a load around you; you are born with some of it because of what your father and mother were and their fathers . . . seems as if it goes right back, like it says in the Bible about the sins being visited. Then when you're a kid the load gets bigger; all the things you need to do and can't; and then all the things you do. They get you either way.' He leant his sad killer's face on his hands. 'It's like confessing to a priest. Only when you've confessed you go and do it all over again. I mean you tell these doctors everything, every dream you have, and afterwards you don't *want* to do it. But you have to tell them everything.'

'Even the flying pigs?' Anne said.

'Everything. And when you've told everything it's gone.'

'It sounds phoney to me,' Anne said.

'I don't suppose I've told it right. But it's what I read. I thought that maybe it might be worth a trial.'

'Life's full of funny things. Me and you being here. You thinking you wanted to kill me. Me thinking we can stop a war. Your psicko isn't any funnier than that.'

'You see it's getting rid of it all that counts,' Raven said. 'It's not what the doctor does. That's how it seemed to me. Like when I told you about the home, and the bread and water and the prayers, they didn't seem so important afterwards.' He swore softly and obscenely, under his breath. 'I'd always said I wouldn't go soft on a skirt. I always thought my lip'd save me. It's not safe to go soft. It makes you slow. I've seen it happen to other fellows. They've always landed in gaol or got a razor in their guts. Now I've gone soft, as soft as all the rest.'

'I like you,' Anne said. 'I'm your friend – '

'I'm not asking anything,' Raven said. 'I'm ugly and I know it. Only one thing. Be different. Don't go to the police. Most skirts do. I've seen it happen. But maybe you aren't a skirt. You're a girl.'

'I'm *someone*'s girl.'

'That's all right with me,' he exclaimed with painful pride in the coldness and the dark. 'I'm not asking anything but that, that you don't grass on me.'

'I'm not going to the police,' Anne said. 'I promise you I won't. I like you as well as any man – except my friend.'

'I thought as how perhaps I could tell you a thing or two – dreams – just as well as any doctor. You see I know doctors. You can't trust them. I went to one before I came down here. I wanted him to alter this lip. He tried to put me to sleep with gas. He was going to call the police. You can't trust them. But I could trust you.'

'You can trust me all right,' Anne said. 'I won't go to the police. But you'd better sleep first and tell me your dreams after if you want to. It's a long night.'

His teeth suddenly chattered uncontrollably with the cold and Anne heard him. She put out a hand and touched his coat. 'You're cold,' she said. 'You've given me all the sacks.'

'I don't need 'em. I've got a coat.'

'We're friends, aren't we?' Anne said. 'We are in this together. You take two of these sacks.'

He said, 'There'll be some more about. I'll look,' and he struck a match and felt his way round the wall. 'Here are two,' he said, sitting down farther away from her, empty-handed, out of reach. He said, 'I can't sleep. Not properly. I had a dream just now. About the old man.'

'What old man?'

'The old man that got murdered. I dreamed I was a kid with a catapult and he was saying, "Shoot me through the eyes," and I was crying and he said, "Shoot me through the eyes, dear child."'

'Search *me* for a meaning,' Anne said.

'I just wanted to tell it you.'

'What did he look like?'

'Like he did look.' Hastily he added, 'Like I've seen in the photographs.' He brooded over his memories with a low passionate urge towards confession. There had never in his life been anyone he could trust till now. He said, 'You don't mind hearing these things?' and listened with a curious deep happiness to her reply, 'We are friends.' He said, 'This is the best night I've ever had.' But there were things he still couldn't tell her. His happiness was incomplete till she knew everything, till he had shown his trust completely. He didn't want to shock or pain her; he led slowly towards the central revelation. He said, 'I've had other dreams of being a kid. I've dreamed I opened a door, a kitchen door, and there was my mother – she'd cut her throat – she looked ugly – her head nearly off – she sawn at it – with a bread knife – '

Anne said, 'That wasn't a dream.'

'No,' he said, 'you're right, that wasn't a dream.' He waited. He could feel her sympathy move silently towards him in the dark. He said, 'That was ugly, wasn't it? You'd think you couldn't beat that for ugliness, wouldn't you? She hadn't even thought enough of me to lock the door so as I shouldn't see. And after that, there was a Home. You know all about that. You'd say that was ugly too, but it wasn't as ugly as *that* was. And they educated me too properly so as I could understand the things I read in the papers. Like this psicko business. And write a good hand and speak the King's English. I got beaten a lot at the start, solitary confinement, bread and water, all the rest of the homey stuff. But that didn't go on when they'd educated me. I was too clever for them after that. They could never put a thing on me. They suspected all right, but they never had the proof. Once the chaplain tried to frame me. They were right when they told us the day we left about it was like life. Jim and me and a bunch of soft kids.' He said bitterly, 'This is the first time they've had anything on me and I'm innocent.'

'You'll get away,' Anne said. 'We'll think up something together.'

'It sounds good your saying "together" like that, but they've got me this time. I wouldn't mind if I could get that Chol-mon-deley and his boss first.' He said with a kind of nervous pride, 'Would you be surprised if I'd told you I'd killed a man?' It was like the first fence; if he cleared that, he would have confidence . . .

'Who?'

'Did you ever hear of Battling Kite?'

'No.'

He laughed with a sacred pleasure. 'I'm trusting you with my life now. If you'd told me twenty-four hours ago that I'd trust my life to . . . but of course I haven't given you any *proof*. I was doing the races then. Kite had a rival gang. There wasn't anything else to do. He'd tried to bump my boss off on the course. Half of us took a fast car back to town. He thought we were on the train with him. But we were on the platform, see, when the train came in. We got round him directly he got outside the carriage. I cut his throat and the others held him up till we were all through the barrier in a bunch. Then we dropped him by the bookstall and did a bolt.' He said, 'You see it was his lot or our lot. They'd had razors out on the course. It was war.'

After a while Anne said, 'Yes. I can see that. He had his chance.'

'It sounds ugly,' Raven said, 'Funny thing is, it wasn't ugly. It was natural.'

'Did you stick to that game?'

'No. It wasn't good enough. You couldn't trust the others. They either went soft or else they got reckless. They didn't use their brains.' He said, 'I wanted to tell you about Kite. I'm not sorry. I haven't got religion. Only you said about being friendly and I don't want you to get any wrong ideas. It was that mix-up with Kite brought me up against Chol-mon-deley. I can see now, he was only in the racing game so as he could meet people. I thought he was a mug.'

'We've got a long way from dreams.'

'I was coming back to them,' Raven said. 'I suppose killing Kite like that made me nervous.' His voice trembled very slightly from fear and hope, hope because she had accepted one killing so quietly and might, after all, take back what she had said: ('Well done', 'I wouldn't raise a finger'); fear because he didn't really believe that you could put such perfect trust in another and not be deceived. But it'd be fine, he thought, to be able to tell everything, to know that another person knew and didn't care; it would be like going to sleep for a long while. He said, 'That spell of sleep I had just now was the first for two – three – I don't know how many nights. It looks as if I'm not tough enough after all.'

'You seem tough enough to me,' Anne said. 'Don't let's hear any more about Kite.'

'No one will hear any more about Kite. But if I was to tell you – ' he ran away from the revelation. 'I've been dreaming a lot lately it was an old woman I killed, not Kite. I heard her calling out through a door and I tried to open the door, but she held the handle. I shot at her through the wood, but she held the handle tight, I had to kill her to open the door. Then I dreamed she was still alive and I shot her through the eyes. But even that – it wasn't *ugly*.'

'You are tough enough in your dreams,' Anne said.

'I killed an old man too in that dream. Behind his desk. I had a silencer. He fell behind it. I didn't want to hurt him. He didn't mean anything to me. I pumped him full. Then I put a bit of paper in his hand. I didn't have to take anything.'

'What do you mean – you didn't have to take?'

Raven said, 'They hadn't paid me to take anything. Chol-mon-deley and his boss.'

'It wasn't a dream.'

'No. It wasn't a dream.' The silence frightened him. He began to talk rapidly to fill it. 'I didn't know the old fellow was one of us. I wouldn't have touched him if I'd known he was like that. All this talk of war. It doesn't mean a thing to me. Why should I care if there's a war? There's always been a war for me. You talk a lot about the kids. Can't you have a bit of pity for the men? It was me or him. Two hundred pounds when I got back and fifty pounds down. It's a lot of money. It was only Kite over again. It was just as easy as it was with Kite.' He said, 'Are you going to leave me now?' and in silence Anne could hear his rasping anxious breath. She said at last, 'No. I'm not going to leave you.'

He said, 'That's good. Oh, that's good,' putting out his hand, feeling hers cold as ice on the sacking. He put it for a moment against his unshaven cheek; he wouldn't touch it with his malformed lip. He said, 'It feels good to trust someone with everything.'

2

Anne waited for a long time before she spoke again. She wanted her voice to sound right, not to show her repulsion. Then she tried it on him, but all she could think of to say was again, 'I'm not going to leave you.' She remembered very clearly in the dark all she had read of the crime: the old woman secretary shot through the eyes lying in the passage, the brutally smashed skull of the old Socialist. The papers had called it the worst political murder since the day when the King and Queen of Serbia were thrown through the windows of their palace to ensure the succession of the war-time hero king.

Raven said again, 'It's good to be able to trust someone like this,' and suddenly his mouth which had never before struck her as particularly ugly came to mind and she could have retched at the memory. Nevertheless, she thought, I must go on with this, I mustn't let him know, he must find Chol- mondeley and Cholmondeley's boss and then . . . She shrank from him into the dark.

He said, 'They are out there waiting now. They've got cops down from London.'

'From London?'

'It was all in the papers,' he said with pride. 'Detective- Sergeant Mather from the Yard.'

She could hardly restrain a cry of desolation and horror. 'Here?'

'He may be outside now.'

'Why doesn't he come in?'

'They'd never get me in the dark. And they'll know by now that *you* are here. They wouldn't be able to shoot.'

'And you – you would?'

'There's no one *I* mind hurting,' Raven said.

'How are you going to get out when it's daylight?'

'I shan't wait till then. I only want just light enough to see my way. And see to shoot. *They* won't be able to fire first; they won't be able to shoot to kill. That's what gives me a break. I only want a few clear hours. If I get away, they'll never guess where to find me. Only you'll know I'm at Mid- land Steel.'

She felt a desperate hatred. 'You'll just shoot like that in cold blood?'

'You said you were on my side, didn't you?'

'Oh yes,' she said warily, 'yes,' trying to think. It was get- ting too much to have to save the world – *and* Jimmy. If it came to a show-down the world would have to take second place. And what, she wondered, is Jimmy thinking? She knew his heavy humourless rectitude; it would take more than Raven's head on a platter to make him understand why she had acted as she had with Raven and Cholmondeley. It sounded weak and fanciful even to herself to say that she wanted to stop a war.

'Let's sleep now,' she said. 'We've got a long, long day ahead.'

126

'I think I could sleep now,' Raven said. 'You don't know how good it seems . . .' It was Anne now who could not sleep. She had too much to think about. It occurred to her that she might steal his pistol before he woke and call the police in. That would save Jimmy from danger, but what was the use? They'd never believe her story; they had no proof that he had killed the old man. And even then he might escape. She needed time and there was no time. She could hear very faintly droning up from the south, where the military aerodrome was, a flight of planes. They passed very high on special patrol, guarding the Nottwich mines and the key industry of Midland Steel, tiny specks of light the size of fireflies travelling fast in formation, over the railway, over the goods yard, over the shed where Anne and Raven lay, over Saunders beating his arms for warmth behind a truck out of the wind's way, over Acky dreaming that he was in the pulpit of St Luke's, over Sir Marcus sleepless beside the tape machine.

Raven slept heavily for the first time for nearly a week, holding the automatic in his lap. He dreamed that he was building a great bonfire on Guy Fawkes day. He threw in everything he could find: a saw-edged knife, a lot of racing cards, the leg of a table. It burnt warmly, deeply, beautifully. A lot of fireworks were going off all round him and again the old War Minister appeared on the other side of the fire. He said, 'It's a good fire,' stepping into it himself. Raven ran to the fire to pull him out, but the old man said, 'Let me be. It's warm here,' and then he sagged like a Guy Fawkes in the flames.

A clock struck. Anne counted the strokes, as she had counted them all through the night; it must be nearly day and she had no plan. She coughed; her throat was stinging; and suddenly she realized with joy that there was fog outside: not one of the black upper fogs, but a cold damp yellow fog from the river, through which it would be easy, if it was thick enough, for a man to escape. She put out her hand unwillingly, because he was now so repulsive to her, and touched Raven. He woke at once. She said, 'There's a fog coming up.'

'What a break!' he said, 'what a break!' laughing softly.

'It makes you believe in Providence, doesn't it?' They could just see each other in the pale earliest light. He was shivering now that he was awake. He said, 'I dreamed of a big fire'. She saw that he had no sacks to cover him, but she felt no pity at all. He was just a wild animal who had to be dealt with carefully and then destroyed. 'Let him freeze,' she thought. He was examining the automatic; she saw him put down the safety catch. He said, 'What about you? You've been straight with me. I don't want you to get into any trouble. I don't want them to think,' he hesitated and went on with questioning humility, 'to know that we are in this together.'

'I'll think up something,' Anne said.

'I ought to knock you out. They wouldn't know then. But I've gone soft. I wouldn't hurt you not if I was paid.'

She couldn't resist saying, 'Not for two hundred and fifty pounds?'

'He was a stranger,' Raven said. 'It's not the same. I thought he was one of the high and mighties. You're – ' he hesitated again, glowering dumbly down at the automatic, 'a friend.'

'You needn't be afraid,' Anne said. 'I'll have a tale to tell.'

He said with admiration, 'You're clever.' He watched the fog coming in under the badly fitting door, filling the small shed with its freezing coils. 'It'll be nearly thick enough now to take a chance.' He held the automatic in his left hand and flexed the fingers of the right. He laughed to keep his courage up. 'They'll never get me now in this fog.'

'You'll shoot?'

'Of course I'll shoot.'

'I've got an idea,' Anne said. 'We don't want to take any risks. Give me your overcoat and hat. I'll put them on and slip out first and give them a run for their money. In this fog they'll never notice till they've caught me. Directly you hear the whistles blow count five slowly and make a bolt. I'll run to the right. You run to the left.'

'You've got nerve,' Raven said. He shook his head. 'No. They might shoot.'

'You said yourself they wouldn't shoot first.'

'That's right. But you'll get a couple of years for this.'

'Oh,' Anne said, 'I'll tell them a tale. I'll say you forced me.' She said with a trace of bitterness, 'This'll give me a lift out of the chorus. I'll have a speaking part.'

Raven said shyly, 'If you made out you were my girl, they wouldn't pin it on you. I'll say that for them. They'd give a man's girl a break.'

'Got a knife?'

'Yes.' He felt in all his pockets; it wasn't there; he must have left it on the floor of Acky's best guest-chamber.

Anne said, 'I wanted to cut up my skirt. I'd be able to run easier.'

'I'll try and tear it,' Raven said, kneeling in front of her, taking a grip, but it wouldn't tear. Looking down she was astonished at the smallness of his wrists; his hands had no more strength or substance than a delicate boy's. The whole of his strength lay in the mechanical instrument at his feet. She thought of Mather and felt contempt now as well as repulsion for the thin ugly body kneeling at her feet.

'Never mind,' she said. 'I'll do the best I can. Give me the coat.'

He shivered, taking it off, and seemed to lose some of his sour assurance without the tight black tube which had hidden a very old, very flamboyant check suit in holes at both the elbows. It hung on him uneasily. He looked under-nourished. He wouldn't have impressed anyone as dangerous now. He pressed his arms to his sides to hide the holes. 'And your hat,' Anne said. He picked it up from the sacks and gave it her. He looked humiliated, and he had never accepted humiliation before without rage. 'Now,' Anne said, 'remember. Wait for the whistles and then count.'

'I don't like it,' Raven said. He tried hopelessly to express the deep pain it gave him to see her go; it felt too much like the end of everything. He said, 'I'll see you again – some time,' and when she mechanically reassured him, 'Yes,' he laughed with his aching despair, 'Not likely, after I've killed – ' but he didn't even know the man's name.

Chapter 6

1

SAUNDERS had half fallen asleep; a voice at his side woke him. 'The fog's getting thick, sir.'

It was already dense, with the first light touching it with dusty yellow, and he would have sworn at the policeman for not waking him earlier if his stammer had not made him chary of wasting words. He said, 'Pass the word round to move in.'

'Are we going to rush the place, sir?'

'No. There's a girl there. We can't have any sh-sh-shooting. Wait till he comes out.'

But the policeman hadn't left his side when he noticed, 'The door's opening.' Saunders put his whistle in his mouth and lowered his safety catch. The light was bad and the fog deceptive; but he recognized the dark coat as it slipped to the right into the shelter of the coal trucks. He blew his whistle and was after it. The black coat had half a minute's start and was moving quickly into the fog. It was impossible to see at all more than twenty feet ahead. But Saunders kept doggedly just in sight blowing his whistle continuously. As he hoped, a whistle blew in front; it confused the fugitive; he hesitated for a moment and Saunders gained on him. They had him cornered, and this Saunders knew was the dangerous moment. He blew his whistle urgently three times into the fog to bring the police round in a complete circle and the whistle was taken up in the yellow obscurity, passing in a wide invisible circle.

But he had lost pace, the fugitive spurted forward and was lost. Saunders blew two blasts: 'Advance slowly and keep in touch.' To the right and in front a single long whistle announced that the man had been seen, and the police converged on the sound. Each kept in touch with a policeman on either hand. It was impossible as long as the circle was kept closed for the man to escape. But the circle drew in and there was no

130

sign of him; the short single exploratory blasts sounded petulant and lost. At last Saunders gazing ahead saw the faint form of a policeman come out of the fog a dozen yards away. He halted them all with a whistled signal: the fugitive must be somewhere just ahead in the tangle of trucks in the centre. Revolver in hand Saunders advanced and a policeman took his place and closed the circle.

Suddenly Saunders spied his man. He had taken up a strategic position where a pile of coal and an empty truck at his back made a wedge which guarded him from surprise. He was invisible to the police behind him, and he had turned sideways like a duellist and presented only a shoulder to Saunders, while a pile of old sleepers hid him to the knees. It seemed to Saunders that it meant only one thing, that he was going to shoot it out; the man must be mad and desperate. The hat was pulled down over the face; the coat hung in an odd loose way; the hands were in the pockets. Saunders called at him through the yellow coils of fog, 'You'd better come quietly.' He raised his pistol and advanced, his finger ready on the trigger. But the immobility of the figure scared him. It was in shadow half hidden in the swirl of fog. It was he who was exposed, with the east, and the pale penetration of early light, behind him. It was like waiting for execution, for he could not fire first. But all the same, knowing what Mather felt, knowing that this man was mixed up with Mather's girl, he did not want much excuse to fire. Mather would stand by him. A movement would be enough. He said sharply without a stammer, 'Put up your hands!' The figure didn't move. He told himself again with a kindling hatred for the man who had injured Mather: I'll plug him if he doesn't obey: they'll all stand by me: one more chance. 'Put up your hands!' and when the figure stayed as it was with its hands hidden, a hardly discernible menace, he fired.

But as he pressed the trigger a whistle blew, a long urgent blast which panted and gave out like a rubber animal, from the direction of the wall and the road. There could be no doubt whatever what that meant, and suddenly he saw it all – he had shot at Mather's girl; she'd drawn them off. He screamed

131

at the men behind him, 'Back to the gate!' and ran forward. He had seen her waver at his shot. He said, 'Are you hurt?' and knocked the hat off her head to see her better.

'You're the third person who's tried to kill me,' Anne said weakly, leaning hard against the truck. 'Come to sunny Nottwich. Well, I've got six lives left.'

Saunders's stammer came back: 'W-w-w-w.'

'This is where you hit,' Anne said, 'if that's what you want to know,' showing the long yellow sliver on the edge of the truck. 'It's only an outer. You don't even get a box of chocolates.'

Saunders said, 'You'll have to c-c-come along with me.'

'It'll be a pleasure. Do you mind if I take off this coat? I feel kind of silly.'

At the gate four policeman stood round something on the ground. One of them said, 'We've sent for an ambulance.'

'Is he dead?'

'Not yet. He's shot in the stomach. He must have gone on whistling – '

Saunders had a moment of vicious rage. 'Stand aside, boys,' he said, 'and let the lady see.' They drew back in an embarrassed unwilling way as if they'd been hiding a dirty chalk picture on the wall and showed the white drained face which looked as if it had never been alive, never known the warm circulation of blood. You couldn't call the expression peaceful; it was just nothing at all. The blood was all over the trousers the men had loosened, was caked on the charcoal of the path. Saunders said, 'Two of you take this lady to the station. I'll stay here till the ambulance comes.'

2

Mather said, 'If you want to make a statement I must warn you. Anything you say may be used in evidence.'

'I haven't got a statement to make,' Anne said. 'I want to talk to you, Jimmy.'

Mather said, 'If the superintendent had been here, I should have asked him to take the case. I want you to understand

132

that I'm not letting personal – that my not having charged you doesn't mean – '

'You might give a girl a cup of coffee,' Anne said. 'It's nearly breakfast time.'

Mather struck the table furiously. 'Where was he going?'

'Give me time,' Anne said, 'I've got plenty to tell. But you won't believe it.'

'You saw the man he shot,' Mather said. 'He's got a wife and two children. They've rung up from the hospital. He's bleeding internally.'

'What's the time?' Anne said.

'Eight o'clock. It won't make any difference your keeping quiet. He can't escape us now. In an hour the air raid signals go. There won't be a soul on the streets without a mask. He'll be spotted at once. What's he wearing?'

'If you'd give me something to eat. I haven't had a thing for twenty-four hours. I could think then.'

Mather said, 'There's only one chance you won't be charged with complicity. If you make a statement.'

'Is this the third degree?' Anne said.

'Why do you want to shelter him? Why keep your word to him when you don't – ?'

'Go on,' Anne said. 'Be personal. No one can blame you. I don't. But I don't want you to think I'd keep my word to him. He killed the old man. He told me so.'

'What old man?'

'The War Minister.'

'You've got to think up something better than that,' Mather said.

'But it's true. He never stole those notes. They double-crossed him. It was what they'd paid him to do the job.'

'He spun you a fancy yarn,' Mather said. 'But *I* know where those notes came from.'

'So do I. I can guess. From somewhere in this town.'

'He told you wrong. They came from United Rail Makers in Victoria Street.'

Anne shook her head. 'They didn't start from there. They came from Midland Steel.'

133

'So that's where he's going, to Midland Steel – in the Tanneries?'

'Yes,' Anne said. There was a sound of finality about the word which daunted her. She hated Raven now, the policeman she had seen bleeding on the ground called at her heart for Raven's death, but she couldn't help remembering the hut, the cold, the pile of sacks, his complete and hopeless trust. She sat with bowed head while Mather lifted the receiver and gave his orders. 'We'll wait for him there,' he said. 'Who is it he wants to see?'

'He doesn't know.'

'There might be something in it,' Mather said. 'Some connection between the two. He's probably been double-crossed by some clerk.'

'It wasn't a clerk who paid him all that money, who tried to kill me just because I knew – '

Mather said, 'Your fairy tale can wait.' He rang a bell and told the constable who came, 'Hold this girl for further inquiries. You can give her a sandwich and a cup of coffee now.'

'Where are you going?'

'To bring in your boy friend,' Mather said.

'He'll shoot. He's quicker than you are. Why can't you let the others – ?' She implored him, 'I'll make a full statement. How he killed a man called Kite too.'

'Take it,' Mather said to the constable. He put on his coat. 'The fog's clearing.'

She said, 'Don't you see that if it's true – only give him time to find his man and there won't be – war.'

'He was telling you a fairy story.'

'He was telling me the truth – but, of course, you weren't there – you didn't hear him. It sounds differently to you. I thought I was saving – everyone.'

'All you did,' Mather said brutally, 'was get a man killed.'

'The whole thing sounds so differently in here. Kind of fantastic. But he believed. Maybe,' she said hopelessly, 'he was mad.'

Mather opened the door. She suddenly cried to him, 'Jimmy, he wasn't mad. They tried to kill *me*.'

He said, 'I'll read your statement when I get back,' and closed the door.

Chapter 7

1

THEY were all having the hell of a time at the hospital. It was the biggest rag they'd had since the day of the street collection when they kidnapped old Piker and ran him to the edge of the Weevil and threatened to duck him if he didn't pay a ransom. Good old Fergusson, good old Buddy, was organizing it all. They had three ambulances out in the courtyard and one had a death's-head banner on it for the dead ones. Somebody shrieked that Mike was taking out the petrol with a nasal syringe, so they began to pelt him with flour and soot; they had it ready in great buckets. It was the unofficial part of the programme: all the casualties were going to be rubbed with it, except the dead ones the death's-head ambulance picked up. *They* were going to be put in the cellar where the refrigerating plant kept the corpses for dissection fresh.

One of the senior surgeons passed rapidly and nervously across a corner of the courtyard. He was on the way to a Caesarian operation, but he had no confidence whatever that the students wouldn't pelt him or duck him; only five years ago there had been a scandal and an inquiry because a woman had died on the day of a rag. The surgeon attending her had been kidnapped and carried all over town dressed as Guy Fawkes. Luckily she wasn't a paying patient, and, though her husband had been hysterical at the inquest, the coroner had decided that one must make allowance for youth. The coroner had been a student himself once and remembered with pleasure the day when they had pelted the Vice-Chancellor of the University with soot.

The senior surgeon had been present that day too. Once safely inside the glass corridor he could smile at the memory. The Vice-Chancellor had been unpopular; he had been a classic which wasn't very suitable for a provincial university. He had translated Lucan's *Pharsalia* into some complicated metre of his own invention. The senior surgeon remembered something vaguely about stresses. He could still see the little wizened frightened Liberal face trying to smile when his pince-nez broke, trying to be a good sportsman. But anyone could tell that he wasn't really a good sportsman. That was why they pelted him so hard.

The senior surgeon, quite safe now, smiled tenderly down at the rabble in the courtyard. Their white coats were already black with soot. Somebody had got hold of a stomach pump. Very soon they'd be raiding the shop in the High Street and seizing their mascot, the stuffed and rather moth-eaten tiger. Youth, youth, he thought, laughing gently when he saw Colson, the treasurer, scuttle from door to door with a scared expression: perhaps they'll catch him: no, they've let him by: what a joke it all was, 'trailing clouds of glory', 'turn as swimmers into cleanness leaping'.

Buddy was having the hell of a time. Everyone was scampering to obey his orders. He was the leader. They'd duck or pelt anyone he told them to. He had an enormous sense of power; it more than atoned for unsatisfactory examination results, for surgeons' sarcasms. Even a surgeon wasn't safe today if *he* gave an order. The soot and water and flour were his idea; the whole gas practice would have been a dull sober official piece of routine if he hadn't thought of making it a 'rag'. The very word 'rag' was powerful; it conferred complete freedom from control. He'd called a meeting of the brighter students and explained. 'If anyone's on the streets without a gas-mask he's a conchie. There are people who want to crab the practice. So when we get 'em back to the hospital we'll give 'em hell.'

They boiled round him. 'Good old Buddy.' 'Look out with that pump.' 'Who's the bastard who's pinched my stetho-scope?' 'What about Tiger Tim?' They surged round Buddy Fergusson, waiting for orders, and he stood superbly above them on the step of an ambulance, his white coat apart, his fingers in the pockets of his double-breasted waistcoat, his square squat figure swelling with pride, while they shouted, 'Tiger Tim! Tiger Tim! Tiger Tim!'

'Friends, Romans and Countrymen,' he said and they

roared with laughter: Good old Buddy. Buddy always had the right word. He could make any party go. You never knew what Buddy would say next. 'Lend me your – ' They shrieked with laughter. He was a dirty dog, old Buddy. Good old Buddy.

Like a great beast which is in need of exercise, which has fed on too much hay, Buddy Fergusson was aware of his body. He felt his biceps; he strained for action. Too many exams, too many lectures, Buddy Fergusson wanted action. While they surged round him he imagined himself a leader of men. No Red Cross work for him when war broke: Buddy Fergusson, company commander, Buddy Fergusson, the daredevil of the trenches. The only exam he had ever successfully passed was Certificate A in the school O.T.C.

'Some of our friends seem to be missing,' Buddy Fergusson said. 'Simmons, Aitkin, Mallowes, Watt. They are bloody conchies, every one, grubbing up anatomy while we are serving our country. We'll pick 'em up in town. The flying squad will go to their lodgings.'

'What about the women, Buddy?' someone screamed, and everyone laughed and began to hit at each other, wrestle and mill. For Buddy had a reputation with the women. He spoke airily to his friends of even the super-barmaid at the Metropole, calling her Juicy Juliet and suggesting to the minds of his hearers amazing scenes of abandonment over high tea at his digs.

Buddy Fergusson straddled across the ambulance step. 'Deliver 'em to me. In war-time we need more mothers.' He felt strong, coarse, vital, a town bull; he hardly remembered himself that he was a virgin, guilty only of a shame-faced unsuccessful attempt on the old Nottwich tart; he was sustained by his reputation, it bore him magically in imagination into every bed. He knew women, he was a realist.

'Treat 'em rough,' they shrieked at him, and 'You're telling me,' he said magnificently, keeping well at bay any thought of the future: the small provincial G.P.'s job, the panel patients in dingy consulting rooms, innumerable midwife cases, a lifetime of hard underpaid fidelity to one dull wife. 'Got your

137

gas-masks ready?' he called to them, the undisputed leader, daredevil Buddy. What the hell did examinations matter when you were a leader of men? He could see several of the younger nurses watching him through the panes. He could see the little brunette called Milly. She was coming to tea with him on Saturday. He felt his muscles taut with pride. What scenes, he told himself, *this* time there would be of disreputable revelry, forgetting the inevitable truth known only to himself and each girl in turn: the long silence over the muffins, the tentative references to League results, the peck at empty air on the doorstep.

The siren at the glue factory started its long mounting whistle rather like a lap dog with hysteria and everyone stood still for a moment with a vague reminiscence of Armistice Day silences. Then they broke into three milling mobs, climbing on to the ambulance roofs, fixing their gas-masks, and drove out into the cold empty Nottwich streets. The ambulances shed a lot of them at each corner, and small groups formed and wandered down the streets with a predatory disappointed air. The streets were almost empty. Only a few errand boys passed on bicycles, looking in their gas-masks like bears doing a trick cycle act in a circus. They all shrieked at each other because they didn't know how their voices sounded outside. It was as if each of them were enclosed in a separate sound-proof telephone cabinet. They stared hungrily through their big mica eye-pieces into the doorways of shops, wanting a victim. A little group collected round Buddy Fergusson and proposed that they should seize a policeman who, being on point duty, was without a mask. But Buddy vetoed the proposal. He said this wasn't an ordinary rag. What they wanted were people who thought so little about their country that they wouldn't even take the trouble to put on a gas-mask. 'They are the people,' he said, 'who avoid boat-drill. We had great fun with a fellow once in the Mediterranean who didn't turn up to boat-drill.'

That reminded them of all the fellows who weren't helping, who were probably getting ahead with their anatomy at that moment. 'Watt lives near here,' Buddy Fergusson said, 'let's get Watt and debag him.' A feeling of physical well-being came over him just as if he had drunk a couple of pints of bitter. 'Down the Tanneries,' Buddy said. 'First left. First right. Second left, Number twelve. First floor.' He knew the way, he said, because he'd been to tea several times with Watt their first term before he'd learned what a hound Watt was. The knowledge of his early mistake made him unusually anxious to do something to Watt physically, to mark the severance of their relationship more completely than with sneers.

They ran down the empty Tanneries, half a dozen masked monstrosities in white coats smutted with soot; it was impossible to tell one from another. Through the great glass door of Midland Steel they saw three men standing by the lift talking to the porter. There were a lot of uniformed police about, and in the square ahead they saw a rival group of fellow-students, who had been luckier than they, carrying a little man (he kicked and squealed) towards an ambulance. The police watched and laughed, and a troop of planes zoomed overhead, diving low over the centre of the town to lend the practice verisimilitude. First left. First right. The centre of Nottwich to a stranger was full of sudden contrasts. Only on the edge of the town to the north, out by the park, were you certain of encountering street after street of well-to-do middle-class houses. Near the market you changed at a corner from modern chromium offices to little cats'-meat shops, from the luxury of the Metropole to seedy lodgings and the smell of cooking greens. There was no excuse in Nottwich for one half of the world being ignorant of how the other half lived.

Second left. The houses on one side gave way to bare rock and the street dived steeply down below the Castle. It wasn't really a castle any longer; it was a yellow brick municipal museum full of flint arrowheads and pieces of broken brown pottery and a few stags' heads in the zoological section suffering from moths and one mummy brought back from Egypt by the Earl of Nottwich in 1843. The moths left that alone, but the custodian thought he had heard mice inside. Mike, with a nasal douche in his breast pocket, wanted to climb up the rock. He shouted to Buddy Fergusson that the custodian was outside, without a mask, signalling to enemy aircraft. But Buddy and the others ran down the hill to number twelve.

The landlady opened the door to them. She smiled winningly and said Mr Watt was in; she thought he was working; she buttonholed Buddy Fergusson and said she was sure it would be good for Mr Watt to be taken away from his books for half an hour. Buddy said, 'We'll take him away.'

'Why, that's Mr Fergusson,' the landlady said. 'I'd know your voice anywhere, but I'd never 'ave known you without you spoke to me, not in them respiratorories. I was just going out when Mr Watt minded me as 'ow it was the gas practice.'

'Oh, he remembers, does he?' Buddy said. He was blushing inside the mask at having been recognized by the landlady. It made him want to assert himself more than ever.

'He said I'd be taken to the 'ospital.'

'Come on, men,' Buddy said and led them up the stairs. But their number was an embarrassment. They couldn't all charge through Watt's door and seize him in a moment from the chair in which he was sitting. They had to go through one at a time after Buddy and then bunch themselves in a shy silence beside the table. This was the moment when an experienced man could have dealt with them, but Watt was aware of his unpopularity. He was afraid of losing dignity. He was a man who worked hard because he liked the work; he hadn't the excuse of poverty. He played no games because he didn't like games, without the excuse of physical weakness. He had a mental arrogance which would ensure his success. If he suffered agony from his unpopularity now as a student it was the price he paid for the baronetcy, the Harley Street consulting room, the fashionable practice of the future. There was no reason to pity him; it was the others who were pitiable, living in their vivid vulgar way for five years before the long provincial interment of a lifetime.

Watt said, 'Close the door, please. There's a draught,' and his scared sarcasm gave them the chance they needed, to resent him.

Buddy said, 'We've come to ask why you weren't at the hospital this morning?'

'That's Fergusson, isn't it?' Watt said. 'I don't know why you want to know.'

'Are you a conchie?'

'How old-world your slang is,' Watt said. 'No. I'm not a conchie. Now I'm just looking through some old medical books, and as I don't suppose they'd interest you, I'll ask you to show yourselves out.'

'Working? That's how fellows like you get ahead, working while others are doing a proper job.'

'It's just a different idea of fun, that's all,' Watt said. 'It's my pleasure to look at these folios, it's yours to go screaming about the streets in that odd costume.'

That let them loose on him. He was as good as insulting the King's uniform. 'We're going to debag you,' Buddy said.

'That's fine. It'll save time,' Watt said, 'if I take them off myself,' and he began to undress. He said, 'This action has an interesting psychological significance. A form of castration. My own theory is that sexual jealousy in some form is at the bottom of it.'

'You dirty tyke,' Buddy said. He took the inkpot and splashed it on the wallpaper. He didn't like the word 'sex'. He believed in barmaids and nurses and tarts, and he believed in love, something rather maternal with deep breasts. The word sex suggested that there was something in common between the two: it outraged him. 'Wreck the room!' he bawled and they were all immediately happy and at ease, exerting themselves physically like young bulls. Because they were happy again they didn't do any real damage, just pulled the books out of the shelves and threw them on the floor; they broke the glass of a picture frame in puritanical zeal because it contained the reproduction of a nude girl. Watt watched them; he was scared, and the more scared he was the more sarcastic he became. Buddy suddenly saw him as he was, standing there in his pants marked from birth for distinction, for success, and hated him. He felt impotent; he hadn't 'class' like Watt, he hadn't the brains, in a very few years nothing he could do or say would affect the fortunes or the happiness of the Harley Street specialist, the woman's physician, the baronet. What was the good of talking about free will? Only war and death could save Buddy from the confinements, the provincial practice, the one dull wife and the bridge parties. It seemed to him that he could be happy if he had the strength to impress himself on Watt's memory. He took the inkpot and poured it over the open title-page of the old folio on the table.

'Come on, men,' he said. 'This room stinks,' and led his party out and down the stairs. He felt an immense exhilaration; it was as if he had proved his manhood.

Almost immediately they picked up an old woman. She didn't in the least know what it was all about. She thought it was a street collection and offered them a penny. They told her she had to come along to the hospital; they were very courteous and one offered to carry her basket; they reacted from violence to a more than usual gentility. She laughed at them. She said, 'Well I never, what you boys will think up next!' and when one took her arm and began to lead her gently up the street, she said, 'Which of you's Father Christmas?' Buddy didn't like that: it hurt his dignity: he had suddenly been feeling rather noble: 'women and children first': 'although bombs were falling all round he brought the woman safely . . .' He stood still and let the others go on up the street with the old woman; she was having the time of her life; she cackled and dug them in the ribs: her voice carried a long distance in the cold air. She kept on telling them to 'take off them things and play fair', and just before they turned a corner out of sight she was calling them Mormons. She meant Mohammedans, because she had an idea that Mohammedans went about with their faces covered up and had a lot of wives. An aeroplane zoomed overhead and Buddy was alone in the street with the dead and dying until Mike appeared. Mike said he had a good idea. Why not pinch the mummy in the Castle and take it to the hospital for not wearing a gas-mask? The fellows with the death's-head ambulance had already got Tiger Tim and were driving round the town crying out for old Piker.

'No,' Buddy said, 'this isn't an ordinary rag. This is serious,' and suddenly at the entrance to a side street he saw a man without a mask double back at the sight of him. 'Quick. Hunt him down,' Buddy cried, 'Tallyho,' and they pelted up the street in pursuit. Mike was the faster runner: Buddy was already a little inclined to fatness, and Mike was soon leading by ten yards. The man had a start, he was round one corner and out of sight. 'Go on,' Buddy shouted, 'hold him till I come.' Mike was out of sight too when a voice from a doorway spoke as he passed. 'Hi,' it said, 'you. What's the hurry?'

Buddy stopped. The man stood there with his back pressed to a house door. He had simply stepped back and Mike in his hurry had gone by. There was something serious and planned and venomous about his behaviour. The street of little Gothic villas was quite empty.

'You were looking for me, weren't you?' the man said.

Buddy demanded sharply, 'Where's your gas-mask?'

'Is this a game?' the man asked angrily.

'Of course it's not a game,' Buddy said. 'You're a casualty. You'll have to come along to the hospital with me.'

'I will, will I?' the man said, pressed back against the door, thin and undersized and out-at-elbows.

'You'd better,' Buddy said. He inflated his chest and made his biceps swell. Discipline, he thought, discipline. The little brute didn't recognize an officer when he saw one. He felt the satisfaction of superior physical strength. He'd punch his nose for him if he didn't come quietly.

'All right,' the man said, 'I'll come.' He emerged from the dark doorway, mean vicious face, hare-lip, a crude check suit, ominous and aggressive in his submission. 'Not that way,' Buddy said, 'to the left.'

'Keep moving,' the small man said, covering Buddy through his pocket, pressing the pistol against his side. '*Me* a casualty,' he said, 'that's a good one,' laughing without mirth. 'Get in through that gate or you'll be the casualty – ' (they were opposite a small garage; it was empty; the owner had driven to his office, and the little bare box stood open at the end of a few feet of drive).

Buddy blustered, 'What the hell!' but he had recognized the face of which the description had appeared in both the local papers, and there was a control in the man's action which horribly convinced Buddy that he wouldn't hesitate to shoot. It was a moment in his life that he never forgot; he was not allowed to forget it by friends who saw nothing wrong in what he did. All through his life the tale cropped up in print in the most unlikely places: serious histories, symposiums of famous crimes: it followed him from obscure practice to obscure practice. Nobody saw anything important in what he did: nobody doubted that he would have done the same: walked into the garage, closed the gates at Raven's orders. But friends didn't realize the crushing nature of the blow: they hadn't just been standing in the street under a hail of bombs, they had not looked forward with pleasure and excitement to war, they hadn't been Buddy, the daredevil of the trenches one minute, before genuine war in the shape of an automatic in a thin desperate hand pressed on him.

'Strip!' Raven said, and obediently Buddy stripped. But he was stripped of more than his gas-mask, his white coat, his green tweed suit. When it was over he hadn't a hope left. It was no good hoping for a war to prove him a leader of men. He was just a stout flushed frightened young man shivering in his pants in the cold garage. There was a hole in the seat of his pants and his knees were pink and clean-shaven. You could tell that he was strong, but you could tell too in the curve of his stomach, the thickness of his neck, that he was beginning to run to seed. Like a mastiff he needed more exercise than the city could afford him, even though several times a week undeterred by the frost he would put on shorts and a singlet and run slowly and obstinately round the park, a little red in the face but undeterred by the grins of nursemaids and the shrill veracious comments of unbearable children in prams. He was keeping fit, but it was a dreadful thought that he had been keeping fit for this: to stand shivering and silent in a pair of holed pants, while the mean thin undernourished city rat, whose arm he could have snapped with a single twist, put on his clothes, his white coat and last of all his gas-mask.

'Turn round,' Raven said, and Buddy Fergusson obeyed. He was so miserable now that he would have missed a chance even if Raven had given him one, miserable and scared as well. He hadn't much imagination; he had never really visualized danger as it gleamed at him under the garage globe in a long grey wicked-looking piece of metal charged with pain and death. 'Put your hands behind you.' Raven tied together the pink strong ham-like wrists with Buddy's tie: the striped chocolate-and-yellow old boys' tie of one of the obscurer public schools. 'Lie down,' and meekly Buddy Fergusson obeyed and Raven tied his feet together with a handkerchief and gagged him with another. It wasn't very secure, but it would have to do. He'd got to work quickly. He left the garage and pulled the doors softly to behind him. He could hope for several hours' start now, but he couldn't count on as many minutes.

He came quietly and cautiously up under the Castle rock, keeping his eye open for students. But the gangs had moved on; some were picketing the station for train arrivals, and the others were sweeping the streets which led out northwards towards the mines. The chief danger now was that at any moment the sirens might blow the 'All Clear'. There were a lot of police about: he knew why, but he moved unhesitatingly past them and on towards the Tanneries. His plan carried him no further than the big glass doors of Midland Steel. He had a kind of blind faith in destiny, in a poetic justice; somehow when he was inside the building he would find the way to the man who had double-crossed him. He came safely round into the Tanneries and moved across the narrow roadway, where there was only room for a single stream of traffic, towards the great functional building of black glass and steel. He hugged the automatic to his hip with a sense of achievement and exhilaration. There was a kind of lightheartedness now about his malice and hatred he had never known before; he had lost his sourness and bitterness; he was less personal in his revenge. It was almost as if he were acting for someone else.

Behind the door of Midland Steel a man peered out at the parked cars and the deserted street. He looked like a clerk.

Raven crossed the pavement. He peered back through the panes of the mask at the man behind the door. Something made him hesitate: the memory of a face he had seen for a moment outside the Soho café where he lodged. He suddenly started away again from the door, walking in a rapid scared way down the Tanneries. The police were there before him.

It meant nothing, Raven told himself, coming out into a silent High Street empty except for a telegraph boy in a gas-mask getting on to a bicycle by the Post Office. It merely meant that the police too had noted a connection between the office in Victoria Street and Midland Steel. It didn't mean that the girl was just another skirt who had betrayed him. Only the faintest shadow of the old sourness and isolation touched his spirits. She's straight, he swore with almost perfect conviction, *she* wouldn't grass, we are together in this, and he remembered with a sense of doubtful safety how she had said, 'We are friends.'

2

The producer had called a rehearsal early. He wasn't going to add to the expenses by buying everyone gas-masks. They would be in the theatre by the time the practice started and they wouldn't leave until the 'All Clear' had sounded. Mr Davis had said he wanted to see the new number, and so the producer had sent him notice of the rehearsal. He had it stuck under the edge of his shaving mirror next a card with the telephone numbers of all his girls.

It was bitterly cold in the modern central-heated bachelor's flat. Something, as usual, had gone wrong with the oil engines, and the constant hot water was barely warm. Mr Davis cut himself shaving several times and stuck little tufts of cotton-wool all over his chin. His eye caught Mayfair 632 and Museum 798. Those were Coral and Lucy. Dark and fair, nubile and thin. His fair and dark angel. A little early fog still yellowed the panes, and the sound of a car back-firing made him think of Raven safely isolated in the railway yard surrounded by armed police. He knew that Sir Marcus was arranging everything and he wondered how it felt to be waking to your last day. 'We know not the hour,' Mr Davis thought happily, plying his styptic pencil, sticking the cotton-wool on the larger wounds, but if one knew, as Raven must know, would one still feel irritation at the failure of central heating, at a blunt blade? Mr Davis's mind was full of great dignified abstractions, and it seemed to him a rather grotesque idea that a man condemned to death should be aware of something so trivial as a shaving cut. But then, of course, Raven would not be shaving in his shed.

Mr Davis made a hasty breakfast – two pieces of toast, two cups of coffee, four kidneys and a piece of bacon sent up by lift from the restaurant, some sweet 'Silver Shred' marmalade. It gave him a good deal of pleasure to think that Raven would not be eating such a breakfast – a condemned man in prison, possibly, but not Raven. Mr Davis did not believe in wasting anything; he had paid for the breakfast, so on the second piece of toast he piled up all the remains of the butter and the marmalade. A little of the marmalade fell off on to his tie.

There was really only one worry left, apart from Sir Marcus's displeasure, and that was the girl. He had lost his head badly: first in trying to kill her and then in not killing her. It had all been Sir Marcus's fault. He had been afraid of what Sir Marcus would do to him if he learnt of the girl's existence. But now everything would be all right. The girl had come out into the open as an accomplice; no court would take a criminal's story against Sir Marcus's. He forgot about the gas practice, as he hurried down to the theatre for a little relaxation now that everything really seemed to have been tidied up. On the way he got a sixpenny packet of toffee out of a slot machine.

He found Mr Collier worried. They'd already had one rehearsal of the new number and Miss Maydew, who was sitting at the front of the stalls in a fur coat, had said it was vulgar. She said she didn't mind sex, but this wasn't in the right class. It was music-hall; it wasn't revue. Mr Collier didn't care a damn what Miss Maydew thought, but it might mean that Mr Cohen . . . He said, 'If you'd tell me what's vulgar . . . I just don't see . . .'

Mr Davis said, 'I'll tell you if it's vulgar. Have it again,' and he sat back in the stalls just behind Miss Maydew with the warm smell of her fur and her rather expensive scent in his nostrils, sucking a toffee. It seemed to him that life could offer nothing better than this. And the show was his. At any rate forty per cent of it was his. He picked out his forty per cent as the girls came on again in blue shorts with a red stripe and bras and postmen's caps, carrying cornucopias: the dark girl with the oriental eyebrows on the right, the fair girl with the rather plump legs and the big mouth (a big mouth was a good sign in a girl). They danced between two pillar-boxes, wriggling their little neat hips, and Mr Davis sucked his toffee.

'It's called "Christmas for Two",' Mr Collier said.

'Why?'

'Well, you see, those cornucops are meant to be Christmas presents made sort of classical. And "For Two" just gives it a little sex. Any number with "For Two" in it goes.'

'We've already got "An Apartment for Two",' Miss Maydew said, 'and "Two Make a Dream".'

'You can't have too much of "For Two",' Mr Collier said. He appealed pitiably, 'Can't you tell me what's vulgar?'

'Those cornucopias, for one thing.'

'But they are classical,' Mr Collier said. 'Greek.'

'And the pillar-boxes, for another.'

'The pillar-boxes,' Mr Collier exclaimed hysterically. 'What's wrong with the pillar-boxes?'

'My dear man,' Miss Maydew said, 'if you don't know what's wrong with the pillar-boxes, I'm not going to tell you. If you like to get a committee of matrons I wouldn't mind telling *them*. But if you *must* have them, paint them blue and let them be air mail.'

Mr Collier said, 'Is this a game or what is it?' He asked bitterly, 'What a time you must have when you write a letter.' The girls went patiently on behind his back to the jingle of the piano, offering the cornucopias, offering their collar-stud bottoms. He turned on them fiercely. 'Stop that, can't you? and let me think.'

Mr Davis said, 'It's fine. We'll have it in the show.' It made him feel good to contradict Miss Maydew, whose perfume he was now luxuriously taking in. It gave him in a modified form the pleasure of beating her or sleeping with her: the pleasure of mastery over a woman of superior birth. It was the kind of dream he had indulged in adolescence, while he carved his name on the desk and seat in a grim Midland board school.

'You really think that, Mr Davenant?'

'My name's Davis.'

'I'm sorry, Mr Davis.' Horror on horror, Mr Collier thought; he was alienating the new backer now.

'I think it's lousy,' Miss Maydew said. Mr Davis took another piece of toffee. 'Go ahead, old man,' he said. 'Go ahead.' They went ahead: the songs and dances floated agreeably through Mr Davis's consciousness, sometimes wistful, sometimes sweet and sad, sometimes catchy. Mr Davis liked the sweet ones best. When they sang, 'You have my mother's way', he really did think of his mother: he was the ideal audience. Somebody came out of the wings and bellowed at Mr Collier. Mr Collier screamed, 'What do you say?' and a young man in a pale blue jumper went on mechanically singing:

> 'Your photograph
> Is just the sweetest half . . .'

'Did you say Christmas tree?' Mr Collier yelled.

> 'In your December
> I shall remember . . .'

Mr Collier screamed, 'Take it away.' The song came abruptly to an end with the words *Another mother*. The young man said, 'You took it too fast,' and began to argue with the pianist.

'I can't take it away,' the man in the wings said. 'It was ordered.' He wore an apron and a cloth cap. He said, 'It took

149

a van and two horses. You'd better come and have a look.' Mr Collier disappeared and returned immediately. 'My God!' he said, 'it's fifteen feet high. Who can have played this fool trick?' Mr Davis was in a happy dream: his slippers had been warmed by a log fire in a big baronial hall, a little exclusive perfume like Miss Maydew's was hovering in the air, and he was just going to go to bed with a good but aristocratic girl to whom he had been properly married that morning by a bishop. She reminded him a little of his mother. *'In your December . . .'*

He was suddenly aware that Mr Collier was saying, 'And there's a crate of glass balls and candles.'

'Why,' Mr Davis said, 'has my little gift arrived?'

'*Your* – little – ?'

'I thought we'd have a Christmas party on the stage,' Mr Davis said. 'I like to get to know all you artistes in a friendly homey way. A little dancing, a song or two,' there seemed to be a visible lack of enthusiasm, 'plenty of pop.' A pale smile lit Mr Collier's face. 'Well,' he said, 'it's very kind of you, Mr Davis. We shall certainly appreciate it.'

'Is the tree all right?'

'Yes, Mr Daven – Davis, it's a magnificent tree.' The young man in the blue jumper looked as if he was going to laugh and Mr Collier scowled at him. 'We all thank you very much, Mr Davis, don't we, girls?' Everybody said in refined and perfect chorus as if the words had been rehearsed, '*Rather*, Mr Collier,' except Miss Maydew, and a dark girl with a roving eye who was two seconds late and said, 'You bet.'

That attracted Mr Davis's notice. Independent, he thought approvingly, stands out from the crowd. He said, 'I think I'll step behind and look at the tree. Don't let me be in the way, old man. Just you carry on,' and made his way into the wings where the tree stood blocking the way to the changing rooms. An electrician had hung some of the baubles on for fun and among the litter of properties under the bare globes it sparkled with icy dignity. Mr Davis rubbed his hands, a buried childish delight came alive. He said, 'It looks lovely.' A kind of Christmas peace lay over his spirit: the occasional memory of Raven

150

was only like the darkness pressing round the little lighted crib:

'That's a tree all right,' a voice said. It was the dark girl. She had followed him into the wings; she wasn't wanted on the stage for the number they were rehearsing. She was short and plump and not very pretty; she sat on a case and watched Mr Davis with gloomy friendliness.

'Gives a Christmas feeling,' Mr Davis said.

'So will a bottle of pop,' the girl said.

'What's your name?'

'Ruby.'

'What about meeting me for a spot of lunch after the rehearsal's over?'

'Your girls sort of disappear, don't they?' Ruby said. 'I could do with a steak and onions, but I don't want any conjuring. I'm not a detective's girl.'

'What's that?' Mr Davis said sharply.

'She's the Yard man's girl. He was round here yesterday.'

'That's all right,' Mr Davis said crossly, thinking hard, 'you're safe with me.'

'You see, I'm unlucky.'

Mr Davis, in spite of his new anxiety, felt alive, vital: this wasn't *his* last day. The kidneys and bacon he had had for breakfast returned a little in his breath. The music came softly through to them: *'Your photograph is just the sweetest half . . .'* He licked a little grain of toffee on a back tooth and said, 'You're in luck now. You couldn't have a better mascot than me.'

'You'll have to do,' the girl said with her habitual gloomy stare.

'The Metropole? At one sharp?'

'I'll be there. Unless I'm run over. I'm the kind of girl who *would* get run over before a free feed.'

'It'll be fun.'

'It depends what you call fun,' the girl said and made room for him on the packing case. They sat side by side staring at the tree. *'In your December, I shall remember.'* Mr Davis put his hand on her bare knee. He was a little awed by the tune,

151

the Christmas atmosphere. His hand fell flatly, reverently, like a bishop's hand on a choirboy's head.

'Sinbad,' the girl said.

'Sinbad?'

'I mean Bluebeard. These pantos get one all mixed up.'

'You aren't frightened of *me*?' Mr Davis protested, leaning his head against the postman's cap.

'If any girl's going to disappear, it'll be me for sure.'

'She shouldn't have left me,' Mr Davis said softly, 'so soon after dinner. Made me go home alone. She'd have been safe with me.' He put his arm tentatively round Ruby's waist and squeezed her, then loosed her hastily as an electrician came along. 'You're a clever girl,' Mr Davis said, 'you ought to have a part. I bet you've got a good voice.'

'Me a voice? I've got as much voice as a peahen.'

'Give me a little kiss?'

'Of course I will.' They kissed rather wetly. 'What do I call you?' Ruby asked. 'It sounds silly to me to call a man who's standing me a free feed Mister.'

Mr Davis said, 'You could call me – Willie?'

'Well,' Ruby said, sighing gloomily, 'I hope I'll be seeing you, Willie. At the Metropole. At one. I'll be there. I only hope *you*'ll be there or bang'll go a good steak and onions.' She drifted back towards the stage. She was needed. *What did Aladdin say* . . . She said to the girl next her. 'He fed out of my hand.' *When he came to Pekin?* 'The trouble is,' Ruby said, 'I can't keep them. There's too much of this love-and-ride-away business. But it looks as if I'll get a good lunch, anyway.' She said, 'There I go again. Saying that and forgetting to cross my fingers.'

Mr Davis had seen enough; he had got what he'd come for; all that had to be done now was to shed a little light and comradeship among the electricians and other employees. He made his way slowly out by way of the dressing-rooms exchanging a word here and there, offering his gold cigarette-case. One never knew. He was fresh to this backstage theatre and it occurred to him that even among the dressers he might find – well, youth and talent, something to be encouraged, and fed too, of course, at the Metropole. He soon learnt better; all the dressers were old; they couldn't understand what he was after and one followed him round everywhere to make sure that he didn't hide in any of the girls' rooms. Mr Davis was offended, but he was always polite. He departed through the stage door into the cold tainted street waving his hand. It was about time anyway that he looked in at Midland Steel and saw Sir Marcus.

The High Street was curiously empty except that there were more police about than was usual; he had quite forgotten the gas practice. No one attempted to interfere with Mr Davis, his face was well known to all the force, though none of them could have said what Mr Davis's occupation was. They would have said, without a smile at the thin hair, the heavy paunch, the plump and wrinkled hands, that he was one of Sir Marcus's young men. With an employer so old you could hardly avoid being one of the young men by comparison. Mr Davis waved gaily to a sergeant on the other pavement and took a toffee. It was not the job of the police to take casualties to hospital and no one would willingly have obstructed Mr Davis. There was something about his fat good nature which easily turned to malevolence. They watched him with covert amusement and hope sail down the pavement towards the Tanneries, rather as one watches a man of some dignity approach an icy slide. Up the street from the Tanneries a medical student in a gas-mask was approaching.

It was some while before Mr Davis noticed the student and the sight of the gas-mask for a moment quite shocked him. He thought: these pacifists are going too far: sensational nonsense, and when the man halted Mr Davis and said something which he could not catch through the heavy mask, Mr Davis drew himself up and said haughtily, 'Nonsense. We're well prepared.' Then he remembered and became quite friendly again; it wasn't pacifism after all, it was patriotism. 'Well, well,' he said, 'I quite forgot. Of course, the practice.' The anonymous stare through the thickened eyepieces, the muffled voice made him uneasy. He said jocularly, 'You won't be taking *me* to the hospital now, will you? I'm a busy man.' The student seemed lost in thought with his hand on Mr Davis's arm. Mr Davis saw a policeman go grinning down the opposite pavement and he found it hard to restrain his irritation. There was a little fog still left in the upper air and a flight of planes drove through it, filling the street with their deep murmur, out towards the south and the aerodrome. 'You see,' Mr Davis said, keeping his temper, 'the practice is over. The sirens will be going any moment now. It would be too absurd to waste a morning at the hospital. You know me. Davis is the name. Everyone in Nottwich knows me. Ask the police there. No one can accuse *me* of being a bad patriot.'

'You think it's nearly over?' the man said.

'I'm glad to see you boys enthusiastic,' Mr Davis said. 'I expect we've met some time at the hospital. I'm up there for all the big functions and I never forget a voice. Why,' Mr Davis said, 'it was me who gave the biggest contribution to the new operating theatre.' Mr Davis would have liked to walk on, but the man blocked his way and it seemed a bit undignified to step into the road and go round him. The man might think he was trying to escape: there might be a tussle, and the police were looking on from the corner. A sudden venom spurted up into Mr Davis's mind like the ink a cuttlefish shoots, staining his thoughts with its dark poison. That grinning ape in uniform ... I'll have him dismissed ... I'll see Calkin about it. He talked on cheerily to the man in the gas-mask, a thin figure, little more than a boy's figure on which the white medical coat hung loosely. 'You boys,' Mr Davis said, 'are doing a splendid work. There's no one appreciates that more than I do. If war comes – '

'You call yourself Davis,' the muffled voice said.

Mr Davis said with sudden irritation, 'You're wasting my time. I'm a busy man. Of course I'm Davis.' He checked his rising temper with an effort. 'Look here. I'm a reasonable man. I'll pay anything you like to the hospital. Say, ten pounds ransom.'

'Yes,' the man said, 'where is it?'

'You can trust me,' Mr Davis said, 'I don't carry that much on me,' and was amazed to hear what sounded like a laugh.

154

This was going too far. 'All right,' Mr Davis said, 'you can come with me to my office and I'll pay you the money. But I shall expect a proper receipt from your treasurer.'

'You'll get your receipt,' the man said in his odd toneless mask-muffled voice and stood on one side to let Mr Davis lead the way. Mr Davis's good humour was quite restored. He prattled on. 'No good offering you a toffee in that thing,' he said. A messenger boy passed in a gas-mask with his cap cocked absurdly on the top of it; he whistled derisively at Mr Davis. Mr Davis went a little pink. His fingers itched to tear the hair, to pull the ear, to twist the wrist. 'The boys enjoy themselves,' he said. He became confiding; a doctor's presence always made him feel safe and oddly important: one could tell the most grotesque things to a doctor about one's digestion and it was as much material for them as an amusing anecdote was for a professional humourist. He said, 'I've been getting hiccups badly lately. After every meal. It's not as if I eat fast . . . but, of course, you're only a student still. Though you know more about these things than I do. Then too I get spots before my eyes. Perhaps I ought to cut down my diet a bit. But it's difficult. A man in my position has a lot of entertaining to do. For instance – ' he grasped his companion's unresponsive arm and squeezed it knowingly – 'it would be no good my promising you that I'd go without my lunch today. You medicos are men of the world and I don't mind telling you I've got a little girl meeting me. At the Metropole. At one.' Some association of ideas made him feel in his pocket to make sure his packet of toffee was safe.

They passed another policeman and Mr Davis waved his hand. His companion was very silent. The boy's shy, Mr Davis thought, he's not used to walking about town with a man like me: it excused a certain roughness in his behaviour; even the suspicion Mr Davis had resented was probably only a form of gawkiness. Mr Davis, because the day was proving fine after all, a little sun sparkling through the cold obscured air, because the kidneys and bacon had really been done to a turn, because he had asserted himself in the presence of Miss Maydew, who was the daughter of a peer, because he had a date at

155

the Metropole with a little girl of talent, because too by this time Raven's body would be safely laid out on its icy slab in the mortuary, for all these reasons Mr Davis felt kindness and Christmas in his spirit; he exerted himself to put the boy at his ease. He said, 'I feel sure we've met somewhere. Perhaps the house surgeon introduced us.' But his companion remained glumly unforthcoming. 'A fine sing-song you all put on at the opening of the new ward.' He glanced again at the delicate wrists. 'You weren't by any chance the boy who dressed up as a girl and sang that naughty song?' Mr Davis laughed thickly at the memory, turning into the Tanneries, laughed as he had laughed more times than he could count over the port, at the club, among the good fellows, at the smutty masculine jokes, 'I was tickled to death.' He put his hand on his companion's arm and pushed through the glass door of Midland Steel.

A stranger stepped out from round a corner and the clerk behind the inquiries counter told him in a strained voice, 'That's all right. That's Mr Davis.'

'What's all this?' Mr Davis asked in a harsh no-nonsense voice, now that he was back where he belonged.

The detective said, 'We are just keeping an eye open.'

'Raven?' Mr Davis asked in a rather shrill voice. The man nodded. Mr Davis said, 'You let him escape? What fools . . .'

The detective said, 'You needn't be scared. He'll be spotted at once if he comes out of hiding. He can't escape this time.'

'But why,' Mr Davis said, 'are you here? Why do you expect . . .'

'We've got our orders,' the man said.

'Have you told Sir Marcus?'

'He knows.'

Mr Davis looked tired and old. He said sharply to his companion, 'Come with me and I'll give you the money. I haven't any time to waste.' He walked with lagging hesitating feet down a passage paved with some black shining composition to the glass lift-shaft. The man in the gas-mask followed him down the passage and into the lift; they moved slowly and steadily upwards together, as intimate as two birds caged. Floor by floor the great building sank below them, a clerk in a black coat hurrying on some mysterious errand which required a lot of blotting paper, a girl standing outside a closed door with a file of papers whispering to herself, rehearsing some excuse, an errand boy walking erratically along a passage balancing a bundle of new pencils on his head. They stopped at an empty floor.

There was something on Mr Davis's mind. He walked slowly, turned the handle of his door softly, almost as if he feared that someone might be waiting for him inside. But the room was quite empty. An inner door opened, and a young woman with fluffy gold hair and exaggerated horn spectacles said, 'Willie', and then saw his companion. She said, 'Sir Marcus wants to see you, Mr Davis.'

'That's all right, Miss Connett,' Mr Davis said. 'You might go and find me an ABC.'

'Are you going away – at once?'

Mr Davis hesitated. 'Look me up what trains there are for town – after lunch.'

'Yes, Mr Davis.' She withdrew and the two of them were alone. Mr Davis shivered slightly and turned on his electric fire. The man in the gas-mask spoke and again the muffled coarse voice pricked at Mr Davis's memory. 'Are you scared of something?'

'There's a madman loose in this town,' Mr Davis said. His nerves were alert at every sound in the corridor outside, a footstep, the ring of a bell. It had needed more courage than he had been conscious of possessing to say 'after lunch', he wanted to be away at once, clear away from Nottwich. He started at the scrape of a little cleaner's platform which was being lowered down the wall of the inner courtyard. He padded to the door and locked it; it gave him a better feeling of security to be locked into his familiar room, with his desk, his swivel chair, the cupboard where he kept two glasses and a bottle of sweet port, the bookcase, which contained a few technical works on steel, a *Whitaker's*, a *Who's Who* and a copy of *His Chinese Concubine*, than to remember the detective in the hall. He took everything in like something seen for the first time, and it was true enough that he had never so realized the peace and comfort of his small room. Again he started at the creak of the ropes from which the cleaner's platform hung. He shut down his double window. He said in a tone of nervous irritation, 'Sir Marcus can wait.'

'Who's Sir Marcus?'

'My boss.' Something about the open door of his secretary's room disturbed him with the idea that anyone could enter that way. He was no longer in a hurry, he wasn't busy any more, he wanted companionship. He said, 'You aren't in any hurry. Take that thing off, it must be stuffy, and have a glass of port.' On his way to the cupboard he shut the inner door and turned the key. He sighed with relief, fetching out the port and the glasses, 'Now we are *really* alone, I want to tell you about these hiccups.' He poured two brimming glasses, but his hand shook and the port ran down the sides. He said, 'Always just after a meal . . .'

The muffled voice said, 'The money . . .'

'Really,' Mr Davis said, 'you are rather impudent. You can trust *me*. I'm Davis.' He went to his desk and unlocked a drawer, took out two five-pound notes and held them out. 'Mind,' he said, 'I shall expect a proper receipt from your treasurer.'

The man put them away. His hand stayed in his pocket. He said, 'Are these phoney notes, too?' A whole scene came back to Mr Davis's mind: a Lyons' Corner House, the taste of an Alpine Glow, the murderer sitting opposite him trying to tell him of the old woman he had killed. Mr Davis screamed: not a word, not a plea for help, just a meaningless cry like a man gives under an anaesthetic when the knife cuts the flesh. He ran, bolted, across the room to the inner door and tugged at the handle. He struggled uselessly as if he were caught on barbed wire between trenches.

'Come away from there,' Raven said. 'You've locked the door.'

Mr Davis came back to his desk. His legs gave way and he sat on the ground beside the waste-paper basket. He said,

'I'm sick. You wouldn't kill a sick man.' The idea really gave him hope. He retched convincingly.

'I'm not going to kill you yet,' Raven said. 'Maybe I won't kill you if you keep quiet and do what I say. This Sir Marcus, he's your boss?'

'An old man,' Mr Davis protested, weeping beside the waste-paper basket.

'He wants to see you,' Raven said. 'We'll go along.' He said, 'I've been waiting days for this – to find the two of you. It almost seems too good to be true. Get up. Get up,' he repeated furiously to the weak flabby figure on the floor.

Mr Davis led the way. Miss Connett came down the passage carrying a slip of paper. She said, 'I've got the trains, Mr Davis. The best is the three-five. The two-seven is really so slow that you wouldn't be up more than ten minutes earlier. Then there's only the five-ten before the night train.'

'Put them on my desk,' Mr Davis said. He hung about there in front of her in the shining modern plutocratic passage as if he wanted to say good-bye to a thousand things if only he had dared, to this wealth, this comfort, this authority; lingering there ('Yes, put them on my desk, May') he might even have been wanting to express at the last some tenderness that had never before entered his mind in connection with 'little girls'. Raven stood just behind him with his hand in his pocket. Her employer looked so sick that Miss Connett said, 'Are you feeling well, Mr Davis?'

'Quite well,' Mr Davis said. Like an explorer going into strange country he felt the need of leaving some record behind at the edge of civilization, to say to the next chance comer, 'I shall be found towards the north' or 'the west'. He said, 'We are going to Sir Marcus, May.'

'He's in a hurry for you,' Miss Connett said. A telephone bell rang. 'I shouldn't be surprised if that's him now.' She pattered down the corridor to her room on very high heels and Mr Davis felt again the remorseless pressure on his elbow to advance, to enter the lift. They rose another floor and when Mr Davis pulled the gates apart he retched again. He wanted to fling himself to the floor and take the bullets in his back.

159

The long gleaming passage to Sir Marcus's study was like a mile-long stadium track to a winded runner.

Sir Marcus was sitting in his Bath chair with a kind of bed-table on his knees. He had his valet with him and his back to the door, but the valet could see with astonishment Mr Davis's exhausted entrance in the company of a medical student in a gas-mask. 'Is that Davis?' Sir Marcus whispered. He broke a dry biscuit and sipped a little hot milk. He was fortifying himself for a day's work.

'Yes, sir.' The valet watched with astonishment Mr Davis's sick progress across the hygienic rubber floor; he looked as if he needed support, as if he was about to collapse at the knees.

'Get out then,' Sir Marcus whispered.

'Yes, sir.' But the man in the gas-mask had turned the key of the door; a faint expression of joy, a rather hopeless expectation, crept into the valet's face as if he were wondering whether something at last was going to happen, something different from pushing Bath chairs along rubber floors, dressing and undressing an old man, not strong enough to keep himself clean, bringing him the hot milk or the hot water or the dry biscuits.

'What are you waiting for?' Sir Marcus whispered.

'Get back against the wall,' Raven suddenly commanded the valet.

Mr Davis cried despairingly, 'He's got a gun. Do what he says.' But there was no need to tell the valet that. The gun was out now and had them all three covered, the valet against the wall, Mr Davis dithering in the middle of the room, Sir Marcus who had twisted the Bath chair round to face them.

'What do you want?' Sir Marcus said.

'Are you the boss?'

Sir Marcus said, 'The police are downstairs. You can't get away from here unless I – ' The telephone began to ring. It rang on and on and on, and then ceased.

Raven said, 'You've got a scar under that beard, haven't you? I don't want to make a mistake. He had your photograph. You were in the home together,' and he glared angrily round the large rich office room comparing it in mind with his

160

own memories of cracked bells and stone stairs and wooden benches, and of the small flat too with the egg boiling on the ring. This man had moved further than the old Minister.

'You're mad,' Sir Marcus whispered. He was too old to be frightened; the revolver represented no greater danger to him than a false step in getting into his chair, a slip in his bath. He seemed to feel only a faint irritation, a faint craving for his interrupted meal. He bent his old lip forward over the bed-table and sucked loudly at the rim of hot milk.

The valet suddenly spoke from the wall. 'He's got a scar,' he said. But Sir Marcus took no notice of any of them, sucking up his milk untidily over his thin beard.

Raven twisted his gun on Mr Davis. 'It was him,' he said. 'If you don't want a bullet in your guts tell me it was him.'

'Yes, yes,' Mr Davis said in horrified subservient haste, 'he thought of it. It was his idea. We were on our last legs here. We'd got to make money. It was worth more than half a million to him.'

'Half a million!' Raven said. 'And he paid me two hundred phoney pounds.'

'I said to him we ought to be generous. He said: "Stop your mouth."'

'I wouldn't have done it,' Raven said, 'if I'd known the old man was like he was. I smashed his skull for him. And the old woman, a bullet in both eyes.' He shouted at Sir Marcus, 'That was your doing. How do you like that?' but the old man sat there apparently unmoved: old age had killed the imagination. The deaths he had ordered were no more real to him than the deaths he read about in the newspapers. A little greed (for his milk), a little vice (occasionally to put his old hand inside a girl's blouse and feel the warmth of life), a little avarice and calculation (half a million against a death), a very small persistent, almost mechanical, sense of self-preservation: these were his only passions. The last made him edge his chair imperceptibly towards the bell at the edge of his desk. He whispered gently, 'I deny it all. You are mad.'

Raven said, 'I've got you now where I want you. Even if the police kill me,' he tapped the gun, 'here's my evidence. This is

161

the gun I used. They can pin the murder to this gun. You told me to leave it behind, but here it is. It would put you away a long, long time even if I didn't shoot you.'

Sir Marcus whispered gently, imperceptibly twisting his silent rubbered wheels, 'A Colt No. 7. The factories turn out thousands.'

Raven said angrily, 'There's nothing the police can't do now with a gun. There are experts – ' He wanted to frighten Sir Marcus before he shot him; it seemed unfair to him that Sir Marcus should suffer less than the old woman he hadn't wanted to kill. He said, 'Don't you want to pray? You're a Jew, aren't you? Better people than you,' he said, 'believe in a God,' remembering how the girl had prayed in the dark cold shed. The wheel of Sir Marcus's chair touched the desk, touched the bell, and the dull ringing came up the well of the lift, going on and on. It conveyed nothing to Raven until the valet spoke. 'The old bastard,' he said, with the hatred of years, 'he's ringing the bell.' Before Raven could decide what to do, someone was at the door, shaking the handle.

Raven said to Sir Marcus, 'Tell them to keep back or I'll shoot.'

'You fool,' Sir Marcus whispered, 'they'll only get you for theft. If you kill me, you'll hang.' But Mr Davis was ready to clutch at any straw. He screamed to the man outside, 'Keep away. For God's sake keep away.'

Sir Marcus said venomously, 'You're a fool, Davis. If he's going to kill us anyway – ' While Raven stood pistol in hand before the two men, an absurd quarrel broke out between them. 'He's got no cause to kill me,' Mr Davis screamed. 'It's you who've got us into this. I only acted for you.'

The valet began to laugh. 'Two to one on the field,' he said.

'Be quiet,' Sir Marcus whispered venomously back at Mr Davis. 'I can put you out of the way at any time.'

'I defy you,' Mr Davis screamed in a high peacock voice. Somebody flung himself against the door.

'I have the West Rand Goldfields filed,' Sir Marcus said, 'the East African Petroleum Company.'

A wave of impatience struck Raven. They seemed to be disturbing some memory of peace and goodness which had been on the point of returning to him when he had told Sir Marcus to pray. He raised his pistol and shot Sir Marcus in the chest. It was the only way to silence them. Sir Marcus fell forward across the bed-table, upsetting the glass of warm milk over the papers on his desk. Blood came out of his mouth.

Mr Davis began to talk very rapidly. He said, 'It was all him, the old devil. You heard him. What could I do? He had me. You've got nothing against me.' He shrieked, 'Go away from that door. He'll kill me if you don't go,' and immediately began to talk again, while the milk dripped from the bed-table to the desk drop by drop. 'I wouldn't have done a thing if it hadn't been for him. Do you know what he did? He went and told the Chief Constable to order the police to shoot you on sight.' He tried not to look at the pistol which remained pointed at his chest. The valet was white and silent by the wall; he watched Sir Marcus's life bleeding away with curious fascination. So this was what it would have been like, he seemed to be thinking, if he himself had had courage . . . any time . . . during all these years.

A voice outside said, 'You had better open this door at once or we'll shoot through it.'

'For God's sake,' Mr Davis screamed, 'leave me alone. He'll shoot me,' and the eyes watched him intently through the panes of the gas-mask, with satisfaction. 'There's not a thing I've done to you,' he began to protest. Over Raven's head he could see the clock: it hadn't moved more than three hours since his breakfast, the hot stale taste of the kidneys and bacon was still on his palate: he couldn't believe that this was really the end: at one o'clock he had a date with a girl: you didn't die before a date. 'Nothing,' he murmured, 'nothing at all.'

'It was you,' Raven said, 'who tried to kill . . .'

'Nobody. Nothing,' Mr Davis moaned.

Raven hesitated. The word was still unfamiliar on his tongue. 'My friend.'

'I don't know. I don't understand.'

'Keep back,' Raven cried through the door, 'I'll shoot him if you fire.' He said, 'The girl.'

Mr Davis shook all over. He was like a man with St Vitus's dance. He said, 'She wasn't a friend of yours. Why are the police here if she didn't . . . who else could have known . . .?'

Raven said, 'I'll shoot you for that and nothing else. She's straight.'

'Why,' Mr Davis screamed at him, 'she's a policeman's girl. She's the Yard man's girl. She's Mather's girl.'

Raven shot him. With despair and deliberation he shot his last chance of escape, plugged two bullets in where one would do, as if he were shooting the whole world in the person of stout moaning bleeding Mr Davis. And so he was. For a man's world is his life and he was shooting that: his mother's suicide, the long years in the home, the race-course gangs, Kite's death and the old man's and the woman's. There was no other way; he had tried the way of confession, and it had failed him for the usual reason. There was no one outside your own brain whom you could trust: not a doctor, not a priest, not a woman. A siren blew up over the town its message that the sham raid was over, and immediately the church bells broke into a noisy Christmas carol: the foxes have their holes, but the son of man . . . A bullet smashed the lock of the door. Raven, with his gun pointed stomach-high, said, 'Is there a bastard called Mather out there? He'd better keep away.'

While he waited for the door to open he couldn't help remembering many things. He did not remember them in detail; they fogged together and formed the climate of his mind as he waited there for the chance of a last revenge: a voice singing above a dark street as the sleet fell: *They say that's a snowflower a man brought from Greenland*, the cultivated unlived voice of the elderly critic reading *Maud: Oh, that 'twere possible after long grief*, while he stood in the garage and felt the ice melt at his heart with a sense of pain and strangeness. It was as if he were passing the customs of a land he had never entered before and would never be able to leave: the girl in the café saying, 'He's bad and ugly . . .', the little plaster child lying in its mother's arms waiting the double-cross, the whips, the nails. She had said to him, 'I'm your friend. You can trust me.' Another bullet burst in the lock.

The valet, white-faced by the wall, said, 'For God's sake, give it up. They'll get you anyway. He was right. It *was* the girl. I heard them on the 'phone.'

I've got to be quick, Raven thought, when the door gives, I must shoot first. But too many ideas besieged his brain at once. He couldn't see clearly enough through the mask and he undid it clumsily with one hand and dropped it on the floor.

The valet could see now the raw inflamed lip, the dark and miserable eyes. He said, 'There's the window. Get on to the roof.' He was talking to a man whose understanding was dulled, who didn't know whether he wished to make an effort or not, who moved his face so slowly to see the window that it was the valet who noticed first the painter's platform swinging down the wide tall pane. Mather was on the platform, but the detective had not allowed for his own inexperience. The little platform swung this way and that; he held a rope with one hand and reached for the window with the other; he had no hand free for his revolver as Raven turned. He dangled outside the window six floors above the narrow Tanneries, a defenceless mark for Raven's pistol.

Raven watched him with bemused eyes, trying to take aim. It wasn't a difficult shot, but it was almost as if he had lost interest in killing. He was only aware of a pain and despair which was more like a complete weariness than anything else. He couldn't work up any sourness, any bitterness, at his betrayal. The dark Weevil under the storm of frozen rain flowed between him and any human enemy. *Ah, Christ! that it were possible*, but he had been marked from his birth for this end, to be betrayed in turn by everyone until every avenue into life was safely closed: by his mother bleeding in the basement, by the chaplain at the home, by the shady doctor off Charlotte Street. How could he have expected to have escaped the commonest betrayal of all: to go soft on a skirt? Even Kite would have been alive now if it hadn't been for a skirt. They all went soft at some time or another: Penrith and Carter, Jossy and Ballard, Barker and the Great Dane. He took aim slowly,

165

absent-mindedly, with a curious humility, with almost a sense of companionship in his loneliness: the Trooper and Mayhew. They had all thought at one time or another that their skirt was better than other men's skirts, that there was something exalted in *their* relation. The only problem when you were once born was to get out of life more neatly and expeditiously than you had entered it. For the first time the idea of his mother's suicide came to him without bitterness, as he reluctantly fixed his aim and Saunders shot him in the back through the opening door. Death came to him in the form of unbearable pain. It was as if he had to deliver this pain as a woman delivers a child, and he sobbed and moaned in the effort. At last it came out of him and he followed his only child into a vast desolation.

Chapter 8

1

THE smell of food came through into the lounge whenever somebody passed in or out of the restaurant. The local Rotarians were having a lunch in one of the private rooms up-stairs and when the door opened Ruby could hear a cork pop and the scrap of a limerick. It was five-past one. Ruby went out and chatted to the porter. She said, 'The worst of it is I'm one of the girls who turn up on the stroke. One o'clock he said and here I am panting for a good meal. I know a girl ought to keep a man waiting, but what do you do if you're hungry? He might go in and start.' She said, 'The trouble is I'm unlucky. I'm the kind of girl who daren't have a bit of fun because she'd be dead sure to get a baby. Well, I don't mean I've had a baby, but I did catch mumps once. Would you believe a grown man could give a girl mumps? But I'm that kind of girl.' She said, 'You look fine in all that gold braid with those medals. You might say something.'

The market was more than usually full, for everyone had come out late to do their last Christmas shopping now that the gas practice was over. Only Mrs Alfred Piker, as Lady Mayoress, had set an example by shopping in a mask. Now she was walking home, and Chinky trotted beside her, trailing his low fur and the feathers on his legs in the cold slush, carrying her mask between his teeth. He stopped by a lamp-post and dropped it in a puddle. 'O, Chinky, you bad little thing,' Mrs Piker said. The porter in his uniform glared out over the market. He wore the Mons medal and the Military Medal. He had been three times wounded. He swung the glass door as the business men came in for their lunch, the head traveller of Crosthwaite and Crosthwaite, the managing director of the big grocery business in the High Street. Once he darted out into the road and disentangled a fat man from a taxi. Then he came back and stood beside Ruby and listened to her with expressionless good humour.

'Ten minutes late,' Ruby said, 'I thought he was a man a girl could trust. I ought to have touched wood or crossed my fingers. It serves me right. I'd rather have lost my honour than that steak. Do you know him? He flings his weight about a lot. Called Davis.'

'He's always in here with girls,' the porter said.

A little man in pince-nez bustled by. 'A Merry Christmas, Hallows.'

'A Merry Christmas to you, sir.' The porter said, 'You wouldn't have got far with him.'

'I haven't got as far as the soup,' Ruby said.

A newsboy went by calling out a special midday edition of the *News*, the evening edition of the *Journal*, and a few minutes later another newsboy went past with a special edition of the *Post*, the evening edition of the more aristocratic *Guardian*. It was impossible to hear what they were shouting and the north-east wind flapped their posters, so that on one it was only possible to read the syllable '– gedy' and on the other the syllable '– der'.

'There are limits,' Ruby said, 'a girl can't afford to make herself cheap. Ten minutes' wait is the outside limit.'

'You've waited more than that now,' the porter said.

Ruby said, 'I'm like that. You'd say I fling myself at men, wouldn't you? That's what I think, but I never seem to hit them.' She added with deep gloom, 'The trouble is I'm the kind that's born to make a man happy. It's written all over me. It keeps them away. I don't blame them. I shouldn't like it myself.'

'There goes the Chief Constable,' the porter said. 'Off to get a drink at the police station. His wife won't let him have them at home. The best of the season to you, sir.'

'He seems in a hurry.' A newspaper poster flapped 'Trag –' at them. 'Is he the kind that would buy a girl a good rump steak with onions and fried potatoes?'

'I tell you what,' the porter said. 'You wait around another five minutes and then I shall be going off for lunch.'

'That's a date,' Ruby said. She crossed her fingers and touched wood. Then she went and sat inside and carried on a long conversation with an imaginary theatrical producer whom she imagined rather like Mr Davis, but a Mr Davis who kept his engagements. The producer called her a little woman with talent, asked her to dinner, took her back to a luxurious flat and gave her several cocktails. He asked her what she would think of a West-End engagement at fifteen pounds a week and said he wanted to show her his flat. Ruby's dark plump gloomy face lightened; she swung one leg excitedly and attracted the angry attention of a business man who was making notes of the midday prices. He found another chair and muttered to himself. Ruby, too, muttered to herself. She was saying, 'This is the dining-room. And through there is the bathroom. And this – elegant, isn't it? – is the bedroom.' Ruby said promptly that she'd like the fifteen pounds a week, but need she have the West-End engagement? Then she looked at the clock and went outside. The porter was waiting for her.

'What?' Ruby said. 'Have I got to go out with that uniform?'

'I only get twenty minutes,' the porter said.

'No rump steak then,' Ruby said. 'Well, I suppose sausages would do.'

They sat at a lunch counter on the other side of the market and had sausages and coffee. 'That uniform,' Ruby said, 'makes me embarrassed. Everyone'll think you're a guards-man going with a girl for a change.'

'Did you hear the shooting?' the man behind the counter said.

'What shooting?'

'Just round the corner from you at Midland Steel. Three dead. That old devil Sir Marcus, and two others.' He laid the midday paper open on the counter, and the old wicked face of Sir Marcus, the plump anxious features of Mr Davis, stared up at them beyond the sausages, the coffee cups, the pepper-pot, beside the hot-water urn. 'So that's why he didn't come,' Ruby said. She was silent for a while reading.

'I wonder what this Raven was after,' the porter said. 'Look here,' and he pointed to a small paragraph at the foot of the column which announced that the head of the special political department of Scotland Yard had arrived by air and gone straight to the offices of Midland Steel. 'It doesn't mean a thing to me,' Ruby said.

The porter turned the pages looking for something. He said, 'Funny thing, isn't it? Here we are just going to war again, and they fill up the front page with a murder. It's driven the war on to a back page.'

'Perhaps there won't be a war.'

They were silent over their sausages. It seemed odd to Ruby that Mr Davis, who had sat on the box with her and looked at the Christmas tree, should be dead, so violently and painfully dead. Perhaps he had meant to keep the date. He wasn't a bad sort. She said, 'I feel sort of sorry for him.'

'Who? Raven?'

'Oh no, not him. Mr Davis, I mean.'

'I know how you feel. I almost feel sorry too – for the old man. I was in Midland Steel myself once. He had his moments. He used to send round turkeys at Christmas. He wasn't too bad. It's more than they do at the hotel.'

'Well,' Ruby said, draining her coffee, 'life goes on.'

'Have another cup.'

'I don't want to sting you.'

'That's all right.' Ruby leant against him on the high stool;

their heads touched; they were a little quietened because each had known a man who was suddenly dead, but the knowledge they shared gave them a sense of companionship which was oddly sweet and reassuring. It was like feeling safe, like feeling in love without the passion, the uncertainty, the pain.

2

Saunders asked a clerk in Midland Steel the way to a lavatory. He washed his hands and thought, 'That job's over.' It hadn't been a satisfactory job; what had begun as a plain robbery had ended with two murders and the death of the murderer. There was a mystery about the whole affair; everything hadn't come out. Mather was up there on the top floor now with the head of the political department; they were going through Sir Marcus's private papers. It really seemed as if the girl's story might be true.

The girl worried Saunders more than anything. He couldn't help admiring her courage and impertinence at the same time as he hated her for making Mather suffer. He was ready to hate anyone who hurt Mather. 'She'll have to be taken to the Yard,' Mather said. 'There may be a charge against her. Put her in a locked carriage on the three-five. I don't want to see her until this thing's cleared up.' The only cheerful thing about the whole business was that the constable whom Raven had shot in the coal-yard was pulling through.

Saunders came out of Midland Steel into the Tanneries with an odd sensation of having nothing to do. He went into a public-house at the corner of the market and had half a pint of bitter and two cold sausages. It was as if life had sunk again to the normal level, was flowing quietly by once more between its banks. A card hanging behind the bar next a few cinema posters caught his eye. 'A New Cure for Stammerers.' Mr Montague Phelps, M.A., was holding a public meeting in the Masonic Hall to explain his new treatment. Entrance was free, but there would be a silver collection. Two o'clock sharp. At one cinema Eddie Cantor. At another George Arliss. Saunders didn't want to go back to the police station until it was time to take the girl to the train. He had tried a good many cures for stammering; he might as well try one more.

It was a large hall. On the walls hung large photographs of masonic dignitaries. They all wore ribbons and badges of strange significance. There was an air of oppressive well-being, of successful groceries, about the photographs. They hung, the well-fed, the successful, the assured, over the small gathering of misfits, in old mackintoshes, in rather faded mauve felt hats, in school ties. Saunders entered behind a fat furtive woman and a steward stammered at him, 'T-t-t – ?' 'One,' Saunders said. He sat down near the front and heard a stammered conversation going on behind him, like the twitters of two Chinamen. Little bursts of impetuous talk and then the fatal impediment. There were about fifty people in the hall. They eyed each other rather as an ugly man eyes himself in shop windows: from this angle, he thinks, I am really not too bad. They gained a sense of companionship; their mutual lack of communication was in itself like a communication. They waited together for a miracle.

Saunders waited with them: waited as he had waited on the windless side of the coal truck, with the same patience. He wasn't unhappy. He knew that he probably exaggerated the value of what he lacked; even if he could speak freely, without care to avoid the dentals which betrayed him, he would probably find it no easier to express his admiration and his affection. The power to speak didn't give you words.

Mr Montague Phelps, M.A., came on to the platform. He wore a frock-coat and his hair was dark and oiled. His blue chin was lightly powdered and he carried himself with a rather aggressive sangfroid, as much as to say to the depressed inhibited gathering, 'See what you too might become with a little more self-confidence, after a few lessons from me.' He was a man of about forty-two who had lived well, who obviously had a private life. One thought in his presence of comfortable beds and heavy meals and Brighton hotels. For a moment he reminded Saunders of Mr Davis who had bustled so importantly into the offices of Midland Steel that morning and had died very painfully and suddenly half an hour later.

It almost seemed as if Raven's act had had no consequences: as if to kill was just as much an illusion as to dream. Here was Mr Davis all over again; they were turned out of a mould, and you couldn't break the mould, and suddenly over Mr Montague Phelps's shoulder Saunders saw the photograph of the Grand Master of the Lodge, above the platform: an old face and a crooked nose and a tuft of beard, Sir Marcus.

3

Major Calkin was very white when he left Midland Steel. He had seen for the first time the effect of violent death. That was war. He made his way as quickly as he could to the police station and was glad to find the superintendent in. He asked quite humbly for a spot of whisky. He said, 'It shakes you up. Only last night he had dinner at my house. Mrs Piker was there with her dog. What a time we had stopping him knowing the dog was there.'

'That dog,' the superintendent said, 'gives us more trouble than any man in Nottwich. Did I ever tell you the time it got in the women's lavatory in Higham Street? That dog isn't much to look at, but every once in a while it goes crazy. If it wasn't Mrs Piker's we'd have had it destroyed many a time.'

Major Calkin said, 'He wanted me to give orders to your men to shoot this fellow on sight. I told him I couldn't. Now I can't help thinking we might have saved two lives.'

'Don't you worry, sir,' the superintendent said, 'we couldn't have taken orders like that. Not from the Home Secretary himself.'

'He was an odd fellow,' Major Calkin said. 'He seemed to think I'd be certain to have a hold over some of you. He promised me all kinds of things. I suppose he was what you'd call a genius. We shan't see his like again. What a waste.' He poured himself out some more whisky. 'Just at a time, too, when we need men like him. War – ' Major Calkin paused with his hand on his glass. He stared into the whisky, seeing things, the remount depot, his uniform in the cupboard. He would never be a colonel now, but on the other hand Sir Marcus could not prevent . . . but curiously he felt no elation at the thought of once more presiding over the tribunal. He said, 'The gas practice seems to have gone off well. But I don't know that it was wise to leave so much to the medical students. They don't know where to stop.'

'There was a pack of them,' the superintendent said, 'went howling past here looking for the Mayor. I don't know how it is Mr Piker seems to be like catmint to those students.'

'Good old Piker,' Major Calkin said mechanically.

'They go too far,' the superintendent said. 'I had a ring from Higginbotham, the cashier at the Westminster. He said his daughter went into the garage and found one of the students there without his trousers.'

Life began to come back to Major Calkin. He said, 'That'll be Rose Higginbotham, I suppose. Trust Rose. What did she do?'

'He said she gave him a dressing down.'

'Dressing down's good,' Major Calkin said. He twisted his glass and drained his whisky. 'I must tell that to old Piker. What did you say?'

'I told him his daughter was lucky not to find a murdered man in the garage. You see that's where Raven must have got his clothes and his mask.'

'What was the boy doing at the Higginbothams' anyway?' Major Calkin said. 'I think I'll go and cash a cheque and ask old Higginbotham that.' He began to laugh; the air was clear again; life was going on quite in the old way: a little scandal, a drink with the super., a story to tell old Piker. On his way to the Westminster he nearly ran into Mrs Piker. He had to dive hastily into a shop to avoid her, and for a horrible moment he thought Chinky, who was some way ahead of her, was going to follow him inside. He made motions of throwing a ball down the street, but Chinky was not a sporting dog and anyway he was trailing a gas-mask in his teeth. Major Calkin had to turn his back abruptly and lean over a counter. He found it was a small haberdasher's. He had never been in the shop before. 'What can I get you, sir?'

'Suspenders,' Major Calkin said desperately. 'A pair of suspenders.'

'What colour, sir?' Out of the corner of his eye Major Calkin saw Chinky trot on past the shop door followed by Mrs Piker. 'Mauve,' he said with relief.

4

The old woman shut the front door softly and trod on tiptoe down the little dark hall. A stranger could not have seen his way, but she knew exactly the position of the hat rack, of the what-not table, and the staircase. She was carrying an evening paper, and when she opened the kitchen door with the very minimum of noise so as not to disturb Acky, her face was alight with exhilaration and excitement. But she held it in, carrying her basket over to the draining board and unloading there her burden of potatoes, a tin of pineapple chunks, two eggs and a slab of cod.

Acky was writing a long letter on the kitchen table. He had pushed his wife's mauve ink to one side and was using the best blue-black and a fountain pen which had long ceased to hold ink. He wrote slowly and painfully, sometimes making a rough copy of a sentence on another slip of paper. The old woman stood beside the sink watching him, waiting for him to speak, holding her breath in, so that sometimes it escaped in little whistles. At last Acky laid down his pen. 'Well, my dear?' he said.

'Oh, Acky,' the old woman said with glee, 'what do you think? Mr Cholmondeley's dead. Killed.' She added, 'It's in the paper. And that Raven too.'

Acky looked at the paper. 'Quite horrible,' he said with satisfaction. 'Another death as well. A holocaust.' He read the account slowly.

'Fancy a thing like that 'appening 'ere in Nottwich.'

'He was a bad man,' Acky said, 'though I wouldn't speak ill of him now that he's dead. He involved us in something of which I was ashamed. I think perhaps now it will be safe for us to stay in Nottwich.' A look of great weariness passed over his face as he looked down at the three pages of small neat classical handwriting.

'Oh, Acky, you've been tiring yourself.'

'I think,' Acky said, 'this will make everything clear.'

'Read it to me, love,' the old woman said. Her little old vicious face was heavily creased with tenderness as she leant back against the sink in an attitude of infinite patience. Acky began to read. He spoke at first in a low hesitating way, but he gained confidence from the sound of his own voice, his hand went up to the lapel of his coat. '"My lord bishop" . . .' He said, 'I thought it best to begin formally, not to trespass at all on my former acquaintanceship.'

'That's right, Acky, you are worth the whole bunch.'

'"I am writing to you for the fourth time . . . after an interval of some eighteen months."'

'Is it so long, love? It was after we took the trip to Clacton.'

'"Sixteen months . . . I am quite aware what your previous answers have been, that my case has been tried already in the proper Church Court, but I cannot believe, my lord bishop, that your sense of justice, if once I convince you of what a deeply injured man I am, will not lead you to do all that is in your power to have my case reheard. I have been condemned to suffer all my life for what in the case of other men is regarded as a peccadillo, a peccadillo of which I am not even guilty."'

'It's written lovely, love.'

'At this point, my dear, I come down to particulars. "How, my lord bishop, could the hotel domestic swear to the identity of a man seen once, a year before the trial, in a darkened chamber, for in her evidence she agreed that he had not allowed her to draw up the blind? As for the evidence of the porter, my lord bishop, I asked in court whether it was not true that money had passed from Colonel and Mrs Mark Egerton into his hands, and my question was disallowed. Is this justice, founded on scandal, misapprehension, and perjury?"'

The old woman smiled with tenderness and pride. 'This is the best letter you've written, Acky, so far.'

'"My lord bishop, it was well known in the parish that Colonel Mark Egerton was my bitterest enemy on the church council, and it was at his instigation that the inquiry was held. As for Mrs Mark Egerton she was a bitch."'

'Is that wise, Acky?'

'Sometimes, dear, one reaches an impasse, when there is nothing to be done but to speak out. At this point I take the evidence in detail as I have done before, but I think I have sharpened my arguments more than a little. And at the end, my dear, I address the worldly man in the only way he can understand.' He knew this passage off by heart; he reeled it fierily off at her, raising his crazy sunken flawed saint's eyes. '"But even assuming, my lord bishop, that this perjured and bribed evidence were accurate, what then? Have I committed the unforgivable sin that I must suffer all my life long, be deprived of my livelihood, depend on ignoble methods to raise enough money to keep myself and my wife alive? Man, my lord bishop, and no one knows it better than yourself – I have seen you among the flesh-pots at the palace – is made up of body as well as soul. A little carnality may be forgiven even to a man of my cloth. Even you, my lord bishop, have in your time no doubt sported among the haycocks."' He stopped, he was a little out of breath; they stared back at each other with awe and affection.

Acky said, 'I want to write a little piéce, dear, now about you.' He took in with what could only have been the deepest and purest love the black sagging skirt, the soiled blouse, the yellow wrinkled face. 'My dear,' he said, 'what I should have done without –' He began to make a rough draft of yet another paragraph, speaking the phrases aloud as he wrote them. '"What I should have done during this long trial – no, martyrdom – I do not know – I cannot conceive – if I had not been supported by the trust and the unswerving fidelity – no, fidelity and unswerving trust of my dear wife, a wife whom Mrs Mark Egerton considered herself in a position to despise. As if Our Lord had chosen the rich and well-born to serve him. At least this trial – has taught me to distinguish between my friends and enemies. And yet at my trial *her* word, the

word of the woman who loved and believed in me, counted –
for nought beside the word – of that – that – trumpery and
deceitful scandalmonger."'

The old woman leant forward with tears of pride and importance in her eyes. She said, 'That's lovely. Do you think
the bishop's wife will read it? Oh, dear, I know I ought to go
and tidy the room upstairs (we might be getting some young
people in), but some'ow, Acky dear, I'd just like to stay right
'ere with you awhile. What you write makes me feel kind of
'oly.' She slumped down on the kitchen chair beside the sink
and watched his hand move on, as if she were watching some
unbelievably lovely vision passing through the room, something which she had never hoped to see and now was hers.
'And finally, my dear,' Acky said, 'I propose to write: "In a
world of perjury and all manner of uncharitableness one
woman remains my sheet anchor, one woman I can trust until
death and beyond."'

'They ought to be ashamed of themselves. Oh, Acky, my
dear,' she wept, 'to think they've treated you that way. But
you've said true. I won't ever leave you. I won't leave you,
not even when I'm dead. Never, never, never,' and the two old
vicious faces regarded each other with the complete belief, the
awe and mutual suffering of a great love, while they affirmed
their eternal union.

5

Anne cautiously felt the door of the compartment in which
she had been left alone. It was locked, as she had thought it
would be in spite of Saunders's tact and his attempt to hide
what he was doing. She stared out at the dingy Midland station with dismay. It seemed to her that everything which made
her life worth the effort of living was lost; she hadn't even got
a job, and she watched, past an advertisement of Horlick's for
night starvation and a bright blue-and-yellow picture of the
Yorkshire coast, the weary pilgrimage which lay before her
from agent to agent. The train began to move by the waiting-
rooms, the lavatories, the sloping concrete into a waste of
rails.

What a fool, she thought, I have been, thinking I could save us from a war. Three men are dead, that's all. Now that she was herself responsible for so many deaths, she could no longer feel the same repulsion towards Raven. In this waste through which she travelled, between the stacks of coal, the tumbledown sheds, abandoned trucks in sidings where a little grass had poked up and died between the cinders, she thought of him again with pity and distress. They had been on the same side, he had trusted her, she had given her word to him, and then she had broken it without even the grace of hesitation. He must have known of her treachery before he died: in that dead mind she was preserved for ever with the chaplain who had tried to frame him, with the doctor who had telephoned to the police.

Well, she had lost the only man she cared a damn about: it was always regarded as some kind of atonement, she thought, to suffer too: lost him for no reason at all. For *she* couldn't stop a war. Men were fighting beasts, they needed war; in the paper that Saunders had left for her on the opposite seat she could read how the mobilization in four countries was complete, how the ultimatum expired at midnight; it was no longer on the front page, but that was only because to Nottwich readers there was a war nearer at hand, fought out to a finish in the Tanneries. How they love it, she thought bitterly, as the dusk came up from the dark wounded ground and the glow of furnaces became visible beyond the long black ridge of slag-heaps. This was war too: this chaos through which the train moved slowly, grinding over point after point like a dying creature dragging itself painfully away through No-Man's Land from the scene of battle.

She pressed her face against the window to keep her tears away: the cold pressure of the frosting pane stiffened her resistance. The train gathered speed by a small neo-Gothic church, a row of villas, and then the country, the fields, a few cows making for an open gate, a hard broken lane and a cyclist lighting his lamp. She began to hum to keep her spirits up, but the only tunes she could remember were 'Aladdin' and 'It's only Kew'. She thought of the long bus-ride home, the voice on the telephone, and how she couldn't get to the window to wave to him and he had stood there with his back to her while the train went by. It was Mr Davis even then who had ruined everything.

And it occurred to her, staring out at the bleak frozen countryside, that perhaps even if she had been able to save the country from a war, it wouldn't have been worth the saving. She thought of Mr Davis and Acky and his old wife, of the producer and Miss Maydew and the landlady at her lodging with the bead of liquid on her nose. What had made her play so absurd a part? If she had not offered to go out to dinner with Mr Davis, Raven probably would be in gaol and the others alive. She tried to remember the watching anxious faces studying the sky-signs in Nottwich High Street, but she couldn't remember them with any vividness.

The door into the corridor was unlocked and staring through the window into the grey fading winter light she thought: more questions. Will they never stop worrying me? She said aloud, 'I've made my statement, haven't I?'

Mather's voice said, 'There are still a few things to discuss.'

She turned hopelessly towards him. 'Need *you* have come?'

'I'm in charge of this case,' Mather said, sitting down opposite to her with his back to the engine, watching the country which she could see approach flow backwards over her shoulder and disappear. He said, 'We've been checking what you told us. It's a strange story.'

'It's true,' she repeated wearily.

He said: 'We've had half the Embassies in London on the 'phone. Not to speak of Geneva. And the Commissioner.'

She said with a flicker of malice, 'I'm sorry you've been troubled.' But she couldn't keep it up; her formal indifference was ruined by his presence, the large clumsy, once friendly hand, the bulk of the man. 'Oh, I'm sorry,' she said. 'I've said it before, haven't I? I'd say it if I'd spilt your coffee, and I've got to say it after all these people are killed. There are no other words, are there, which mean more? It all worked out wrong; I thought everything was clear. I've failed. I didn't mean to hurt you ever. I suppose the Commissioner . . .' She began to cry without tears; it was as if those ducts were frozen.

He said, 'I'm to have promotion. I don't know why. It seems to me as if I'd bungled it.' He added gently and pleadingly, leaning forward across the compartment, 'We could get married – at once – though I dare say you don't want to now, you'll do all right. They'll give you a grant.'

It was like going into the manager's office expecting dismissal and getting a rise instead – or a speaking part, but it never happened that way. She stared silently back at him.

'Of course,' he said gloomily, 'you'll be the rage now. You'll have stopped a war. I know I didn't believe you. I've failed. I thought I'd always trust – We've found enough already to prove what you told me and I thought was lies. They'll have to withdraw their ultimatum now. They won't have any choice.' He added with a deep hatred of publicity, 'It'll be the sensation of a century,' sitting back with his face heavy and sad.

'You mean,' she said with incredulity, 'that when we get in – we can go off straight away and be married?'

'Will you?'

She said, 'The taxi won't be fast enough.'

'It won't be as quick as all that. It takes three weeks. We can't afford a special licence.'

She said, 'Didn't you tell me about a grant? I'll blow it on the licence,' and suddenly as they both laughed it was as if the past three days left the carriage, were whirled backward down the metals to Nottwich. It had all happened there, and they need never go back to the scene of it. Only a shade of disquiet remained, a fading spectre of Raven. If his immortality was to be on the lips of living men, he was fighting now his last losing fight against extinction.

'All the same,' Anne said, as Raven covered her with his sack: Raven touched her icy hand, 'I failed.'

'Failed?' Mather said. 'You've been the biggest success,' and it seemed to Anne for a few moments that this sense of failure would never die from her brain, that it would cloud a

180

little every happiness; it was something she could never explain: her lover would never understand it. But already as his face lost its gloom, she was failing again – failing to atone. The cloud was blown away by his voice; it evaporated under his large and clumsy and tender hand.

'Such a success.' He was as inarticulate as Saunders, now that he was realizing what it meant. It was worth a little publicity. This darkening land, flowing backwards down the line, was safe for a few more years. He was a countryman, and he didn't ask for more than a few years' safety at a time for something he so dearly loved. The precariousness of its safety made it only the more precious. Somebody was burning winter weeds under a hedge, and down a dark lane a farmer rode home alone from the hunt in a queer old-fashioned bowler hat on a horse that would never take a ditch. A small lit village came up beside his window and sailed away like a pleasure steamer hung with lanterns; he had just time to notice the grey English church squatted among the yews and graves, the thick deaths of centuries, like an old dog who will not leave his corner. On the wooden platform as they whirled by a porter was reading the label on a Christmas tree.

'You haven't failed,' he said.

London had its roots in her heart: she saw nothing in the dark countryside, she looked away from it to Mather's happy face. 'You don't understand,' she said, sheltering the ghost for a very short while longer, 'I *did* fail.' But she forgot it herself completely when the train drew in to London over a great viaduct under which the small bright shabby streets ran off like the rays of a star with their sweet shops, their Methodist chapels, their messages chalked on the paving stones. Then it was she who thought: this is safe, and wiping the glass free from steam, she pressed her face against the pane and happily and avidly and tenderly watched, like a child whose mother has died watches the family *she* must rear without being aware at all that the responsibility is too great. A mob of children went screaming down a street, she could tell they screamed because she was one of them, she couldn't hear their voices or see their mouths; a man was selling hot chestnuts at a corner, and it was on *her* face that his little fire glowed, the sweet shops were full of white gauze stockings crammed with cheap gifts. 'Oh,' she said with a sigh of unshadowed happiness, 'we're home.'

THE HISTORY OF VINTAGE

The famous American publisher Alfred A. Knopf (1892–1984) founded Vintage Books in the United States in 1954 as a paperback home for the authors published by his company. Vintage was launched in the United Kingdom in 1990 and works independently from the American imprint although both are part of the international publishing group, Random House.

Vintage in the United Kingdom was initially created to publish paperback editions of books acquired by the prestigious hardback imprints in the Random House Group such as Jonathan Cape, Chatto & Windus, Hutchinson and later William Heinemann, Secker & Warburg and The Harvill Press. There are many Booker and Nobel Prize-winning authors on the Vintage list and the imprint publishes a huge variety of fiction and non-fiction. Over the years Vintage has expanded and the list now includes great authors of the past – who are published under the Vintage Classics imprint – as well as many of the most influential authors of the present.

For a full list of the books Vintage publishes, please visit our website
www.vintage-books.co.uk

For book details and other information about the classic authors we publish, please visit the Vintage Classics website
www.vintage-classics.info